T4-AJQ-923

s p l e n d i d   o m e n s

THOMAS DUNNE BOOKS

ST. MARTIN'S PRESS

New York

splendid omens

■

ROBLEY WILSON

THOMAS DUNNE BOOKS.
An imprint of St. Martin's Press.

A portion of this novel appeared in altered form
in *TriQuarterly* as "A Day of Splendid Omens"; it was later
included under that title in *The Book of Lost Fathers,* published
by The Johns Hopkins University Press, and is here reprinted
with the permission of the publisher.

www.stmartins.com

BOOK DESIGN BY JENNIFER ANN DADDIO

Library of Congress Cataloging-in-Publication Data

Wilson, Robley.
  Splendid omens / Robley Wilson.—1st ed.
    p. cm.
  ISBN 0-312-32167-8
  1. Santa Barbara (Calif.)—Fiction.   2. Middle-aged men—
Fiction.   3. Male friendship—Fiction.   4. Birth fathers—
Fiction.   5. Young women—Fiction.   6. Deception—Fiction.
7. Widowers—Fiction.   I. Title.

PS3573.I4665S65 2004
813'.54—dc22

                                                    2003058544

First Edition: February 2004

10   9   8   7   6   5   4   3   2   1

acknowledgments

WHEN A DOZEN YEARS PASS between an author's first novel and his second, it's plain that he needs certain assistance in maintaining his patience and his writerly good humor. A number of people have served me well in this regard, notably my wife, Susan, and her daughters, Kate and Clare, who have shown plenty of patience of their own throughout this long literary haul. I'm indebted for their early encouragements to Kitty Florey and Ann Beattie, Jerry Klinkowitz and Barry Sanders, and for its later encouragement, to the Corporation of Yaddo—an institution with a human heart. I'm especially grateful to my agent, Rob Preskill, who always believed in this book despite the argument of much rejection, and to my editor, John Parsley, who was persuaded to share this risky faith.

s p l e n d i d   o m e n s

o n e

■

I'M ON MY WAY to a September wedding in Scoggin, a small town in Maine not far from Portland. It's Webster—Webb, my closest friend since the days when we were at Bowdoin together—who's getting married. He's marrying Prudence, who will become either his fourth or his fifth wife; I haven't met all of them, and I can't keep track, partly because I have a tendency not to pay attention to people's names—I've had thousands of students in my courses over the years, and I forget all their names as soon as each year ends. Memory—it's one of the reasons I took early retirement.

Webb and Pru have lived together for a little more than five years, even have a daughter who must be about three now. When Webb called me in Evanston to ask me if I'd stand up for him, he mumbled something about making an honest man of himself—he'd had a few drinks—and I felt a funny twinge of I don't know what. Envy, possibly; or, on the other side of it, maybe a curious sort of disapproval. Webb is sixty-two, the same age I am, and I suppose some Puritan part of me rose up and clucked its tongue at the idea of a man as old as Webb marrying a woman as young—I think she's early thirties—as Pru. What if we'd known when we were in college, dating the girls from Holyoke and Smith and Jackson and Bradford Junior, that one of us might eventually love and impregnate and get married to someone not even born yet? I'm thinking about that as I make the left turn away from the lake where Webb and I used to sit and drink beer while the two kids—brother and sister—from his first marriage ran around in their birthday suits and splashed water on each other and tried to catch minnows in their hands.

WEBB IS AN ARTIST—a good one, I think, but not a successful one. He moved to Maine after his last divorce and managed to buy a run-down farmhouse for back taxes. Then he spent the next few years making it livable—patching the roof of the house and the barnlike ell, shoring up the foundation, replacing broken windowpanes; he dug a new well, put in a septic tank so he could have an indoor toilet. He was alone during all that rehabilitation, living a life so organized it hardly seemed possible this was the Webster Hartley I'd known at school. He got up with the sun, went into his makeshift studio carrying a cup of coffee spiked with Jameson's, and painted for two, three hours; he gave over the rest of the daylight to being a carpenter, an electrician, a journeyman plumber. Then in the hours after dark, before Prudence Mackenzie came into his life, he drank until he fell into bed. It was edifying—I told him this—to see a man take up the disconnected pieces of his life and use them to build a house. "If *I* could do that," I said, "I'd have a castle as big as San Simeon." I felt then, still so close to the death of my wife, that my own life had smashed into a lot more pieces than Webb's.

Prudence worked at the Coop, in Cambridge—when she came to Maine and joined Webb, it was only logical and practical that she should be hired on at the Scoggin bookstore, the Open Stack—and to hear Webb describe their first meeting, it was clearly love at first glimpse. He wrote me about her:

> *She's a little taller than me, and I reckon that's part of the*
> *attraction, someone I can look up to after years of lording it over*
> *so many women smaller and weaker and easily intimidated. But*
> *there's something more, something almost uncanny, that*
> *captivates me. I see in her bits and pieces of all the women I've*
> *known—that won't surprise you, I'm sure—but I also see*
> *myself in her, as if she were some beautiful mirror of my life.*
> *She's got long red-brown hair—a glorious earth tone—and the*
> *straightest teeth I've ever seen. She's a quiet one, but when she*
> *does speak, her voice—Hell, it's indescribable, but if one of*
> *those Botticelli women ever opened her mouth to speak she'd*

*sound like her, a low, gentle voice that would remind you of
someone crooning lullabies. Seriously, I'm smitten. Or I'm
seriously smitten. Same thing.*

At first I kidded him—that he'd fallen for this woman because she could get him a discount on the kind of art books he
used to steal when we were in school, or that he was looking
for a mother-figure, or a daughter-figure, or just a cheap model.
I couldn't take the relationship seriously at first—obviously—
Webb being so much older than Pru. "What can she see in
you?" I asked him once. He shrugged. "Potential," he said.
"What else?"

I can only imagine what they've lived on; I suppose on what
she makes at the bookstore, since Webb's income as a painter
occupies a range from slim to none—though nowadays when
he does sell a picture, he tells me he often gets something up
in the four-figure neighborhood. Perhaps he sells two pieces a
year, three in a super-good year. He doesn't have savings. He
never did.

But the two of them are happy. I visited them a couple of
summers ago, pulling into the yard on a Sunday afternoon in
August, the day sweltering and hazy-gold. There were white
chickens in the driveway, a fat, lazy orange cat asleep on the
porch railing, a rusty pickup truck and a vintage Chevy sedan
parked between the house and a rickety barn. Webb came out
of the house in torn tennis shoes and swim trunks, Pru in the
shadows behind him, barefoot, wearing a long-tailed man's shirt
that might have been all she had on. The baby, Melinda—she
was walking, but just barely, so she must have been what? not

quite a year old?—was in cotton underpants, tottering against her father's hairy legs.

You have to spend a lot of time with Webb Hartley to know him. He's not tall, but he's big and he seems tall. He's broad shouldered, stocky, with hands so huge that if somebody asked you you'd presume that if he were any kind of artist he had to be a sculptor, and ever since he entered his thirties he's worn a beard so red and so unruly he looks like a scruffy Viking warrior. Outrageous—that's how you might describe him, first meeting him. But it wouldn't be long before you realized you were in the presence of a painfully shy man, and you'd forget you thought him outrageous in favor of thinking him reticent, or self-effacing, or politely anti-social. He has a squint to his eyes that suggests the wariness he feels in the company of other humans; I've seen that squint disappear only when he's in front of a new canvas, or looking at Pru across the dinner table, or sitting on the porch steps by himself, petting the indolent orange cat in an absent fashion, his mind a million miles away.

And yet he has a temper. It isn't quick—you have to really rile him—and you can always see it coming, building slowly and ominously behind the squint, behind the camouflage of the tousled beard, until his face seems to be taking on the beard-color, reddening, and the squint looks like the evidence of genuine madness. He doesn't strike out at you from this impressive rage; he doesn't yell or curse. He boils and churns, he broods the way gods brood. He is, I'm certain, holding himself in check just at the horrible edge of murder. There—if you needed it: Webb is a man always at the very boundary of himself.

IT'S LATE AFTERNOON when I arrive at the farmhouse.
The ceremony is scheduled for six, but the reception is before
the wedding and I'm looking forward to some hefty eating and
drinking and clowning around for the newlyweds' benefit. The
day—in fact it's the first day of autumn, the equinox—is superb.
The sky is absolutely unclouded, is perfectly, flawlessly blue; the
air is warm and moves with the slightest of breezes, only enough
to keep you from feeling uncomfortable; you can smell the
grasses—not the humid scent of fresh-cut green, but more subtle, drier, mingled with a distant suspicion of cow and horse
from some unobtrusive neighbor's farm. A knockout day to
declare love unto death, a day of splendid omens.

Oddly, there's nobody around. I sit for a few minutes in the
rented car, surveying the farmyard, the house and the extended
ell with its shake shingles bi-colored where Webb has patched,
wondering why no one strolls out to greet me. The car window
is down, the breeze touches my face, but no sounds blow in.
No laughter, no clink of glasses, no background of a hired mu-
sician tuning his fiddle. No cars belonging to guests—only the
Hartley pickup, rustier than ever. I leave my gift-wrapped package on the car's passenger seat—the package contains a pair of
sterling napkin rings engraved with the first names of the bride
and groom, my usual unimaginative wedding gift—and climb
out of the car. I'm surrounded by rare silence—or what passes
for silence in a noisy world: a soft thunder we hear that science
says is the rush of blood through our bodies; a thin whine alleged to be the electric current that drives the nervous system.

Then other sounds disturb the quiet. The chirp of a cricket. A fly's buzz. A barely audible rustle of leaves in the birches. A crow calling, distant, like a rusty hinge. But no human noise. I go to the farmhouse, cross the porch to the screen door, and knock. Knock harder. Open the screen door and tap on the glass of the inside door with the car key. The sharp noise of the key echoes into the birches, and the echo comes back sounding like someone far off swinging an ax against a tree, cutting it down. I push the door open—Webb has never locked anything in his life—and call Webb's name, get no response, close the door and turn away. I wonder if I have the wrong day, or only the wrong hour.

Walking around the house, I meet a first sign of human habitation: a pet, a small brown-and-white terrier who is over-joyed to meet me, who jumps up to lick my hands, whose tail wags nonstop. "Hey, little guy," I say. "Hello, boy. Where's the party?" I follow the dog around the end of the ell; he's limping, and I see that his right hind leg is deformed, as if it might have been caught in a trap meant for something wild. At the end of the long, sloping lawn the farm pond shows a few dimples where dragonflies touch and dance away; otherwise the water is quiet and unruffled.

In the backyard, finally things look festive. Three picnic ta-bles, covered with red-checkered tablecloths, have been set end to end and laden with bowls of potato salad, macaroni salad, corn chips, raw vegetables, a variety of dips—all of them cov-ered over with plastic wrap for protection from insects and air. At the end of one table are glass cups arranged in a circle that suggests they're intended to surround a missing punch bowl.

On a pair of card tables nearby—also draped in red-checkered cloths—are paper plates, a few styrofoam cups, an aluminum coffeemaker. On the lawn, pushed into the shade of a fair-sized oak tree, are a couple of galvanized iron washtubs filled with ice and canned beer, and I can see the corked necks of wine bottles looking aloof among the cans. The trunk of the tree is wrapped with pink and white crepe streamers. Tubular aluminum chairs with bright-colored plastic seats and backs are scattered about; a few emptied beer cans are in evidence, standing alongside the chairs or tipped over into the grass. On the top step under the back door of the house sits an old-fashioned wind-up Victrola, its lid open, its varnished horn aimed across the yard; a stack of shellac records is on a step below.

But no people. I stroll through the party scene with the terrier wagging at my heels, open a can of Narragansett, slip my fingers under transparent plastic to withdraw a stark cerebrum of cauliflower. I eat the blossom, toss the stem to the dog, who sniffs it and then gives me a puzzled look. I sip the beer and wonder what Webb is up to. Perhaps after a toast or two in champagne he has proposed to his guests a walk in the countryside, a procession, a one-time ritual—the wedding party tramping through the late-summer meadows to put on the last of the wildflower pollens, breathe the faint and fading perfumes of the dying season—that will lead back to the ceremony itself. That would be like him: nothing raucous, nothing orgiastic; just a simplicity of shared sociableness, because anything complicated would have annoyed him, spoiled the point of this day intended only to solemnize his love for Pru and hers for him.

That explanation satisfies me, and I sit on the steps next to the Victrola, drinking my beer, waiting for the party to return.

The dog makes several circles, slumps into the grass at the foot of the steps and rests his head on his forepaws. I remember someone once told me that the point of the old RCA Victor trademark—"His Master's Voice"—is that what the terrier is sitting on, head cocked to listen, is a coffin, and the Master is dead inside it. Webb would enjoy this scene at the back of his house, the rearrangement of the trademark, its elements fragmented but the reference still clear; this is the kind of still life subject he looks for in the world, the sort of thing that ignites his imagination and sends him into his studio. I pick a phonograph record off the top of the pile at my feet—*Vocalion,* I can read, but the gilt lettering is too worn for me to read the fine print of the label—and put it on the green felt of the turntable. I lift the arm and turn it down to rest the needle at the edge of the record; the turntable begins moving, but too slowly to make melody. I crank the phonograph; the turntable speeds up, the music wavers and rises and becomes intelligible—a tenor voice, a sentimental song: "Believe Me, If All Those Endearing Young Charms."

TIME PASSES. The day cools, the sun has made its descent into autumn, the shadows lengthen and climb the shingles of the house, the breeze drops off to nothing. The orange cat— I'd wondered if it was still a familiar of this place—puts in a tardy appearance, passing through, doing a tentative but deliberate high-step through the taller grass at the edge of the yard, ignoring me, ignoring the dog, absorbed in selfish, cattish concerns.

By now I'm sinking into concerns of my own. Where *are*

Webb and Pru? Where are the wedding guests? What was it that called all of them away from celebration? I walk around to the front of the house, the terrier at my heels, and sit in a Boston rocker at the end of the porch—a vantage point from which I can look down the narrow gravel road, see what's coming toward me. For a long time I sit on Webb's porch, rubbing the ears of the dog at my feet, crooning nonsense words. I remember a society page headline I saw, years ago: HER NUPTIALS HELD. I tell the dog about it and his tail thumps the porch floor. Dumb animals—they seem always starved for affection, for any sort of mindless attention. Where in the hell is Pru? Why isn't she here to have her nuptials held? The dog raises his head and laughs up at me.

In the distance is a glitter of chrome—a car coming. I scowl down the length of the road, the low sun in my eyes, a cloud of dust behind the car colored like gold, boiling, molten. It's a blue Ford, a newish sedan that could stand washing, and it speeds past, its driver a middle-aged man, straw-hatted, with his hands holding the wheel at 10 and 2 o'clock.

"False alarm," I say to the terrier. I fold my hands in my lap; the dog drops his head onto his paws and heaves an almost human sigh. I lean back in the rocker, close my eyes, try not to speculate. I wonder what happened to the white chickens. I wonder if Melinda—Mindy—is old enough to be the flower girl for her parents, and how they will dress her—or *if* they will dress her. I wonder if Webb's grown children are invited, and if they have come to Scoggin to meet yet another stepmother. I wonder if his other wives have kept track of him.

Now another car is approaching, not as fast, and behind it

is a second. They slow as they come near, the dust clouds behind them diminishing, flattening in light no longer direct. I stand; the dog startles to his feet. I walk down the two porch steps to meet the new arrivals. Because it is dusk by now, the lead car has its parking lights on.

Both cars turn into the farmyard—the first stopping in the driveway, almost running up on the lawn in front of the porch, and the second going past it to park beside the truck. The driver's-side doors open simultaneously, like something choreographed, and two men appear. Neither one is Webb. The man from the car nearest me trots to the passenger side and opens the door. He offers his hand; a young woman takes it and he helps her to stand. Pru. She is dressed in a pale blue dress whose fullness suggests that she may be carrying Webb's newest child; the color of the dress is almost neutralized by the failing of the daylight, and her high-heeled shoes are likewise pale blue. She is bareheaded, but in one hand she carries a flowered hat and a sheer white scarf. She leans heavily on the man, who steers her toward the house. Only then does she turn in my direction and I see her face—a young woman's face such as I have seen up-lifted a hundred times from among my seas of students.

"Alec," she says.

"What's the matter?" I say. "What's going on?"

She puts her free hand to her face as if she is going to brush aside a stray lock of her long hair, but the hair is pulled severely, formally, back. The hand seems to flutter at her eyes, her mouth.

"Webb," she says.

"What about him?" I take a step toward her. I wish I knew who this man was who suddenly seems so proprietary, who

stiffens and turns his shoulder so that Pru is shielded from my
question. Pru anticipates me.

"This is the minister," she says. "This is the man who was
going to marry us."

"Was?"

"Webster Hartley's dead," the man says. He embraces Pru's
shoulders and steers her past me. "Let's get you inside," he says
to her.

By now the man from the other car has come up.

"Alec," he says, almost jovial. He holds out his hand; I take
it—a reflex—my mind still grappling with the words "Webster
Hartley's dead," wondering if I heard correctly. "Bob Hartley,"
he says. "Webb's kid brother. We met once, a couple of Webb
weddings ago."

"What the hell happened?"

"Heart attack."

"Jesus Christ. On his wedding day?" I feel dizzy, and sit on
the top step of the porch. Bob Hartley sits down next to me.

"It was out of the blue," he says. "Right out of left field.
One minute he was hugging Pru and bragging about his good
luck; the next he was on his face, dead as the proverbial door-
nail. It was weird."

"Jesus." It is all I can think of to say. A prayer, a supplication—
I don't know what. *Jesus.* "Are they sure?"

"Sure of what?"

"Are they sure he's dead?" *Jesus,* I keep saying inside my
head. *Jesus Christ.* Does the name give us some kind of relief
from horror? Is that why we keep saying it?

"Yeah, they're sure. They tried CPR. They tried adrenaline." Bob produces a cigarette and lights it. "That electric-shock gizmo. He's dead all right."

"Where is he?"

"Kimball Hospital. The undertaker's supposed to pick him up tonight."

Sweet Jesus. I try to get a purchase on the day, to say anything that suggests I might have some modest control of reality, no matter how tentative. "How's Pru?"

"Destroyed; you saw. She's four months preggy too." He blows smoke into the dusky air. "Isn't *that* a bitch?"

"Where's Mindy?"

"My wife—you remember Theresa— I dropped her and Mindy back at our motel. They were going to watch cartoons."

IT SEEMS TO ME it is the interior of Webb's house that is a cartoon—a caricature of what is expected to happen when someone dies. While I was hearing the facts of the day from Robert Hartley, two more cars pulled into the yard and emptied themselves—a parade of solemn guests passing around and between us, so that by the time he and I come inside, the front parlor feels crowded and there is activity in the kitchen. A screen door slams periodically; someone is ferrying food from the picnic tables to the refrigerator. Bob excuses himself, leaves me, reappears shortly thereafter staggering under the weight of one of the tubs of beer, which he slides noisily onto a kitchen counter. He calls out to the rest of us.

"Who wants a beer?" he asks. "Who wants wine?"

This is a small room, made smaller by its furnishings. An old upright piano occupies most of the far end, bulking so large that it partially blocks a window. A claw-footed couch covered with an afghan sits under the window that looks onto the porch, a long coffee table, littered with magazines and paperback books, slightly askew in front of it. On the facing wall: a leather chair, a brass floor lamp, a magazine rack. The leather is cracked, the lamp shade has a tricorn tear in it and a cloth-insulated cord frayed where it joins the plug—perhaps that explains why the lamp is not plugged in—and the magazine rack is overflowing with brightly colored sheets of construction paper. On the floor is a worn Oriental carpet, mostly dark red with extravagant designs of gray and orange; the pattern is almost obliterated in front of the chair, around the piano bench, between the sofa and the coffee table.

I know all this stuff. In some cases I was there when Webb acquired it; I helped wear it out. The couch belonged to our landlady in Brunswick; when Webb and I graduated, he bought it and carried it away with him. It's hard to believe that the couch has moved everywhere with him, through so much geography, so many landlords and loves, for nearly forty years—all the awkwardness, the pointless possession, the physical burden.

And the lamp. That was from his three-year stint in Baltimore, teaching at an art school whose administration was consistently slow to honor its salary promises and eventually reneged entirely on Webb's third-year contract. "The three foolish years," he called them. The years of buying horse meat, the early years of his first marriage. The lamp—it had a different shade then; the original got torn during a lovers' quarrel—was in the bedroom of the Baltimore apartment; one of Webb's many dogs, not the one that waited with me for the messenger of death, chewed up the insulation on the cord.

The leather chair was the oldest piece. When Webb was a boy he lived with his grandmother—his father's mother—and the chair was in what was known as "the sitting room." There was a parlor, he told me, but nobody used it; it was too fine, with an expensive carpet, a display cabinet of delicate china cups and saucers, a black baby-grand piano. There were pictures on the walls—cherubs and pink, voluptuous nymphs trailing gossamer scarves—and small alabaster statues drawn from tales in Greek or Roman mythology. The doors to the parlor were kept shut; the rare times when his grandmother left the house, Webb would instantly sneak in and play at playing the piano. But the leather chair, he told me, carried the best memories of the otherwise terrible relationship with his grandmother: it was the chair he sat in—knelt in, rather, so he could reach the table—to play Pounce, a double solitaire game, with the old woman. After the grandmother died, there was an auction; Webb was in Mexico when he heard about it from a neighbor, and he claimed to have hitchhiked from San Miguel de Allende to Scoggin for the sole purpose of buying the wonderful chair. Over the years the leather had dried and cracked, and the blue-gray stuffing was everywhere revealed, but sentiment—surely only that—kept the chair prominent in the farmhouse.

It was the piano that was Webb's pride and joy. I was with him when he acquired it—gratis—from the Methodist Church of Holderness, New Hampshire, which wanted it moved out of the basement to make room for a projection-screen television set. Webb was beside himself; he hired half the football team of the Holderness School to do the moving, rented a pickup— he later bought the truck; it's the one that sits in the yard, rusting away even as we settle in to the evening's wake—and brought it here pretending it was a birthday present for half-nude Mindy. He'd play it whenever he'd had too much to drink and the light was too weak for painting. Honky-tonk; that was his specialty, and the piano—out of tune, missing innumerable felts and having a cracked sounding board—was the perfect instrument. Had he not been so happy, so good-hearted, the experience of listening to Webb play would have been excruciating. But as it was, you couldn't help but feel his pleasure. He sang "The Darktown Strutters' Ball," his left hand boom-chucking away, his right hand trilling treble octaves, his voice—his awful voice—bouncing the lyrics off the room's walls and ceiling. He sang "I'll Take You Home Again, Kathleen," tremolo, while tears streamed down his cheeks. He played "House of Blue Lights" until the boogie-woogie bass gave you a headache. But how do you say to a man who's in a heaven of his own making that he should for God's sake give us a rest from all that racket? All at once I feel thirsty and answer Webb's brother's question: "Beer here, please."

SOMEONE HAS TURNED ON the overhead light in the room after someone else has tried the unplugged lamp in vain, and for a moment the brightness is painful. I close my eyes; when I do, the rectangles of pictures on the walls linger on my retinas. I open my eyes. These are Webb's drawings, pencil and charcoal, put up with cellophane tape—sketches that now will never turn into paintings.

Bob Hartley appears, presses a beer into my hand, pausing to make sure I have a grip on it, since I must seem to him not to be paying attention. He says, "O.K., old buddy?" and I snap out of it and nod. The room is suddenly warm, crowded; the cold beer is marvelous, a perverse joy. The wedding guests talk softly, moving between the parlor and the kitchen—the rooms are separated from each other by a countertop and a bank of cupboards—pouring wine, helping themselves to food. The screen door to the backyard creaks open and slaps shut incessantly. Except for the solemn tenor of the conversations, the atmosphere is festive.

I lean back in the leather chair and press the beer can against my forehead. The cold feels sharp-pointed, welcome. Bob returns and sits unsteadily on the chair arm.

"Pru's lying down upstairs," he says. "She'd like to talk with you."

"Now?"

"I think so; yes."

"Shouldn't she rest?"

Bob shrugs. "She took a couple of pills. I think she's about cried out for today."

As I leave the room I have the feeling everyone, all this strange company, is looking at me. *Who's that? Is he a relative?* At the foot of the stairs I wonder if I should carry the beer with me, or finish it down here, or just set it down somewhere and come back to it later. I keep it, go upstairs, muddle around in the hall for a moment before I remember where Webb's bedroom is.

Pru is leaning against two pillows in the center of the brass bed; a patchwork quilt is under her; she's clutching one of the matching pillow shams, holding it against herself like a security blanket, so the swell of her stomach is partly concealed. She's red-eyed, but not crying.

"Alec," she says, her voice small and sweet.

"Bob said I should look in."

"Please." She pats the quilt beside her. "I asked him to find you."

I sit, gently, intending not to shake the bed. "Can I get you anything?"

"Thank you, no." She lowers the sham and lets go of it; she puts out her right hand toward me, but doesn't try to touch me. "Is that beer?"

"Yes."

"Let me have a taste."

"Should you? On top of—whatever?"

"They were only aspirin. Cross my heart. I can't risk anything strong."

I hold out the beer, but instead of taking it from me she puts her hand over mine and steers the can to her mouth. She takes a long swallow, then releases me. "I hate beer," she says. "It's such bitter stuff."

"There's sweeter stuff downstairs."

"I know. I helped buy it." She sighs, leans back, closes her eyes. "I made the punch too. With plenty of vodka. The bowl never made it out of the pantry."

I don't know what to say, or what she wants of me. I let my gaze roam around the bedroom: to her blue heels in the middle of the room, the scarf and hat on a wicker chair under a window, on one of the room's two dressers a beribboned plastic box with flowers inside it.

"You came a long way for nothing," she says.

Her eyes are open, and very green—although I seem to remember that she wears contacts, and the contacts are tinted. On both her cheeks are faint, thin streaks made by tears, and her lipstick is faded almost to nothing. Her hair is loose; the combs are on the nightstand nearby. She is a pretty woman; the delicacy of her young features has always made her seem to me unusually vulnerable, and the tragedy of this day makes her seem terribly in need of care, of protective solace. "Then there's that thing about redheads," Webb said to me once. "They blush so readily. Their faces always tell the truth." I take a swallow of my beer, my mouth where hers has been.

"If I can help," I say, without the slightest idea of how to complete the thought.

"You can," she says. She sits upright, swings her legs over the far side of the bed. "But you have to turn your back while I get into something simple."

I hear her clothing rustle. I hear the blue skirt falling to the floor, the white blouse gliding off her arms. A closet door slides; hangers jangle.

"All right," she says. "I'm decent." She's in tights, a loose pink sweater; she is tying her hair into a ponytail. "In the corner closet," she says, "could you get me that scruffy pair of Tretorns?"

"Where are we going?"

"I want to go to the studio." She finishes tying the tennis shoes, takes my hand to lead me. "Come," she says. "We'll use the back stairs so we miss everybody."

I follow. At the head of the stairs she stops so abruptly I almost collide with her; she turns, throws her arms around my waist and hangs on desperately. Her head is down, her face against my chest. "God," she says. "I didn't want all these people; I wanted you, and Bobby and Terry, just to witness."

"They'll be gone pretty soon."

"They don't know anything about any of this," she says. "They don't have a single clue."

AFTER HE'D PICKED UP the old farmhouse from the Tax Assessor—long after the blond second or third wife had left him, but before Pru came into his life—I visited him here, followed him around while he boasted about what he was going to do, what he'd already done. The studio in those first days was an impressive mess: the ell windows had long been broken out by storms and vandals, and half the animal kingdom of southern Maine must have been wintering in it for years; scat and straw and nests of fur like tumbleweeds corrupted the space—the odor was unbelievably raw—and off and on during my stay various of the previous tenants tried to reassert their squatters' rights. One morning we burst in on a red fox couple, another time a family of raccoons like a band of gypsy thieves surprised around a campfire. Skunks were the riskiest, Webb told me, and when one Sunday he cornered one behind the potbellied stove he'd just hooked up, I opted out—went back inside the house and poured another cup of coffee for myself. "How'd it go?" I wanted to know when he came back to the kitchen. "Piece of cake," Webb said. "I think I've driven that one off before; he was friendlier than most—acted like he knew me."

That was the year I stayed all summer, and by the time I left, Webb had been painting in his new studio for almost three weeks. We'd put in a skylight, caulked all the old window frames, replaced a dozen broken floorboards. We even lugged in three cords of stovewood to take Webb through his first winter. Seeing the studio now, with poor Pru, brought all of that back, and it brought back the time I'd first met her.

The year was melting into springtime then, but there'd been a spectacular ice storm the day I arrived. The driving was ugly—I'd seen cars and trucks tipped off at the side of the roads, and I'd clutched the wheel to my chest like a life vest, praying the rear wheels wouldn't break away every time I came to a curve—but Nature was glorious, encased in ice, glittering like cut crystal. This was still the time before Pru had joined him—barely—but there were already chickens, pecking and scratching in the mud and flattened grass. Webb either saw or heard me coming; by the time I drove into the yard he was standing on the porch—Levi's, green-and-black plaid shirt, the same style of army boots he'd worn for close to forty years—waiting for me. He had a great black skillet—a "spider," he called it—in his right hand, and in his left a couple of brown hen's eggs he held up and waved at me. When I got out of the car, I said, "This the place that's hiring lumberjacks?"

"How many eggs in your omelet?" he said.

"Three."

I trailed him inside a house that was already full of the smell of bacon and too-strong coffee, laid my toilet kit on the magazine rack—it held magazines then—and sat at the kitchen table. The table was a recent find of Webb's; it was old and austere and heavy, made of oak and varnished to an autumnal shade of brown. With its four high-backed chairs it crowded the kitchen and made the place cozy at the same time. Webb poured me a mug of the coffee from a battered aluminum pot and went about his cooking duties, breaking a half-dozen eggs into an outsized measuring cup, adding a healthy splash of water from a faucet at the sink—"Anybody tells you to add milk instead of water has never been intimate with a hen," he said—beating the mix with the tines of a fork and pouring half into the greasy spider.

"I'll remember."

"Cheese?" he said.

"Why not?"

He opened the refrigerator and brought out a fist-sized block of cheddar, grated much of it into the pan, ate most of the rest while he oversaw the omelet. "Sharp," he said. "Nice edge on it." The bacon was draining on a wad of paper towels on the counter, the coffee steamed above its low blue flame at the back of the stove. I remember how secure I felt; it came from being comfortable and attended to and needed. It had been years since I'd lost my wife, and the pleasures of breakfast and smoky morning smells and the joy of a beloved familiar face and voice were long obscured by the numbing horror of Harriet's being in and out of each of those hospitals that had taken yet another scrap of her life. I was still getting used to traveling alone, restless, moving in this direction and that like a hurt animal that thinks it can walk away from its pain.

"This woman I met," Webb told me. It was a statement that sounded abrupt—as if he'd been holding it in until it simply refused any longer to be contained. "This demure damsel such as you found hard to believe. In Boston some months ago." He prodded the omelet, bent down to stove level to adjust the flame under it. "Goes by the old-fashioned name of Prudence."

"How'd you meet her?"

"Luck." He folded the omelet over, danced the spider on the burner for a moment or two, tipped it up so the omelet slid off onto a heavy white plate. He added several strips of the bacon and set the plate before me. "Karma. Life's reward for Good Behavior." He turned his back to me and went to work on the second omelet.

"Sounds serious," I said.

"Maybe it's witchcraft," Webb said. "You remember me telling you about the old woman down on Cat Mousam Road."

"The one you did the scary portrait of—with the cat."

"That's her. Maybe she's rewarding me for my superb eye. My supernatural good taste."

"So what's she do?—this young chickie. Besides turn you on."

Webb scowled at me over his shoulder. "What else does she need to do?" he said.

"Is she rich?"

He seemed to study the question. "I think not," he said after a while. "Not by any worldly definition."

He set his plate on the table, brought over what was left of the bacon on its bed of greasy paper, sat down across from me.

"So you're in love with her," I said.

He took a mouthful of omelet, chewed, swallowed. "There's salt and pepper behind the mustard pot," he said. "I don't know your taste. Or your dietary requirements."

"So you're *not* in love with her?"

"I'm deliberating over the word 'love,' " he said. "There's a connection between us—I can't describe it." He tried his coffee, found it had cooled, went to the stove to add hot. "Maybe it's indescribable. A profound attachment. Like I've been only half human all this time, and Pru is the other half of me."

"Another marriage ahead?" I said.

"No," he said. "Never. She's too good to be made by any man into a mere wife."

"And so?"

He took a sip of coffee, scratched the beard at his chin. "How long are you staying?" he said.

"Till Sunday," I said. "If you'll tolerate me."

"Then you'll meet her. She's moving in with me on Saturday."

ON TODAY'S SAD VISIT the studio has the agreeable clutter it lacked when Webb and I first got it into shape to be used. One end of it is a kind of carpenter's shop smelling of the pungent, fresh-sawn wood waiting to be made into canvas stretchers and frames, and of the thick brown glue kept hot in its electric pot. At the other end, under the skylight stained from years of gray weather and mottled with bird droppings, the smell is sharper, of oil paint, lacquers and thinners, turpentine-soaked rags. Prudence wends her way through the canvases leaned against the workbench, the one-by-twos and one-by-threes of pine and hickory and oak; she pauses, picks up several corner fasteners and spills them with a sound like cracked bells into an open paper box on the bench. "Webb was never neat," she says.

Now we're in the studio proper, where Webb worked. A large easel directly under the skylight, finished canvases and Masonite boards leaned and piled against the end wall, a cabinet with open drawers that reveal paint tubes and brushes of every size. The floor, where years of colors have fallen, is like a Pollock painting. Squat cans of turpentine, spray cans of plastic, line the sills of the two windows that face east. Under those windows sits something like a toychest, open to display its innards—kids' games, thin books with oilcloth covers, a Ouija board, a confusion of wooden blocks belonging to sets for both alphabet and architecture.

"Mindy's things," Pru says. "Webb would paint; Mindy would sit on the floor and play. They'd carry on long, philosophical conversations."

"Precocious," I say.

"You'll like her," Pru says. "She's often easier to get along with than Webb."

"He had his days," I say. "He must have been a challenge to live with."

She lowers her eyes and I understand I shouldn't have said

that—shouldn't in any careless way seem to be trying to demean Webb, even Webb gone.

"Do you have a cigarette on you?" she says.

"No. I didn't know you smoked."

"Not much lately. Not since we started the new baby. Sometimes I sneak a quick drag or two." She stands. "I thought you were a smoker."

I shake my head. "No more."

"I need just one," she says. "I'll be right back."

I touch her arm, gently, to stop her. "I'll find cigarettes. Stay put."

"There's a carton in the kitchen," she says behind me. "To the left of the sink."

A chill is in the air as I cross the breezeway to the house, and the world's sounds have put on darkness. When I open the door I hear the far-off stammer of an owl, the hollow yapping of a farm dog or a fox just waking.

The Saturday morning of Pru's arrival, Webb brought me to the studio to show me his recent work—not something I was much in the mood to do. We'd been up late the night before; Webb had brought out the bottle of Irish, and between us we'd nearly finished it. I had the granddaddy of all hangovers; I felt generally dessicated, like driftwood in the sun, or like one of those cow skulls you see in a movie Western. Webb showed no sympathy. He handed me a tumbler of tomato juice and Tabasco, made his usual pot of vile coffee and dragged me to the studio.

If anyone had asked me a week later if there was anything Webb showed me that I liked, I think I'd have said yes, many things, but that morning I was in no mood—or no condition—for pleasure. I knew that, going in, and I resolved to say as little as possible. Mothers tell their children: "If you can't say something nice, don't say anything." I was going to be a circumspect child in the presence of the morning's artworks.

It drove him crazy. At first he was talkative, wound up, eager as a kid showing off—"Look at this one: look at that contrast!" "How about this, those wild shadows where the green meets the gray!" and on and on. I'd nod; I'd say, "Mmmm." Gradually he ran down, stopped raving about his own cleverness with color or brush stroke or composition. He'd put another piece on the easel without a word, step back to admire it. He'd look at me. I'd stroke my chin and nod.

"For Christ's sake," he said—I suppose we'd been an hour or more going through a couple of dozen paintings—"if you don't like it, say so."

"Hey," I said. "You know I admire your stuff."

It was true—*is* true. I like Webb's work; I like the starkness of it, the blockiness of it. He doesn't deal in subtleties; either he never learned how or he never wanted to. All-night cafeterias, alleys, MTA platforms. He'd spend days, sometimes weeks, on a painting, and you always knew whose work it was because he had a kind of trademark: he outlined certain elements of the picture heavily in black. It jumped the piece from reality into fantasy; the black line was a primitive device, jarring, yet wonderful because it reshaped—refreshed—your attention. I was in a bad mood that morning, but it wasn't because I didn't admire Webb's talent with a brush.

"I wish you'd fucking *show* it," he said.

"I don't know how you want me to show it. You want me to applaud?"

He glared. He didn't say anything; just started putting things back where he'd found them, leaning the canvases and boards face inward against the wall.

Then I did it. He was holding a street scene he'd done, he told me, just a few weeks ago, and I decided to comment on it. Show him I was paying attention.

"That one," I said. I pointed, and he stopped, the canvas in his hand. "That one I particularly liked."

He turned it and lifted it in both hands to ponder it, then propped it back up on the easel. Even after all this time I can see it in my mind's eye: a street corner, after dark, two men under a traffic light, a mailbox behind them, graffiti on a building nearby, a littered street in the foreground. It's been raining; a pale, reflective wash of wetness touches the hard surfaces and the men seem somehow conspiratorial.

"You like it," Webb said.

I nodded. "Mostly," I said.

"Mostly?" He looked at me, at the painting, at me again. "What *don't* you like?"

"It's not important." Something in his posture, the way he leaned a little in my direction, should have alerted me.

"No, tell me," he said. "I value your opinion."

I was cornered; I had to answer. "Maybe the mailbox," I said. My headache was worse than ever. I wanted to go back to the kitchen, drink a glass of water, take a nap.

"What about the mailbox?"

"Well— Everything in the picture is kind of ominous with

greens and blacks and dark reds. I like that. I like the sort of implied threat the two men represent." I stopped. "What is it? A drug deal?"

"You were talking about the mailbox." Under the beard, his jaw was set.

"It seems to stand out." I turned away from it. "I need another cup of coffee," I said.

"How do you mean 'It seems to stand out'?"

"God, Webb— It's just so fucking *blue*."

I waited. He didn't say anything. He took down the painting and leaned it against the wall with the others. Then he said, "Let's get your coffee."

We walked the length of the ell in silence, went through the screen door into the storage pantry and on into the kitchen. I gave Webb my coffee mug; he took it, filled it, handed it back. He sat at the table, across from me. He squinted at his hands, which were working at each other in front of him. You could see him gathering himself, marshaling his anger.

"How many hours a year do you figure you spend looking at paintings?" Webb said at last.

"I don't know."

"Fifty? A hundred? A thousand?"

I thought about it. "I suppose I'm in the Art Institute two or three times a year," I said. It was partly true—I hadn't been there at all that year, but I'd gone several times the year before.

"For how long?"

"How long what?"

"When you visit the Art Institute, how long do you stay?"

"It depends."

"Average," he said.

"I suppose two or three hours. I always go back to their Impressionist stuff, their Picassos—"

He interrupted me. "I make that nine hours."

"What about nine hours?"

"Nine hours of looking at paintings. A total of nine hours *a year.*"

"Well—" I thought: *God help me.* "Give or take."

"You look at paintings for less than nine hours a year, and you have the nerve to tell me my mailbox is too *blue?*"

His diatribe was cut off after a half hour or so by the arrival of Prudence Mackenzie. While it lasted, it was high drama for Webb—pacing, waving his arms, shouting and whispering and pounding the table. Did I know how many hundreds of hours a year he was seeing paintings, studying paintings, making paintings? Did I know how many thousands of hours that added up to over his lifetime? Did I know that painting was his life, not a goddamned hobby the way it was for me? Did I know what a presumptuous s.o.b. I was?

Then the Chevy was in the driveway, and this pretty, red-haired woman was getting out, and we were both at the kitchen window when I said, "Damn it, Webb, you *asked* me what I thought," and Webb, on his way out to take his new love in his arms, only said, "You frigging schoolteacher."

I FIND A CARTON OF SALEMS in the cupboard, and while I'm sliding out a pack for Prudence, Bob appears beside me.

"Where's Pru?"

"In the studio. She wanted a cigarette."

"She O.K.?"

"I think so. She's talking about Webb." I replace the carton, close the cupboard door. "Seems like good therapy."

"Right." He squeezes my shoulder. "Tell her I'm on my way to get Terry and Mindy."

"I will. Are there any matches?"

"That bowl on the counter."

The bowl is full of matchbooks from all over; the one I grab says The Dolphin Striker—it's a restaurant with a Portsmouth address. When I get back to the studio, Pru takes the pack from me, opens it, taps it on the back of her hand to get at a cigarette. I light it for her; again she holds my hand to steer it.

"It wasn't my idea to get married," she says. "If you've wondered. I was against it. I thought we were doing fine as lovers, as people with special 'significance' for each other." She leans against the windowsill. The light from overhead makes unflattering shadows on her face, accents her eye sockets, hollows her cheeks. "Whatever that idiom is," she says.

"He was no stranger to marriage," I say.

"I know." She looks down and her face is all shadow. "I'd have been number four."

"I'd lost count."

"There was Jennifer—the longest of all. Then there was Eleanor. That lasted five weeks; they realized their mistake in the Bahamas, on the honeymoon. And then came—was it Wendy? That was finished nine years ago. He told me all about them, chapter and verse. It wasn't that he was bragging. I think

he really wanted me to know him, make sense of him. He told
me that after Wendy he'd decided never to do marriage again."

"What made him change his mind? Just sentiment?"

"Oh, I think he was trying to be practical. I think that
because he was so much older—and really, he was getting awfully conscious of his age—he wanted me to have whatever
benefits the wedding ceremony might bring with it. Survivor
benefits, insurance, tax breaks. I don't know what."

"Age affects people," I say. Not sarcastic.

"It never bothered me. I mean he never seemed to me to
act old or talk old—or *paint* old." She takes a drag from the
cigarette, inhales deeply—I think, like a father, *I wish she
wouldn't*—and sighs the smoke out. "I suppose, too, he wanted
to make things easier for Mindy."

"He said he wanted to make everybody honest."

"Something like that." She drops the hardly-smoked cigarette to the spattered floor, crushes it with the heel of her tennis
shoe. She looks suddenly forlorn, and for an uneasy moment I
think she's going to just let go, just collapse, as if it's easier to
be unconscious and let the world go on without her for a while.
My wife used to say *I'm tired; today I'm just going to be a passenger.*
Pru raises her hands—a gesture of futility.

"And he actually loved me," she says. "God— You can't
believe how much I already miss him."

I hold her. "I'll miss him for the rest of my life," she says,
and then she cries and cries. I hang on while the sobs shake her,
my right hand pressed against her back, pressed against the light
sweater, through which I can feel her warmth, my left hand
cradling her head to my chest, feeling the stray tendrils of hair

damp against her forehead. I wonder if she can hear my heart, or if her own grief drowns it out. I wonder if an unborn child has a hearable heartbeat at four months. Pru tries to talk through the weeping. "You don't know," she says, and "Nobody knows," over and over.

"It's O.K.," I say, though I've no idea what she means. "It's all right."

After a while she stops crying, her body begins to relax, she wipes at her cheeks with the back of her hand and steps away from me. Her face is mottled and her eyes swollen. She tries to smile.

"We were a strange and wonderful pair," she says.

"You seemed to belong together."

"We did," she says. Then she goes through the motions of pulling herself together—adjusts the tights at her waist, pushes the unruly strands of hair back from her face, takes a facial tissue from a box on Webb's cabinet to dry her cheeks, blow her nose. "God," she says, "I almost forgot why I dragged you out here."

She goes to the pictures leaned against the wall of the studio and slides out the one with the blue mailbox.

"Remember?" she says.

"I'll say."

"I didn't know what I'd walked into, that first time I came to the farm. Anyway, he wanted you to have it. He said you might grow into it."

"Maybe I will," I say.

"Oh, Alec." Now she comes back to me, not to cry but to let us embrace like the friends I believe we are. "You came here to stand up for Webb, and now you've got to stand up for me.

You have to stay. You have to see me through whatever it is that's supposed to happen next."

"I'll do anything I can."

"I don't even know the rules," she says. "I don't know what people do when someone dies. I don't know if Webb should be buried, or cremated, or if I should do what he told me to do."

"What's that?"

"Give his body to a medical school for research." She hangs back from me, looking stricken. "I can't imagine students chopping him up. I don't know if he was serious or teasing me."

"Maybe you should let Bobby and me take care of the arrangements."

She hugs me. "Yes," she says. "Yes, please."

"WEBB WASN'T A PRACTICAL PERSON," Bob Hartley says. "When I found out that he'd never made out a Last Will and Testament, and here he was with this string of ex-wives, and him planning to marry Prudence—God, I could see the complications. Nightmares for everybody, and Pru could end up in the poorhouse."

Bob is a lawyer by profession—something I might have remembered if I hadn't been so staggered by Webb's death—and we are sitting in the kitchen, at the oak table, with papers and envelopes strewn between us. Bob's glasses are pushed up on his head, and he's finally taken off his necktie. At my left elbow is a half-empty bottle of Jameson's, and he and I each have a tumbler full of ice cubes tinctured with whiskey. Prudence is still up with us—it's past midnight, the guests are long gone, Mindy has been put to bed upstairs—and she and Theresa are doing up the serving dishes and silverware.

"Though I'll tell you," Bob says. "She may end up there anyway. My brother didn't have much to give away."

"You can't take it with you," Theresa says. She's a big-boned woman with the kind of voice you can pick out of all the other voices at a restaurant or a cocktail party. "So why own it? I think that was the touchstone of Webb's life."

"Be fair," Bob tells her. "He just needed someone to remind him that he was going alone. That he might leave a survivor or two."

"Is there any estate at all?" I ask.

"Oh, sure." He unfolds the will stapled into its blue cover. "There's this house, which believe it or not is free and clear, and the seventy acres with it. This is a valuable thing—though this is a depressed area and it isn't an especially good time to sell. It's a terrible time, as a matter of fact."

"I won't sell it," Pru says. "Mindy and I live here."

"And there's his paintings."

"Ha," Theresa says.

"Cut it out, Terry," Bob tells her. "Picasso he isn't, but he told me the last thing he sold was for thirty-five hundred. And that was for a painting by a living artist. Dead—"

"God, stop it, Bobby." Pru throws down the dish towel she's been using and runs upstairs.

"Shit," Theresa says. She follows Pru.

"Just as well," Bob says. "Let them cry on each other's shoulders."

"Catharsis," I say. It must be something about Bob that makes me say the obvious.

Bob looks at me. "It's peculiar. Terry didn't much like Webster, but she liked the *idea* of him. She'd like to have rolled us both into one person, Webb's Bohemian flair, my talent for making money."

"She doesn't seem to think much of his paintings."

"I've had divorce clients who act like Terry," he says. "They're still in love with the spouse but they know it won't work anymore, so they snipe at something they may very well be fond of—some habit of the spouse that used to be endearing and now seems to drive them bananas." He flips back the top page of Webb's will. "You know: denial."

I take a drink of the whiskey. When Webb and I were college freshmen, we had to read a story called "In the Midst of Death We Live." I've no idea now what the story was about, but the title resonates in this place.

"It's a real stunner," Bob says, "to see a man drop dead before your eyes. One minute Webb was standing with his arm around Prudence, waving a champagne glass in the air, and he was saying something about how ordinary language was insufficient to express his feelings for this woman by his side. Very formal. The next minute he was on the ground at her feet." He tips back in his chair so it's leaning against the counter behind him. "You know what we did? We laughed."

I can imagine it. I can hear people saying what a joker Webb was.

"Then, of course—" He rocks forward. "Well," he says, "the rest you know." He takes a long swallow of whiskey and sets the drink aside; he brings the glasses down to his nose to read. "Anyway, everything goes to Pru, as you might guess, except one of his paintings is yours—he's specific about it; you don't get to choose."

"Pru told me."

He fishes among the papers in front of him and comes up with a business-size white envelope. "And this." He hands it to me. "The ever-popular 'to-be-opened-in-the-event' letter."

"Thanks." I see that it has my name on it, in Webb's hand, then I fold it in half, tuck it into my back pocket. I want to be alone with whatever it says.

"And the old pickup truck. It goes to some farmer over in West Egypt. Don't ask me why." He shuffles the papers, gathers them, makes them into an even pile. "So much for that."

"Pru's worried about funeral arrangements," I say.

"That's easy. I talked to old man Curtis from a pay phone at the hospital. We just have to choose a casket—something I think you and I should do; I don't think Pru needs to be burdened with that."

"I think her worry has more to do with the body than with the box. Webb apparently said something once about giving his body to science."

"And his brain to Harvard," Bob says scornfully. "I think that's totally unacceptable. My brother isn't going to be some medical student's cadaver. You've heard those horror stories—they cut the body completely in half, for Christ's sake."

"So I've heard." When I was in graduate school, there was gossip about a med student who cut a heart-shaped chunk of flesh out of his cadaver's buttock and sent it to his fiancée on Valentine's Day.

"How would she feel about cremation?"

"I don't know."

"That seems to me the most sensible thing," Bob says. "No fuss, no grave to tend—maybe a marker in one of those commercial mausoleums, but no perpetual-care fee to pay to some cemetery rummy, maybe not even a casket—and then if she wants to scatter his ashes in some appropriate place, someplace symbolic and special—"

"Like the Ganges," I say. "And then she could throw herself on a funeral pyre."

Bob stares at me for a long moment. "Fuck you," he says. "I'm only trying to deal seriously with my brother's remains."

PRU DOESN'T COME BACK to the kitchen; Theresa rejoins us briefly, finds a bottle of Bailey's Irish Cream at the back of the liquor cupboard and pours herself a small glassful. Sitting at the table, she and Bob carry on a wary discussion: should the two of them go back to their motel, or should they stay—both of them measuring my presence—in case Pru wakes in the night and needs the consolation of another woman? My opinion isn't asked for. Finally, Bob gathers up his papers and they leave. I watch the car's taillights diminish in the trailing pink dust of the gravel road. Alone, I wander around downstairs, find a stray punch cup on top of the piano, a wadded-up paper napkin on the floor under the coffee table, an empty beer can balanced on the arm of the leather chair. I rinse the cup under the hot-water faucet and throw the napkin into a wastebasket labeled PAPER. I don't remember if Maine has a can-and-bottle law, and I don't have my glasses on to read the label, so I leave the beer can sitting on the counter.

My usual room is the guest bedroom off the kitchen, but before I turn in for the night I make a proprietary tour of doors and windows, checking locks, making sure the stove controls are turned off. I even climb the stairs—carefully because I'm not sure I remember which ones creak—and on the way back I hear voices from Mindy's room. The door is partly open, and I pause to look inside. Among the dim shadows cast by a light that may be the moon's, I see Prudence. She is lying beside her daughter, one arm holding the child close, the small blond head nested under the mother's chin. Pru is talking softly—so softly, almost a whisper, that I can make out only a word, a phrase, nothing truly connected. I realize she is telling Mindy about Webb and about fathers and about love, and for a moment I think I should slip quietly into the room to hear the whole story for myself—but this is a private time for Webb's two women, and I dare not intrude. Besides, what can I learn about fatherhood at this late date?

I DREAD WHAT'S INSIDE the envelope Webb has left me. Everyone is in bed, the house is as quiet as any silence you can imagine. The sound of my tearing open the flap seems as loud as the ripping of tree roots out of hard earth—I think Pru and Mindy will surely rush downstairs, say *What was that?*—and when I unfold the letter inside, written on heavy stock, it too is unnaturally noisy. I straighten the folds in the paper, find my reading glasses, take a deep breath.

Dear Alec,
If you actually have this, then you must be shocked by my
death. I reckon I must have been pretty shocked too, and if

brother Bob is nearby you can tell him for me that I believe
there must be some substance to the notion of self-fulfilling
prophecy, because ever since I told him I wanted to marry Pru
he has been badgering me to make a will, and he finally
succeeded. It wasn't a very complicated undertaking (ha ha),
because everything goes to Pru and, through her, to Mindy. The
only exceptions as you know by now are the truck and the
picture you admired so ambiguously, the weekend my darling
Pru came to live with me.

I left you the blue mailbox so you can hang it in a prominent
place and remember what an ignorant asshole you can be, and
be reminded of the shameful way you had of insulting me when
you were hung over. Sending guilt from beyond the grave is
going to be my new vocation. To balance that act of unkindness,
I ask you to find the red-witch picture and destroy it—it was in
its way another kind of revenge, and the person it was aimed at
has never deserved its cruelty.

The catch is that in exchange for owning a Hartley painting of
great value you have to do me a favor and go tell Jenny the
news and the circumstances of my death. This has to be a
mission done in person, face to face, it can't be a phone call or a
letter full of heartfelt sympathy and flowery sentiments you
dictated to somebody with readable handwriting. Jenny is raising
horses near Santa Barbara—or was when I wrote this—at a
place called Zodiac Ranch. I don't know any more than that. I
don't know if she owns the place or is Head Wrangler or what.

I know it's been a lot of years since you've seen her or talked to
her, but I trust you to do this for me, to let bygones be truly
bygones among us all. You and I owe each other a lot. But I'm
the one who's dead, and I get to collect first.

If friends can love friends, even if they're both male war
buddies, then I'll end all of this by admitting (ugh) I love you,
Alec. Don't be so damned professorial, and don't ever lose your
capacity, or your willingness, to be surprised.

                                                              Webb

It's dated a couple of months back.

I put Webb's letter back into its envelope and undress for
bed. Then I pad back upstairs to the bathroom as softly as I can
and run water into the sink while I relieve myself. I wonder
why I'm so squeamish in a house filled with women; do I believe women don't go to the bathroom—like Tarzan in the
movies—or that women don't know men do? A crazy question.
I only know, standing there, that I'm embarrassed to imagine
Pru lying awake, listening to my urine splash into the toilet
bowl. Upbringing—the way parents raise their children. Lessons. I think of my mother bathing me long after I was old
enough to bathe myself; how attentive she was to my appearance by washing and combing my hair; how one day when I
had combed my own hair—with pride, because I was barely
nine or ten—my mother cupped my jaw and said, 'Allie, look
at you. The part in your hair looks like a snake's back.' " There
used to be a time when I wondered how Webb's mother might
have treated him—if it was something subtly sexual that ac-

counted for his wives, his affairs—but that was before Webb answered the question for me.

Passing Mindy's room, I look in again through the half-opened door. Pru is gone. Mindy is a dim form under the sheet, one bare leg outside the covering, one arm hung over the edge of the mattress. Across the hall, the door to Pru's room is closed.

For what seems like hours, I lie in the dark and try to make sense of the day just past. The window is open a few inches; the night outside is a long sigh of light wind in the trees nearby, and my thoughts ride with it—a gentle recapitulation of flying and driving, of perplexed waiting and irrational outcomes, of images: the untouched feast, the crippled terrier, the scratchy phonograph record, and Pru—Pru numbed by shock, Pru trying to weep, Pru against me for consolation, perhaps meaning to borrow my strength, not realizing how she has nourished my own perverse desire. Now: Pru being Mindy's mother, her voice made gentle by death and loving. And here I am, deputized by my dead friend, about to become the bridge—an arch across the country and the years—between Pru, Webb's not-quite last wife, and Jennifer, his first.

I ask myself what Webb had in his mind when he wrote my half-jocular, half-serious letter. What sort of request am I fulfilling? Certainly a phone call would tell Jenny all she needs—or, probably, wants—to know about Webb's death. If there really is more to it—"don't ever lose your capacity, or your willingness, to be surprised"—I wonder how eager I am to learn what it is. Are there other letters, to be found and opened and acted on, so that the other wives, the What's-their-names, will get the message? Will I have to find them all?

But I know better. It's Jenny we have in common; it's Jenny holds meaning for us both.

The last time I saw Webb and Jenny and their children as a family was—how long ago? Now I remember it was the summer of the Watergate hearings, for that was a major topic of conversation as we sat in our plastic beach chairs outside the camp on Square Pond, watching Webb's children, Amanda and Will, swim tirelessly back and forth between the shore and the dock that floated a dozen yards out. I can see us as we were then—the silly wide-brimmed cotton hats we wore, Webb's with a plastic window in its brim, turning his face a seasick shade of green; both of us in Bermuda shorts and polo shirts, Webb's legs thick and hairy and tanned, mine scrawny and dead-thing pale; both of us in worn tennis shoes that had never seen a tennis court; both of us sipping highballs of whiskey and water—my bourbon, Webb's eternal Irish.

Ostensibly we were kid-sitters, males performing a guardianship function while the women sat on the porch over iced tea and needlework, catching each other up on the months between visits. Harriet was well then; her cancer was not even a shadow of a shadow on the horizon of our lives, and she was a creature of marvelous energy—a jogger, bicyclist, cross-country skier—who looked forward to our trips to Maine every summer as a chance to swim in what she called "real water," and who enjoyed Jenny Hartley's company as a change of pace from the faculty wives of Evanston, whose talk was filled with the height and depth of their husband's grievances. If it bothered her that Jenny and I had once been lovers, had all but gotten married long ago in Baltimore, the bother never showed.

The truth was, since Harriet and I were childless, that the Hartley kids had over the course of our annual visits become surrogate, the son and daughter we never had—"the joy of parenthood without the burden of it," Harriet would say. Not that we hadn't tried for children of our own, worked at it, fretted over our barrenness, not realizing until long after that final summer before Webb and Jenny's divorce how Harriet's womb was already covertly carrying the death cells that would ripen and mature and devour her. She told me—after the eventual worst-case diagnosis and the certain futility of treatment— that she'd imagined someday losing a breast to cancer, for it was, after all, a commonplace disease in modern American life, and thousands of women went under the knife to arrest it. "It has to be the price we pay for the advantage of being female," she told me one night when we lay in bed, holding each other tightly in the dark of Nature and of fear. But that this cancer should have originated in the radical center of her— *That,* she said, seemed too cruel, even for a male God.

But all of that came later. That summer of political scandal, there they sat in the hot afternoons, Harriet and Jenny, two handsome women in their prime forties, both inextricable from Webb's and my mutual history, leaving the children for an hour or two to our tipsy oversight. I remember sipping my bourbon and branch, thinking how marvelously sweet the whiskey tasted, how balmy was the soft breeze that blew over us off the pond, how pleasant it was to be able to sit and do nothing, say nothing, think nothing. And hear nothing that wasn't delightful and restful: a distant gargle of outboard motor, the lap of water against shore, the giggling of children.

Neither kid had any need of us—or any use for us, for that

matter. Amanda, I think, was eleven, maybe twelve, and Will a couple of years younger, both of them old enough and experienced enough to be masters of their watery environment. Still, they were never out of our sight, never less than constant figures in our idle visions, especially Webb's. I might have dozed off for a moment or two, but I think Webb's watchfulness never flagged.

He doted on Amanda. That's memorable to me, even at this remote and posthumous place in time. There was always more than blood between them—or so it struck me—as if they were not merely father and daughter but a pair of special friends, who rarely spoke but always understood each other. Every so often, that afternoon, she would abruptly stop what she was doing—trying to catch minnows close to shore, swimming a tireless series of laps from land to the dancing green shadow of the dock, instructing her brother in some arcane pond-lore— and trot across the sand to Webb, stand before him for an instant like an adult passing judgment on the drink in his hand, then unexpectedly lean forward and kiss him on the forehead with a loud, wet smack of her lips. Webb always put on a shocked look; he'd raise his hand to his brow and say, "Am I bleeding?" Amanda, each time, laughed and ran away to resume her childhood. "Isn't she something?" Webb would say to me. And then he would shake his head and take a swallow of Irish. "I wonder what," he would add.

LATER, something in the room brings me awake; when I open my eyes, Prudence is standing beside my bed. There is a certain moon now, and in its eerie light through the windows I can see she is wrapped in the patchwork quilt she lay on earlier this evening. For a confused moment or two I'm more concerned with what woke me than with why Pru is here—wondering if a sound was what penetrated my sleep, or the pressure of moonlight when I turned to face the windows, or was it Pru's scent: of soap or faint perfume.

"What is it?" I say. My voice is caught in my throat and I try again. "What's the matter?"

"I woke up," she says. "I couldn't go back to sleep."

I move away from her to make room so she can sit on the bed. "Do you want to talk?"

"I don't know. I don't know what I want." She sits, hugging the quilt around her. "Yes, I do," she says. "I want Webb."

"I'm sorry."

The room fills—with silence, with her insomnia, with my helplessness. She huddles inside her quilt, rocking slightly, forward and back. Her hair is down; its unruliness hides her face.

"I heard you talking to Mindy—or telling a story," I say. "I couldn't quite hear what it was about."

"It was about Webb, a nonsense thing. Love, loss, God and His jokes. I said almost anything that came into my head, but it seemed to make sense to Mindy."

"Child's intuition?"

"She thinks she can still talk to him." Pru says it softly. "What do you think?"

"To Webb? Talk to him how?"

"The two of them used to play with the Ouija board." She shivers—I can feel it as a tremor in the mattress under me. "I don't know if 'play' is the right word. They talk to an intermediary; I forget his name."

Wait a minute, I want to say, *what kind of nonsense are you teaching her?* Instead, I say, "I don't know anything about the Ouija board. Isn't it a party game?"

"Mindy says they ask questions, and the intermediary—I remember: the name is *Bakkar*—Bakkar asks dead people who know the answers."

"But that's just something she and her father did for fun."

She goes on as if I haven't spoken. "That's the way Mindy put it: 'Bakkar asks the dead people. Bakkar can ask Daddy.' "

She turns to look at me. In the dim light her face is a pale oval, almost featureless, like the moon behind a thin mist.

"I know; it's crazy," she says. The cloud, the screen of her hair, covers the moon of her face.

"Not crazy," I say; I regret that I set out to belittle Mindy. "Wishful thinking, maybe; maybe childish; but not crazy."

She rocks. "Mindy and I had a long talk—earlier, after Terry and I first put her to bed. She's much more matter-of-fact about Webb's dying than I am. She's a strong child—an extra-special child—and she loved Webb, was deeply devoted to him. You know what she said to me?"

"What?"

"She said: 'Nobody dies before they're ready to. Daddy doesn't mind being dead.' "

"Huh," I say. How do you respond to something whose reality seems radically different from your own, radically different from what's considered *usual?* In Baltimore, one night twenty-five years ago, I sat with Webb when he was tripping on a tablespoonful of Pearly Gates morning glory seeds. We were in an all-night diner, talking, drinking coffee. Webb had pulled a paper napkin out of the container at the end of the

table and crumpled it in his hand. For all of five minutes afterward he was entirely attentive to the napkin, raving about it—
how beautiful it was, how intricate the design of it, like a complicated white flower, like the most beautiful pattern of lace
he'd ever seen. Of course I couldn't share the pleasure. If it was
only a cheap paper napkin to me, to him it was high art. I
couldn't get him to throw it away; when we finally left
the diner, he was still holding on to it as if it were a treasure.
Not long afterward the seed companies started spraying chemicals on the three morning glory seed varieties that were
hallucinogenic—Heavenly Blue and Flying Saucer were the
other two—and a damned good move it was, I remember
thinking, having Webb's experience freshly in mind. Let him
throw up a few times, learn a lesson.

"I suppose nobody minds being dead, after it's happened,"
is what I say.

Pru stops rocking. "What did you and Bobby decide
about—" she gropes for words "—about what happens next?"

"Bobby thinks cremation is best."

That's a terrible statement. It lies between us like something
palpable—a stone neither of us can lift, a fog neither of us wants
to breathe. Having uttered it—and having *heard* myself utter it—
I think I've now said enough words to last me my lifetime. If
Prudence Mackenzie refuses ever again to share my insensitive
company, I'll understand perfectly. But she surprises me. "That's
good," she says. "I think that's good. I couldn't bear to think
of Webb in the black ground. The damp and dark. The—the
maggots." She turns her face toward me again. "The upheaval,
when the world ends."

Another surprise—thank you, Webb, for alerting me. None of that stuff—the End of the World, Armageddon, the Last Judgment—would have occurred to me, but possibly it's a facet of Pru only tragedy could have discovered. Part of me wants to be coldly rational and mock her; part of me wants to take her in my arms, and believe, and share all those of her sensibilities that Webb's death has harrowed.

It is as if she reads my mind. "Can I lie here for a while, so I don't have to go back to that empty bed?"

"If you want." I move to the far side of the bed to give her room.

"I'll just sleep on top of the covers," she says.

She lies beside me, a summer blanket and sheet between us, the quilt covering her. She nestles against me; she is so close I can smell her hair, her sweet breath, the perfume left over from her wedding day.

"I'm sorry," she says. "I meant: *may* I lie here for a while."

And then she is asleep. It is a sleep something like a cat's, punctuated with small movements, small sounds like an animal's— all of this connected, I'm sure, to whatever dreams assail her. The only other noise is the intermittent start-up of the refrigerator motor in the kitchen.

I lie beside Pru, staring at the ceiling, the half-drawn shades, the dim shadow of the overhead light fixture. Years ago—we'd bought our first house with a G.I. loan, a tract house barely big enough for the two of us—Harriet asked for new kitchen linoleum. It was a birthday, an anniversary—"some sentimental gift," I remember saying—and two men came early in the day to install it. I was on my way to school. "Where do you work?"

one of the men asked me. "The college," I said. "You teach?" "Yes, English." "Uh-oh," the other one said, "we better watch our language." Instantly we were all strangers, as if in our modern culture it is subversive to speak and be revealed as oneself.

Just before I drop off to sleep, I am struck by the eerie notion that Pru's concern for the proper use of *can* and *may* is only Webb Hartley's vicarious way of ridiculing my profession—my former profession—from beyond the grave.

WHEN I WAKE AGAIN, the room is awash with sunlight, its direct rays pouring through the open window and around the edges of the window shades. The wide floorboards glow almost orange with sun, and the ceiling is mottled with its reflected light. The old-fashioned alarm clock on the nightstand—white hands, white numbers—says it is nearly nine o'clock, and when I remember where I am—and, especially, who is on the bed beside me—I have a sudden vision of Bob and Theresa Hartley bounding up the stairs to find us, and to draw the wrongest-possible conclusion from what they think they see.

I leave the bed carefully, cross the room to the chair under the vivid window, and pull my khaki trousers on. Prudence is still asleep, lying on her back, looking unbearably young. The thin quilt that covers her has gone askew, and her breasts are partly revealed above her nightgown—except that by any conventional standard, even in pregnancy, she has no breasts: only nipples, like a boy. I can't explain why Pru, thus discovered, seems so exciting to me. She is young enough to be the child Harriet and I never had, I remind myself, and perhaps that—

mere youth, which I learned when I was still an untenured instructor is easily confused with beauty—is explanation enough. Whatever, I experience an indictable guiltiness for staring at Pru, and on my way to the bathroom I stop and draw the quilt up to cover her. I think I understand something of Webb's affection for her—and hers for him—how the connections between them must have been made myriad by the space between their generations: lover, father-figure, teacher, friend, worshiper of beauty.

The house is quiet. On the way down from the bathroom I notice that Mindy's bed is empty, and I wonder, idly, where she might be, if her curious precociousness extends to making breakfast for the grownups. I'm reaching for my shoes to finish dressing when I realize Pru is awake, looking at me, the quilt drawn around her to her neck.

"Good morning," she says. "It must be late."

I gesture toward the clock. "Almost nine thirty."

She yawns. "This is the date when night and day are supposed to be the same length," she says. "I think I've slept half of each."

"I think you needed it," I say.

"God," she says. She slumps back against the pillow. "Yesterday wasn't a dream, was it?"

"It was real." I go over to the nightstand on my side of the bed, pick up Webb's letter and stuff it into my back pocket. I sit on the bed. "I didn't see Mindy in my travels," I say.

"This was supposed to be the honeymoon," Pru says. She lowers the quilt and frames her belly with her hands; the thin nightgown makes her just decent. "We were looking forward to the prissy desk clerks." Then she says, "Mindy's all right. She's an early riser, and very self-sufficient. Probably she looked in, saw we were both asleep and went out to the studio to amuse herself."

"What must she have thought of—of us two in the same bed?"

Pru laughs. "You're the answer to the question 'Do men blush?' " She leans over and butts my shoulder gently with her forehead. "She's a bright three year old, but she doesn't think like an adult. She isn't knowledgeable about sex stuff, and even if she were she wouldn't know how to be judgmental. She dismissed us from her mind the moment we were out of her sight."

"I apologize," I say. I probably look as sheepish as I feel.

"Accepted." She launches herself off the bed. "Let me shed this clumsy quilt and I'll try to make us some sort of breakfast."

I sit up in bed to wait for her, re-reading the posthumous letter. I think of how long it's been since I last saw Jennifer Grant Hartley, and of how much has changed in all our lives. I think of what I must do for Webb, and I feel a mix of apprehension and not-unpleasant anticipation. There was the time when I loved Jenny deeply; then there was the period when we were very much on the outs—the three of us went way back, as they say, and long friendships between men and women can get hellishly complicated—followed by the years of truce, the years of distance and reluctant summer mellowing.

When Pru comes down to the kitchen—in the ponytail, fresh blouse, the jeans and tennis shoes, looking like anything but a widow—I replace Webb's letter in its envelope and get into my robe to join her at the table.

"I thought you'd at least have started coffee," she says with mock disapproval. Or possibly the disapproval is real. "Webb made it in the old pot, but I prefer the Chemex." She points. "The coffee and the filters are in the cupboard above. One scoop for each cup. I'll put the kettle on."

Thus am I implicated in breakfast, and only the smile she wears as she orders me about persuades me she is teasing me. I think I can see in her face a faint proof of the bromide that when a man and woman live together, they begin to resemble each other; Pru already has the slightly raised left eyebrow that was Webb's skeptic defense against the world, and I suppose that with Webb dead she will gradually lose that resemblance—that for a time she will put on the anonymous masks of disappointment and grief, and then someone else will enter her life and modify her dear familiar features with his own.

I'm scooping coffee into the filter when she says, "He wants you to tell *her,* doesn't he?" She is putting dark bread into the toaster as she speaks. "I didn't read the letter, but isn't that what he asked you to do? Tell her he's dead?"

"Yes."

"That divorce was a thousand years ago, I know," she says. "But you'd be amazed how particularly Jenny came between us, how she was one of our few subjects for argument."

"I didn't think he stayed in touch with her."

"For a while I think he had to. I think he felt it was an obligation not to lose track of women he'd loved." She turns toward me; what I read in her face is not anger, but a kind of perplexity—as if the subject of Webb's first wife is an irritation whose source can't be got at, an itch that can't be scratched. She closes the cellophane wrapper over the half-loaf of bread, turning it inside out like folding a sock just taken from the drier. "I put toast in for you. I'm just going to have yogurt and a cup of coffee, but I'll make whatever you want. Webb wouldn't have liked me to starve you."

"I'll settle for toast and coffee. I'm not much of a breakfast eater." It's true that since I've been living alone I spend precious little time on meals.

"I'll go out later and see what Mindy would like. I think this glass must be hers, so she's already had orange juice."

She joins me at the table and we wait. When the toast pops up, she goes to butter it while I add water to the Chemex. When the coffee is ready, she puts mugs on the counter for me to fill and opens the refrigerator to get yogurt for herself.

"I could explain to you what it is about Jenny in particular," Pru says. "But I sha'n't. It's just something that dug really deep into both of us, and after a few rather bitter discussions he gradually let go of her—to please me, soothe my feelings, I suppose." She stirs the yogurt, looks up at me across the table. "I'm not naïve. Webb did have a lot of women in his life— you know better than anyone. It wasn't that he loved them; it was more like he *collected* them, seeing how many he could attract."

"Yes," I agree, "I saw that side of him."

"And as he got older—seeing if he still *could* attract them." She takes a sip of my coffee and wrinkles her nose in distaste. "I forgot to tell you 'one for the pot,' " she says.

"Sorry if it's weak."

"But that was Webb. It was so much a part of his nature that I couldn't be angry with him, couldn't let myself be hurt by him. Sometimes I plotted to get even with him, but that was childish. He was so much to me in so many other ways."

"Were they always young? These women?"

"Young like me, you mean." She shook her head and smiled ruefully. "I actually think he preferred them in their late thirties, early forties." She goes to the stove and adds coffee to her mug. "Though his tastes were pretty catholic, age-wise. Was it experience he was after, do you suppose?"

"I don't know."

"But that was one of the reasons I didn't want to get married—remember, I told you it was Webb's idea?"

"Yes."

"I thought it was better that he didn't have a broken vow to contend with, every time some new woman went after him."

"You're very modern," I say. The fact is that I'm both baffled and charmed by Prudence Mackenzie, by how easy she is, as if I had always known her—not merely as an occasional visitor to this place. She seems to me wise for one so young, and I wonder if it is simply that I have forgotten how much more quickly women mature—how slow, how galumphing, men are by comparison. I can't imagine dealing with the world around me as objectively—in so measured and pragmatic a way—as Pru seems to.

"I didn't want us to have a baby, either." She looks at me as if she expects a reaction—and of course I've no idea how she wants me to react, or how I ought to.

"Accidents happen," is what I say, and I can see she's actually amused.

"And repeat themselves," she says. "It's nice that you think

I'm *modern* but you must also think I'm pretty weird. The truth is that in the end I somehow always let Webb persuade me into doing the things I didn't think I wanted to do. Mindy wasn't a mistake, and this brother-to-be isn't either; Webb simply sweet-talked me into getting pregnant—or *argued* me into it; it wasn't terribly sweet. The first time, I tried to remind him that when this baby he was so eager for turned—let's say fifteen—he'd be in his seventies, and how did he think he'd cope with the trau-mas of adolescence as a septuagenarian? He said he was thinking of me, and of *us,* and how with his talent and good looks, and my brains and beauty, it was criminal not to bring a child into the world before the ugly morons crowded us out."

"Webb was nothing if not élitist," I say. "I bet he was pleased you gave him a girl." Of course the image of Amanda— the quick kiss, the pixie-like way she dealt with her father— comes to the front of my mind. Mandy. Mindy. That's no co-incidence, I remind myself.

"You know him," she says. "Speaking of which—" She scrapes the last of the yogurt from the plastic cup. "—I'd better take the breakfast menu out to Mindy."

BY THE TIME Pru comes back from the studio, Bob and Theresa have arrived from their motel. They're both casually dressed, and the casualness transforms them, makes them seem almost likable. Theresa is in jeans and a pink blouse, a stone-washed denim jacket over her arm; her Reeboks are so white as to be stark, and she is wearing a single-strand pearl necklace. Bob is in jeans and blue canvas-tops, and he has on an Amherst sweatshirt.

"Where's Prudence?" is Terry's first question, and she surveys the kitchen and front room as if Pru might be hiding—probably naked, possibly bruised—to conceal the acts, ongoing and unspeakable, I have coerced her into.

"Studio," I say around a mouthful of toast. "With Mindy."

Bob is pouring himself a mug of coffee. "We got off to a late start," he says. "I've been on the phone with old man Curtis."

"Disposing of the body," I say.

He sits across from me, sets Pru's coffee cup aside and raises an eyebrow at me. "That's the general idea," he says, "though I'd have put it a little more delicately."

"I'll be delicate around Pru."

"The good news is that Maine doesn't have any strange and stupid laws about cremation. Nothing that requires the survivors to buy a casket or a cemetery plot as if there was an actual body to be buried."

"Which means Maine's undertakers have a weak lobby," Terry says. Bob and I both give her a perplexed look. She puts up her hands defensively. "I was trying to be funny," she says.

Pru comes in through the pantry. "Oh, good," she says. "That was nice timing. Mindy wants scrambled eggs, so I can offer you two the same." She glances at me. "Alec's already had his breakfast."

"Coffee's enough for me," Bob says. "But why did you make it so weak?"

"Eggs sound good," says Theresa. "Do you have any cottage cheese?" Bob makes a face. "It isn't essential," she says.

"Alec and I think cremation is the best plan," Bob says. "Is that agreeable to you?"

Pru is breaking eggs into the spider, and for a moment her

shoulders stiffen and she holds an empty shell over the pan an instant longer than she needs to.

"I'll leave all of that to you two," she says.

"Good." Bob digs through a batch of papers he's produced from somewhere under his sweatshirt. "I knew you'd say O.K.; I told the people at Curtis to go ahead. They'll ship Webb's body over to Saco this morning."

"Why Saco?" I wonder out loud.

"Crematorium. Laurel Hill, I think they called it. Apparently most funeral homes can't afford the luxury of their own furnaces."

Theresa is watching Pru, and now she gestures at Bob as if to shush him. He looks annoyed.

"Can't we talk about this after breakfast?" Terry says.

"Sorry," Bob says. "Sorry, Pru."

"It's all right." Pru stands with her back to the rest of us, stirring the eggs. "It's probably better to get this all out of the way at once."

"That's what *I* think," Bob says. "Besides, Terry and I ought to be back on the road. If not tomorrow, then the day after. The only thing that really has to be decided is do we want—does *Pru* want—a service of some kind?"

"What are the options?" I ask.

"Wide-open. An old-fashioned church funeral, a modest memorial service at the funeral parlor, a ceremony at the cemetery—"

"With no body?" Pru says. She divides the scrambled eggs between two plates, gives the more generous one to Theresa. "I didn't add salt," she tells Terry.

"It's just one of your options," Bob says. "You don't have to do anything at all, if you don't want to. All I'm saying is that if you want some kind of memorial ritual to remember Webb by, you can have it."

Pru adds salt and pepper to the other plate, then stands uncertainly with it in her hand. "Alec," she says. "Would you take this out to Mindy?" I get up from the table and take the eggs. "Wait," she says. She goes to the refrigerator and brings out a half-pint carton of chocolate milk. "Take this. Tell her it's a special treat for being so patient with us grownups."

I head for the studio, glad to get away from the discussion about memorializing Webb. I've sat here through Bob's dogged insistence on making Webb's corpse our breakfast table topic, and now I'm thinking about the people I've buried during my lifetime. My father and my mother, who died far enough apart to allow me to watch my mother live alone for years—and to give me, it occurs to me now, some kind of insight into what Pru may expect if the worst happens, if she determines to love Webb forever and patiently refuses to remarry; my wife, whose service I neglected to attend, out of despair and guilt and a general anger—like today's—at the way we are obliged to dispose of death; a close friend and colleague at my sometime university—a suicide whose life I have always imagined I could have saved if I had been paying attention to the things he confided to me when we drank together.

Behind me I hear Pru telling Bob what she wants. "I think we don't have to do any kind of ritual to remember his death by. Jesus Christ, we all stood there and watched it happen. It's a wonder we don't have eight-by-ten glossy photographs."

————

WHEN THERESA BROUGHT MINDY HOME last night, I scarcely saw her. She was asleep in her aunt's arms, her head on Terry's shoulder, and all I could see was a small, sweet face—eyes closed, cheeks flushed, thumb in mouth—inside an unruly frame of reddish-blond hair, wispy and curly and angelic. I can put that together with my imperfect recollection of the toddler I saw two years ago, topless beside her father, with the same auburn hair like a halo; with huge curious eyes that turned out to be green, like her mother's, and that watched everything with a cool curiosity appropriate to the prodigy she has by all accounts become; with a touchingly usual, unsteady child's body, thin armed and swaybacked and bowlegged. A baby girl, dependent on Daddy. What will she be now—an ancient of three-plus years?

The studio is awash with sunlight that streams through the east windows. In the center of the speckled floor sits Mindy—*Melinda Joanne Hartley;* I remember that her birth announcement, designed by Webb, had been a collision of the symbols for male and female, respectively black and scarlet, with a second female sign emerging from the mix in an aura of ethereal pink. She looks ordinary enough. Pru has dressed her—or she has dressed herself—in red corduroy overalls and a white cotton shirt; her sunlit hair is caught back in a red barrette; she is barefoot and entirely preoccupied. Around her on the floor are an array of crayons, the Ouija board, several sheets of colored construction paper. Her right hand is on the board, making lazy circles over its surface, stopping at different letters of the alphabet. When her hand stops moving for good, she uses one of the crayons to print a word in large block letters on a sheet of the paper.

"It's breakfast time," I say. "Where do you want me to put it?"

"Just a minute," she says. She finishes printing her letters—they spell N-E-V-E-R—and puts down the crayon. "I'm talking to Daddy."

"Are you really ?" I kneel beside her, balancing the eggs and the milk carton. "I wasn't sure if I could believe it when your mother told me that's what you were doing."

She looks at me, squinting against the sunshine. The squint reminds me of Webb; the green eyes are indeed her mother's. "That's what I'm doing," she says. "It isn't really Daddy who answers the questions. It's Bakkar who gets the answers for me."

"Is that so?" I wonder if she understands my skepticism.

"Bakkar is the medium," she says. "He spells the words Daddy sends me."

"How do you know Bakkar is a he?"

She shrugs her small shoulders. "That's what I *think,* but I don't know for sure."

Being closer to her level, closer to the board, I can see that the pointer she is using seems to be a plastic guitar pick. "Don't you have a whatchamacallit? A planchette?"

"That's too heavy for me when I play by myself. I use Daddy's banjo picker."

"Oh."

She slides a low stool toward me. "You can put the plate here," she says. "Is that chocolate milk?"

"I guess your mother thought you'd like a treat."

"That's nice." She sets the milk on the floor beside her. "Do you want me to ask a question for you?"

"A question for your father?"

"You don't *have* to."

I ponder—not what question to ask, but what fantasy of this child's I'll be feeding if I pretend to believe what she believes. I've seen adults, people old enough to know better, play this game at parties, and to the extent they have really seemed convinced they were communicating with another dimension, I pitied them for their gullibility. But Mindy is too young—surely she is—to have the adult resource of reason. If I humor her, will she grow up to be like the pitiable party crowds? Is this like encouraging a belief in Santa Claus? Or is this a problem not even worth my wrestling with? After all, this is only a little girl who misses her dead father.

"Ask him what's the worst thing about being dead," I say. At least I'm not pussyfooting around the fact of death. I didn't say *What's the worst thing about being with the angels?*

"O.K.," she says. She asks the question; the pick under her fingers seems to move, carrying her tiny hand up across the arc of letters, around and around, until it stops at a *T*—not a long stop, but a pause pronounced enough to let a player read the letter—then resumes its circles to the next letter. *E*. In spite of myself, I'm fascinated—not because I believe an unseen power is moving the pointer, but because it's clear that Mindy already has an answer in mind and I wonder what it is, how she arrived at it, how has the fact of her father's death occupied her thoughts. Now another *E*. I've already seen that Mindy doesn't copy the letters as they come, but waits until the message is finished. One more evidence that she knows what the answer will be. A second *T*.

The pointer moves for a long time, and when I finally understand what the word is going to be, I'm amused. It sounds like Webb; it tells me his daughter is heir to his sense of humor.

Mindy prints it out with red crayon on a sheet of yellow paper: *T-E-E-T-O-T-A-L-I-N-G.*

"The worst thing about being dead is teetotaling," I say. "That sounds like your father."

"Does it? What does it mean?"

She seems genuinely perplexed, studying the word she has put down on the paper.

"It means not having anything to drink. No whiskey."

She grins at me—tiny, even teeth, delighted eyes, a baby's face alive with pleasure. "That *does* sound like Daddy," she says.

ALL MORNING LONG, Bob and Theresa and Pru hash over the question of how to commemorate Webb's dying, and at last Pru prevails: they decide to do nothing—no hollow funeral, no formal remembrance, nothing maudlin and mocking that will only make everyone miserable. The ashes will be sent to Pru; she will decide whether to scatter them or save them or flush them down the john; she says she will consult with Mindy, who has a knack for accommodating herself to such illogical problems. I believe it.

Or do I? I believe *something*. Squatting beside Mindy while she made words from the movement of her makeshift planchette—seeing the intensity of concentration on her small features and realizing that it reflected the kind of innocent trust that makes religion more than mumbo jumbo—I found myself thinking: *Could she contact Harriet?* It was only a momentary thought, but there it was, undeniable, undisownable. And what would I have asked, what question relayed through Mindy's androgynous Bakkar? My wife has been dead nearly ten years, and for ten years before that we had less and less to say to each other. Harriet was already ill; the first shadow of cancer had shown up in her vitals, and a year later came the first surgery that was supposed to—and didn't—*get it all*. I suppose I didn't know what to say to her, that if someone had told me what were the magic words I might pronounce to save her life, I surely would have said them. Not knowing them, it was as if I were simply tongue-tied, a man who made his living off language but could not to save his soul—to save *her* soul—apply that language to the life it was intended to represent. If I could say something today across whatever geography separates the living from the dead—and if the dead have feelings—I can imagine the sarcasm Harriet must have saved up for me.

But that's the other world, the world that perhaps exists only in the way the past exists—as history, which like the possibility of an afterlife becomes the creature of our imaginations—our selfish imaginations that excuse and castigate ourselves. *This* world—now—is as real as it can be, and it finds me sitting at the heavy kitchen table while Pru goes about cleaning up the last of the ill-fated reception. Robert and Theresa have already left—"I don't see any point in hanging around, since there's no memorial service," Terry said; she was almost petulant, almost pouting, as if Webb's death were not finished to her taste—and I'm already wondering what to do about a flight from Logan that will land me in Santa Barbara.

Pru—with some help from me—has worried the cut-crystal punch bowl from the pantry to the kitchen counter beside the sink. Half full of punch, it reminded me of emptying the drip pan under my grandmother's icebox, the liquid moving like the tide, drawing me off balance first left, then right.

"Unless I hear a strong vote to the contrary," she says, "I'm just going to dump it down the drain."

"I tasted it last night," I say. "It's pretty sweet stuff."

She tips the bowl, slowly and a little bit gingerly, over the sink. The punch is brownish-yellow, smells fruity even from where I'm sitting, and hisses in the drain. "Let the fish of the Piscataqua get drunk as skunks," Pru says.

"They'll get sick before they get drunk."

She smiles. "Probably." She watches the last of the punch foam away, sets the bowl into the sink and runs water into it from the tap. "It was Terry's recipe. She was in here adding more vodka while Webb was collapsing."

She tears a paper towel from the roll over the sink and wipes her hands.

"Yesterday," she says. She sits across the table from me. "It's amazing how dreamlike it all seems—like a movie I saw once, or like a book I imagined while I was reading it."

"That makes things manageable," I say. I suppose that's true; it's the way I see Harriet's dying: like a scene from an opera—something Italian, too sentimental for tears.

"I wonder." She puts her hands over her eyes for a moment,

then lowers them and shakes her head like someone who doesn't believe what's she's seen. "God," she says.

"Mindy's got it figured out. You're right: she's still talking to him."

"The Ouija. Yes. She and Webb played with the board for hours in the evening before I put her to bed. I suppose she doesn't bother to make distinctions between here and *there*."

"I don't quite know what to make of her," I say.

"No, neither do I," Pru says. "But I don't make fun of her. I tell myself that she and Webb have been having a nonstop dialogue for more than two years, so why should it end now?"

Again I think of Harriet—of that longtime partner Webb's death has made more real for me—and I remember one of our first weekends after we married, the two of us in bed, holding desperately on to each other as if we already had a premonition of the impossibility of spending a full life together. We were confessing our deepest fears; Harriet believed that all the words spoken on earth lasted forever, and she was afraid that when she died she might not be truly dead—that her soul, "or whatever you want to call it," would drift through the universe until the end of time, obliged to listen to those voices, to hear not only every human's sweet declarations of love and cries of happiness, but all their expressions of agony, of pain and loss, of doubt and terror. "Could there be a better definition of Hell?" she wanted to know. "But that's a physical impossibility," I told her. "Sound needs air—molecules—to carry it. In an empty universe there's nothing but silence." "You can't talk about 'physical' impossibility," she said. "We won't *be* physical." How could I argue with that?

"Webb's griping that there's nothing to drink where he is," I tell Pru.

"Is that what Mindy asked him?"

"On my behalf. I asked him what was the worst thing about being dead."

"He should have said, 'Leaving Prudence.'" She gets up from the table. "Coffee? I made a fresh pot; it's a little more like the real thing."

"Sure."

"They were quite a pair," she says. "Actually Mindy's spent far more time with Webb than with me." She sets the mug in front of me, sits down again with her own coffee. "I got to tell the bedtime stories, because Webb was usually asleep after a couple of drinks, but her first word, her first sentence, her first *concept*—if I can say that about a baby—came while she was with him. I always got in on the replay." She looks at me, green eyes glistening, lower lip trembling for a moment. "I'm not complaining. He was dedicated to her."

"That's clear," I say.

"I can even tell you exactly when it started. It started when I went back to work and Webb had to do the baby-sitting. He'd carry Mindy out to the studio in the morning—you know: baby in one hand, coffee in the other—and he'd plop her down on a blanket while he went to work."

"How old was she then?"

"Oh, God—I went back to the bookstore full-time when she was five months. She was talking at nine months—that's not super-unusual—but she had Webb there, and she turned into a really incredible, really eloquent child."

"Only because of Webb?"

"I'm sure." She looks down; it's as if she's looking into a past she didn't actually see: Webb and Mindy in the studio, the light through the skylight descending the wall until it lit the child's golden hair, then climbing again as the afternoon wore on. Webb engrossed in his canvas; Mindy batting at blocks and soft animals; Webb and Mindy consorting when he paused at his work.

"He talked *to* her at first, then *with* her. Once in a while I'd come home early in the afternoon, or come home for lunch. I'd go into the studio, tippy-toe, and watch them. Sometimes they'd be on the blanket together, Webb talking, Mindy— I don't know. Making noises that after a while began to sound like real words. And finally they were."

"Attention," I say. "The presence of another person."

"More than that," Pru says. "If you live alone—and I did for a long time—you talk to pets, you know? God knows *I* did, to this cat I had in Somerville. But we weren't— We weren't *engaged* with each other. There was no give-and-take, no sharing."

"You don't like catnip?"

"Don't poke fun. I think that makes a difference."

"That Webb shared her play?"

"Well, you know Webb, what a kid he was at heart. It was never a case of an adult simply tolerating a child's babble, or an adult saying words so the child would have the illusion she was being taken seriously. And it was a lot more than Ouija. Webb wasn't playing games with a pet; he was always *relating*. He'd stop what he was doing and sit on the floor beside her, and they'd play with blocks, or those bright-colored papers she's crazy about, or the picture books he was always bringing home from secondhand stores—those old-fashioned cloth things you hardly see anymore, and dog-eared volumes on astrology and how to read palms and tea leaves. And he was a whiz at pretend. He loved being the make-believe father of a stuffed monkey, but best of all he loved playing teacher. He'd ask her questions—and he'd insist on sensible answers. In the beginning, sometimes I'd say, 'My God, Webb, she's only a baby,' and he'd say, 'She's got a mind, hasn't she?' "

"You didn't approve?"

"Oh no, I did approve—but I worried he was pushing her too hard, too fast."

"She does seem remarkable."

"Well—" Pru looks in the direction of the pantry as if Mindy might suddenly materialize and overhear. "The truth is, she's not so remarkable as she was a year ago, or two years ago. Nowadays she seems fairly normal to me. But maybe I'm just used to her gift of gab."

"Either way, I bet she'll be a handful for you," I say.

For a moment she appears startled; then she grins in spite of herself. "I know," she says. "I wish she'd write a symphony or something." She reaches across the table and catches my right hand in hers. "But I'll survive," she says, "and so will we all."

So abrupt a gesture. I imagine she is including Jennifer in her scheme of survival, and I wonder how confident she would be if she knew all of the complex history that connects me with Webb's first wife. I wonder if she understands that the complexity of the history is in large part what accounts for my willingness to leave Scoggin—and poor Pru—in such selfish haste.

THAT AFTERNOON I sit on the front porch with the phone book open in my lap to the yellow pages, looking to make arrangements to fly to California, to carry the news to Jennifer. Pru emerges from the house and puts a glass of lemonade into my hand.

"Mindy's down for a nap," she says. She settles into the rocker and sighs. "Though whether or not she'll sleep in this heat wave is another story."

"Indian Summer," I say.

"What?"

"That's what Harriet would have called weather like today's. It's autumn; she wouldn't consider this a heat wave."

Pru smiles and sips her own lemonade. She scarcely looks pregnant. She's wearing a white t-shirt and faded blue cutoffs and dirty tennis shoes without socks. The top button of the cutoffs is unfastened—the only outward sign of Webb's baby growing slowly toward life and light.

She sets the glass on the porch beside her chair and takes up a magazine from a pile on the table between us. "Do you still miss her?" she says.

"Harriet?" I wonder if that's the proper verb. "I don't think I 'miss' her in the sense that I feel a gap, an absence, in my everyday life. Once in a while something happens, or someone says something, that reminds me I had a wife once."

"How long ago?"

I have to think. "She died not quite ten years ago. Ten years in November."

"And things still remind you," Pru says. She looks sad and meditative, not reading her magazine but seeming to watch a family of grackles waddling at the end of the driveway. "I wonder if I'll still be remembering Webster ten years from now—my God, in the twenty-first century."

"Probably, now and then."

"*Two thousand three*," she says. "You saw it on the late show; now live in it." Her eyes glisten; she looks away from me.

"It won't be so bad," I say.

And perhaps it won't. Pru is a lovely young woman; in ten years she'll be in her early forties, she'll have grown into her beauty, surely she'll have found a worthy—faithful—man to love her and her children. She'll forget Webb—he'd be a doddering seventy-two years old by then anyway—and, probably, me.

This last realization shakes me. It's as if I feel I have a claim on her, as if by sharing her grief with me she has become mine in some elusive way—some way in which I am not entirely a disinterested friend, but merely a man, drawn to a pretty woman, a hurt woman. Damsel in distress; white knight to the rescue; the savior absorbing strength and youth from the saved. I watch Pru mastering this latest wave of misery, turning to smile bravely at me.

"Wow," she says. "It's like the old morning sickness, except it wears black."

"It fades," I say.

"It better." She flops open the magazine with a gesture of real intention. "What are *you* reading?"

"The phone directory. The sooner I book a flight to California, the sooner I'll satisfy whatever it is I owe Webb."

"And the sooner you'll come back."

I must look as surprised as I feel, for Pru puts her magazine aside and leans forward, her face serious.

"Please come back here," she says. There is real intensity in the words. "I don't know if you were planning to or not. Maybe you want to get home to the Midwest. But I don't care about that. I need somebody—just for a while. Just to be here, to help me adjust, to get over this thing."

"I could," I say. "But you ought to call a friend—maybe a close woman friend—who'd be more useful than me."

"We never had any friends to speak of. Tim Weems—the town librarian—but he's barely an acquaintance. Edith at the bookshop, but no *real* women friends. Nobody I'd want to stay with me."

"Parents?"

"Especially not parents." She reaches across the table and rests her right hand on my wrist. "Robert's taken care of the legal stuff, the practical stuff. You can have your usual room. You can take care of whatever's left of me. The sick heart," she says, "the guilty dreams."

I STAY AT THE FARM for almost a week, and by the time I'm obliged to leave for the airport I think I'm half in love with Prudence Mackenzie—perhaps more than half. My few days with the two females—one the proper age for my daughter, the other for my granddaughter—are like a rare holiday, a vacation

from responsibilities and judgments. I become almost comfortable with Pru's cutoffs, almost accustomed to her long bare legs,
almost fond of the belly that contains her baby.

I even get used to Mindy—her seriousness, the habit she has
of asking questions one on top of another, as if real truth lies
only at the last link of an exceedingly long chain. We play
checkers together, and then double solitaire, and finally I teach
her to play cribbage because it is the only game I believe will
give me the advantage over her. Even here she is consistently a
winner, intent and ruthless, with an apparent instinct for playing
the right card. Time after time I hear myself saying, "Well, why
didn't you play your seven *first* so I could have made something
out of my eight?" or, "How in the world did you know not
to play the five before the queen?" It's only on the last morning
of my stay that I learn the answers.

"It seems to me," Mindy says offhandedly, "you'd play better if you didn't wear glasses."

"What makes you say that?"

"People can read the cards in your lenses," she says—this,
while she is putting away the deck.

"People?" I say.

"People like me," she says.

"That's cheating, isn't it?"

She puts both hands into her hair and piles it on the very
top of her head; a red bow-ribbon catches between her fingers
and she brings it down to look at it, her lower lip held for a
moment under her teeth.

"Probably it is," she says.

THE DAY I LEAVE, I carry a last vision away with me, just before I toss my suitcase into the rental car and start the trip to Logan.

It is late afternoon of another day that has turned out to be unseasonably warm. As I close up my suitcase, I look out one of the windows of the bedroom where I have slept—where I read Webb's letter, where Pru lay chastely beside me on that first night—and I see Mindy, playing on the circle of grass where the driveway curves out to the road. She is nude, her skin pale with just a trace of an even paler criss-cross of bathing suit visible between her shoulder blades. Pru has turned on a sprinkler in the center of this tiny lawn, and Mindy is running into the circling water jets, then running away from them, laughing with a high sound that seems from my high perch almost like music. On one of her flights to the edge of the circle, she stops and crouches slightly, and then she urinates—a thin, glittering arc that splashes into the grass. It is a vision perfectly childish, perfectly innocent, and it gives me hope that she's not such a prodigy after all.

t w o

■

WHEN WEBB AND I were first at Bowdoin, it was 1949
and the world was different. There were veterans of World War
Two on campus, and I suppose as much "teaching" took place
outside our classes as in. It was difficult at eighteen to consider
death a serious matter, yet here were men in their early twenties
who had already confronted it as a fact, who had lived to tell
us about its closeness and realness—the face it wore, the smell
it carried, the overwhelming weight and the terrible colors of
it. One of my fraternity brothers had been caught up in the

Battle of the Bulge, that last desperate winter of the war in
Europe, and suffered frostbite so harsh that he had lost several
of his toes and walked forever after in a peculiar rolling gait
that made him look as if he ought to be snapping his fingers to
the rhythm of his dancing feet. Another appeared to be in a
state of continuous shock, wild-eyed and slow of speech and
capable of an immobility bordering on catatonia. One night
over a bottle of whiskey in the depths of the Chi Psi bar he
told us about serving with a marine unit on Guadalcanal, and
how he was ordered into the jungle as a sniper, to murder a
navy pilot held prisoner by the Japanese; the pilot had been tied
to a tree for days, was being starved and systematically
tortured—"I put the poor bastard out of his misery," the ex-
marine told us in his measured monotone. "One bullet in the
brain from seventy-five yards." My first-semester roommate in
Winthrop Hall was an air corps pilot who had been shot down
over France and was held in a German prisoner-of-war camp
until the war's end. He was a senior and an Independent, good-
looking and cocky, who treated everything I ever said to him
with an unconcealed skepticism that made me feel I had been
born unreliable—that I was somehow innately untrustworthy.

They were none of them like us, those veterans. They had
served in the war we were too young for—the war we had
followed only by the maps we tacked up on our bedroom walls,
by the pictures of warplanes and the portraits of famous generals
we clipped from magazines and Sunday supplements. At best,
the war was movies. We were innocents, trying in our college
lives to invent our own passably—and of course manageably—
evil world. We were frivolous, we were girl-crazy, we were all-

around silly drunks. We bought benches identical to the benches in the town park, and carried them through the streets after dark until the local police arrested us—then produced bills of sale and threatened to sue for false arrest. We met our Seven-Sisters girlfriends at the Brunswick train station and lay with them in rooms at the Hotel Eagle or in rumpled upstairs beds at the fraternity houses; lay naked together all night, Did Everything But, and could scarcely imagine actual copulation—the exception to that rule being the fortunate couples who were already engaged to be married. "Quaint honor," as a poet in our freshman English reader once pointed out. On weekends—these were the days, the years, before the college admitted women either as students or faculty—you'd see young men stumbling across campus under the school's famous pines, carrying glasses that turned out to hold a mixture of lab alcohol and orange juice.

Through it all, Webb and I were inseparable, as we had been since the first day we met in Ogunquit two years earlier—both of us kitchen help at the Cliff House, a resort within easy walking distance of the pliant girls of another hotel named Sparhawk Hall. Webb was the leader, I was the follower. He taught me to drink, he demonstrated hypnotism for my benefit, he advised me on buying my first prophylactics. When he proposed breaking into the college Selective Service offices to steal blank draft registration cards, I helped boost him through the window and stood lookout. We were twin beings. I even signed up for an art history course with Webb, imagining as I looked at one slide after another that I might become a connoisseur and a collector. *Nine hours a year,* I say to myself; I probably looked at as many paintings in that one semester as I have looked at in the rest of my life since then—and in a way I'm relieved that Webb isn't alive to heap still more scorn on my guilty head.

All this runs through my thoughts as the DC-10 drones toward Los Angeles, the twilight at this high altitude making the universe seem bodiless and starless, the cloud cover below us so uniform there might as well be no land to return to.

I almost wish it.

By the time Webb and I lived together in Baltimore, years had passed. We had both enlisted in the air force when the Korean thing came along—not the kind of war we had dreamed of in our teens, but the only one available—and we had both been assigned to Language School. I had wanted to be an A&E mechanic, wise about aircraft and engines—if they wouldn't let me fly, at least they could let me be near the flying machines— but by the luck of the draw, I was picked to study Russian at Syracuse; deliberately, Webb chose to go to Yale for Chinese because he was taken by the calligraphy, the graceful ideograms. I served in Germany; Webb was sent to Japan. What would have happened to us if we had been stationed together is impossible to know, but I imagine we would have ended our military careers disastrously. Without Webb's lead to follow, I became more settled, more inclined to sense. While my comrades in arms drank in the local Gasthauses, I stayed in the barracks and settled for a bottle of Tuborg and a book from the Special Services library, surrounded by The Finer Things. I shared a room with H. Wallingford Bradley, a Floridian, who introduced me to such singers as Greta Keller and Lotte Lenya, Mabel Mercer and Hugh Shannon; who taught me to make

Martinis; who let me use his MG-TD whenever he was on duty and I was on break. Wally was offering me civilization, and though I was no perfect pupil, his lessons changed me and my appetites.

I also fell in love, and *that* changed me too. For most of my last year in Germany—until her tour was up and she returned to the States—I dated the Special Services librarian who recommended titles for me to take back to my barracks room. She was a year older than I was—a quiet, auburn-haired woman with hazel eyes and a high forehead and a pretty mouth with dimples at each corner. I remember seeing her one summer evening outside the library in her taupe-colored trench coat and black heels, the blue overseas cap jaunty on her head, waiting for the military bus that would take her home to her apartment house; she looked small and self-assured and so beautiful across the benign distance between us that I felt my knees turn liquid under me. That was the first time I realized I was probably in love with Jennifer Grant.

I'M RARELY FORTUNATE in the matter of traveling companions. Webb Hartley, whenever he talked to me at the end of some airline trip he'd taken, was full of stories of stunning women, or rich women, or exciting women who'd sat beside him on the flight. If neither he nor the woman was making a connection—and if she wasn't being met by a husband or a fiancé or a boyfriend, though there were times when even that circumstance didn't matter—they usually ended up spending a night together, a night whose details Webb would recite to me with great energy and humor. Women were his avocation, as painting was his calling; I don't believe it was within his powers to conceive of a relationship between a man and a woman that could not be consummated—indeed, that did not *require* consummation. Even in the adolescent days when we were doing dishes together at the Cliff House, Webb's definition of "Platonic" was already "play for him; tonic for her." It was a high-school joke that propelled him through dalliances and affairs and marriages at a pace that seemed to have slowed only with his meeting Pru, though what she said to me in the farmhouse in Scoggin made it clear it hadn't entirely stopped. "A man has to keep on doing what he does best," he told me once. "That's the only happiness life has for us on Earth."

He was especially adept at taking women away from men they were already attached to. He told me, for instance, of sitting across the aisle from a man in his forties—"a salesman of some kind"—and a woman in her late twenties—"with marvelous shimmery black hair drawn back into a French knot"—and of their talk and actions: "She was the one who'd struck up the conversation—the what-do-you-do?, the where-are-you-from? and all that—and she was the one whose body language was saying aren't-I-worth-noticing? and don't-I-interest-you? and don't-you-want-me? It was a long flight, remember—Seattle to Boston—and I've got to say she made it a fascinating one for the voyeur in me. The woman was pure delight. She played with her earrings—they were gold rings, great circles at the end of gold chains, she did pouty things with her mouth, she stretched, she crossed her legs, very slowly and gracefully, turning her knees in his direction across the empty seat between them. Once she went to the restroom, and when she came back she'd let down her hair—undone the braid and let it flow over her shoulders like a shawl. She was seducing him—no question about that—and all the while the talk was about his job, whatever it was he was selling to make a living, his most recent big commission. Nothing about herself; she was going to be the enigma, the private one, the mysterious and therefore the more desirable. I don't doubt he knew he was being seduced, and that he was willing—I heard him raise the possibility of dinner for two when the plane landed—but he was going about it so damned badly. I felt sorry for him.

"It's a mirror dance, don't you think? The woman does something; the man follows. For every word or gesture *she* puts forth, *he* supplies an echo—he reciprocates. The man can't ignore the woman's lead, because he can't take the lead away from her until he's fallen into the rhythm of *her* dance. This salesman—God knows how he could be making a living at selling; I guarantee he's already unemployed—this salesman was too self-involved to follow all the wonderful little things she was doing; she even went through the ritual of taking off her earrings, tucking them into her purse—Christ, she was *undressing* for him in public! But by the time he got around to mentioning dinner, I could see she'd already written him off. When he went to the john—Jesus, *finally*—I slid over and chatted with her until he came back. If looks could kill, right? Then, when I saw her again at the baggage claim, we decided to have dinner at Zuber's. We had a wonderful night; she was an extraordinary woman."

Webb was always sincere about his encounters: through his

eyes the women were truly remarkable, their charms perfectly arresting, their gestures ballet itself. Even his empathy for the men whose clumsiness interfered with conquest—that too was genuine. If I remember his words, his stories so vividly, perhaps it's because envy makes us attentive.

Or perhaps it's because while I was sitting in my window seat at Logan—my thoughts on Webb as I knew him, the huge plane filling up—a blond-haired, sweet-faced girl, perhaps twelve or thirteen years old, appeared in the aisle beside me, shoved a bright red backpack under the seat ahead, and plopped down next to me. "Tanagers," Webb would have said if he were alive. "Curious baby birds."

But I am not Webb, and though since her appearance the girl and I have been having a lively conversation about boarding schools she has attended in the East and about the difference between American Airlines—which we are on—and United— which the girl prefers—and about music groups I have never heard of, but which she is enthusiastic about, and though I buy her a Diet Coke to drink with her chicken-pie dinner, eventually she excuses herself from my boring company and tilts her seat back so she can nap. I'm left to myself in the dusky silence, free to watch shadows flickering on the movie screen at the front of the cabin and, from time to time, to glance at the girl's delicate profile as she dozes. Webb's advice from beyond the grave about mirror dancing does not apply to me, and it would appear that my seatmate—her name is Esther—is not to be the kind of adventure that for Webb, accustomed to a daughter, might have been as perversely simple as simple can be.

I SHOULD HAVE LEARNED from Webb never to under-
estimate Destiny's inventiveness. When this Esther stretches and
yawns and lets her seat forward, the plane already beginning its
descent into Los Angeles, she is even more talkative than before.
She combs her hair as she chats with me, tells me she has a
brother in Sacramento and another brother at Stanford, confesses
that her parents are divorced—she lives with her mother; her
father owns a motel chain in the East—says that she is on her
way home to Santa Barbara. When I ask if she is booked on
the same commuter flight I'm scheduled for, she fumbles in a
pocket of her backpack to find her ticket and seems pleased to
discover that she is. We are over the city. It is not long after
dark; the sun is gone, but from our altitude the edge of the
world lies under a strange and beautiful orange light that probably comes from the city's famous pollutions. I am amazed and
dazzled by the lights that seem to reach to every horizon—as
many lights on the ground below us as there will be stars in the
darkening sky—a shimmering sprawl that makes me glad I'm
not obliged to live here.

"It looks godawfully crowded," I say to Esther.

"It is," she agrees.

"And all those cars."

"There have to be a lot of cars. Everything's so far away
from everything else."

"I know," I say. "The freeways must be a pain in the neck."

"I love cars," Esther says. "I can't wait to drive."

She is leaning forward and across me, looking out the window at the city as it rises to meet us. Her face is curtained by
the fall of her long blond hair; it smells like summer—earth and
vegetation and flower gardens—and she brushes it back with a

graceful gesture of her right hand as we talk. It is as if she needs
to see my words as well as hear them, and I wonder what curious rapport the two of us unexpectedly may have as the plane
lands. She is a child, but a woman child. I find that I'm out-
rageously aware of her as a sexual being—not only the perfume
of her, but her warmth, her *liveness,* an animal identity artless
yet already potent—and in the fleeting instant of being on the
edge of arousal I say to myself *What is wrong with you?* and I
try to turn my thoughts away to some harmless—some *neutral*—
concern. I wonder if Webb has been corrupting me for as long
as I have known him, like a Borgia feeding me larger and larger
doses of a debilitating poison, and if this present shameful attraction to Esther is one of the consequences. Gliding over the
shimmer of Los Angeles I think about the stories of film people
and country singers and powerful politicians in thrall to their
teen-aged mistresses. I think of a photograph I once saw in a
slick-paper conservation magazine, of a tree in California alive
with hundreds of literal tanagers, the limbs brilliant with yellow
birds, and how I was reminded then, crazily, of Webb's nickname for teenagers, and of all the random women of all ages
who flitted in and out of his life. I think what relief I feel when
the DC-10 makes contact with the runway and Esther sinks
back into her seat away from me.

What was it I envied in Webb, coveted in his behavior?
When I glance again at Esther, surreptitiously, as if I'd rather
not be caught looking, I see a child's profile, a child's clear
forehead and soft chin and too-full mouth, a child's bored impatience with the long taxiing to our eventual gate. I see a
child's feet—in fancy sneakers decorated green and black—

propped on her bright red backpack, and a child's small hands whose fingers beat idle time against her denim-covered thighs. I am back to normal, a responsible adult. What Webb would have seen, what he'd have instantly understood, I can only guess: some subtle sexuality, untapped, unthought of; some fresh beauty on the threshold of blossom, some fragile elegance only an artist—who else but Webb?—could coax to life. When we lived in Baltimore he was invited once to a meeting of Girl Scouts. He was the guest artist, instructing, advising, showing off by doing quick pencil sketches of the troop, and he came back to the apartment in a state of sad rapture. "Mothers and daughters," he said. "The big-eyed daughters, the wise-eyed mothers; the owls who know their disappointments, the day-birds who can't wait to learn them."

"I have to call my mother," Esther says. "To make sure she'll meet me. Is somebody meeting you?"

"No," I say. "I'm renting a car at the airport."

"Don't you have friends in Santa Barbara?"

"Not really. I'm going to look up an old acquaintance, a woman I haven't seen in twenty years."

She looks at me, thoughtful, pondering—or so I imagine—the dimensions of twenty years. "I'll bet she's a *paramour* you wish you'd never left," she says.

I have to laugh at the word. "No," I say. "She married my best friend, and that was fine with me." Half-true.

"So where will you stay?"

"I'll find a motel."

"I bet you could stay with us," she says. "We've got plenty of room."

"That's kind of you," I say, "but I think that would be an imposition."

"I suppose," she says.

We share a brief silence, a conversational impasse, while the plane moves closer to the terminal. I lean my head against the window; the runway lights glide past, green and blue and red. Not that I'm fond of motels; they seem to me the most inhospitable of hospitalities, and in the years since Harriet died they are the places where insomnia attacks me, so that I leave the television turned on all night, sleep only fitfully, and wake in the mornings to the image of muscular young women doing aerobics on vacant beaches.

"Do you like California?" Esther asks.

"I've been here just once before. I don't have enough evidence to answer the question."

She crosses her arms across her chest and puts out her lower lip. "I hate it," she says. "My dad lives in Boston and has a summer place on Martha's Vineyard. I like Massachusetts."

"So do I."

"California has no seasons," she says, and it is her last pronouncement until after we have arrived at the gate and crowded our way to the terminal.

B Y   T H E   T I M E Webb and I returned to Bowdoin in the fall of 1956, the whole world had changed, had entered upon an uneasy equilibrium in which nothing was happening but anything *might* happen. Everything political and social seemed to be in stasis. Korea, the occasion for our wearing America's uni-

form, was settled the way you settle most fights between brothers: you separate them by physical force and hold them at arm's
length from each other. The same with our dealings with Russia
and Sovietized Europe: a constant circling, but no blows struck.
Africa and China and Latin America weren't yet even on the
maps of our consciousness. Webb and I weren't warriors in the
way the veterans of World War Two had been: we wore our
fatigue jackets in cold weather; for a while we kept our dog
tags around our necks—Webb and I had not only consecutive
serial numbers, but the same B-positive blood type; we invented
the best war stories we could.

"We used to sit around in the barracks and drink beer and
argue about preëmptive strikes against the Soviet Union." This
was me, talking with Webb that last September back in
Brunswick—still drinking beer, but in a McKeen Street apartment instead of a barracks. "It seemed perfectly reasonable at
the time."

"Oh, sure," Webb agreed. "We had the bomb; they didn't,
but they were working on it. Why not get them before they
got us?"

"Exactly."

Webb shook his head as if he couldn't believe either one of
us. "What bloodthirsty bastards we were in those days."

"It was only three years ago," I said.

"Bloodthirsty," he repeated.

"War lovers," I said.

"Speaking of which—" He took a long drink from his Narragansett bottle. "Tell me again how you broke your cherry in
Germany."

It was true of Webb when he was young that he could never let well enough alone, and so my confessing to him how, at the late age of twenty-three, I had finally lost my virginity to a woman I met in a bar in Bremerhaven was a bad mistake; he brought it up at every opportunity, on any pretext. "Tell it, Alec," he'd say. "I need cheering up." I think what delighted him was the naïveté I'd brought to the event—how innocent I was, how by Webb's definition I had been "taken in" by the woman. "There are some things I can't repeat in front of Alec," he'd say to a date, some gaunt creature from Bennington or Skidmore. "He's led a sheltered life."

But Erika had not been a happy experience for me. Webb couldn't understand such a thing; for him in those days all sex was pleasurable and conscienceless; for him my failure was all of a piece with my social clumsiness and my aesthetic ignorance. He rode me mercilessly; he made me sorry I'd ever shared a confidence with any fellow human, for who knew when that confidence might be made public and show me up as a fool? "Tell the Erika story," he'd say, and I would shut up for the rest of the evening, all the words I might have said turned into suppressed profanity that churned sickeningly inside my stomach.

Because, truth to tell, I was desperately lonely at college. It was not simply that as veterans we were different from the war survivors we had known when we were freshmen—though we were: less heroic by miles, not carrying with us the aura that comes from having fought a war manifestly between Good and Evil, not seeming, like the returning armies of the Forties, to be able to instruct others in the dimensions of Hell. For one thing, there were more of us on the campus, and for another, the age difference that separated us from those who had not served was far smaller. We were not looked up to; our patriotic accomplishments were ambiguous. And many of us—most of us, I imagined—were married, so that there was an entire social structure unrelated to the campus life we had known the first time around, as if we had outgrown the trivial, unworldly life of fraternity parties and college sports and abstract bull-sessions. I felt I belonged to a generation apart; I was so conscious of being out of place, it was almost as if I had dedicated myself to wallowing in my alienation. I don't think I was alone in that dedication. One night in the basement of the Deke house I danced with the wife of a classmate I knew, vaguely, from bi-ology lab. Both of us were a little drunk—was it a Halloween party? There were crepe streamers, potent artillery punch, can-dlelight reflected from cobwebbed basement windows; probably I had Jennifer Grant on my mind as we circled the small floor. Whatever, I was affected by this woman's perfume, the smell of her hair, the *realness* of her in my embrace; I was acutely sorry for myself because the woman I loved was somewhere far from Brunswick, Maine, but I was giddy with the fact of this stranger. At a moment that seemed almost natural, I kissed her, and she surprised me by kissing back. It was only the one kiss, a single moment of connection instantly broken by the practical world that surrounded it, but it resonated; it made me ecstatic and miserable, both at once, and I felt as if I had known her, sought her, all my life. We never spoke again—I don't believe I ever saw her after that night—but I assumed her vision of the world was like mine, and that she too wished for a connection, a belonging, of a kind that our artificial campus reality denied her.

Probably it was nothing that profound. Probably the kiss meant only that she hated being a student wife, and wanted her husband to get out into the world and make some money.

For me, everything of college life fed a solitary discontent. I made lists of my miseries. Item: I never rejoined my fraternity as an active, but sometimes I was invited to dinner as a guest. The first time I accepted, and the last, I was seated across from a pimply young man with a crewcut, who had apparently been drinking all afternoon; halfway through the fruit cocktail, he backed away from the table, stumbled to his knees, and threw up on my shoes. Item: Webb and I shared an apartment over-looking the railroad tracks—by now it was only an occasional freight train that used them—with Delbert Wallace, a Canadian, who was younger than we were, who *did* have more money, and who was probably crazy. The money was reputed to have come from distilleries and breweries—Webb invented a company: Moose Pee Limited—and Del lavished the wealth on himself. The week after he moved in with us, he bought a red Thunderbird; he never let us drive it or even ride in it. Remember that these were the days when the Thunderbird was a sports car, and if you have an eye for cars you can understand why we disliked him. In return, we were the enemy of his people; we were Americanizing pure Canada. Item: Even the campus had changed for the worse. There were new buildings, new walkways and drives, fewer pines, and, worst of all, no Delta. In the 1940s, the Delta was a triangle of land where Harpswell and Bath Streets met. At the intersection stood Adams

Hall, a classroom building that in ancient times had been the medical school; the rest of the Delta was vacant and was the place for soccer, softball, and all-purpose rowdiness—our untended equivalent of the playing fields of Eton. Now it was gone, Harpswell Street rerouted, buildings put up, sod put down. "All progress is grass," Webb said. "Tell me the Erika story."

I couldn't—wouldn't—but it was an episode of my life that dogged me not only because Webb harped on it, but because it more and more represented a betrayal of Jenny, whom I badly missed. I regretted having had anything to do with Erika, but I dreamed about her, and when I woke from the dreams I wondered how much of a fool I'd actually been. If it was loneliness that intensified my remorse now, it had been loneliness that brought me to bed with Erika in the first place. It was not a question of sex—never mind that at the advanced age of twenty-three I was sensitive about being a virgin, and never mind that I had tried as eloquently and insistently as I knew how to persuade Jenny to make love with me.

In those days Jenny was old-fashioned and adamant: did I want to marry her? I wasn't sure; who knew what my life would be like after I left the air force? and how long would it be before I could support a wife? All I knew was that I was crazy in love with her, that I wanted her in every possible way—as her protector, partner, possessor—and that I believed she loved me. For months in Germany we were yet another case of Everything But; it was my freshman college year all over again. We would undress together and hug each other under the comforter of her small bed, our nakedness itself a comforting. We slept entwined;

our bodies learned not to move, so that we were like twins agreeing instinctively not to disturb each other, breathing in unison, perhaps enjoying the same dreams.

Remember the story of the analyst whose woman patient has told him her dreams for years, and one day when she is several months pregnant she recounts a dream which makes no sense to the analyst, which is wholly out of key with all her earlier scenarios? After a while—I must ask Pru if this has ever happened to her—the analyst realizes it is the fetus's dream she has told him. That might have been the connection I felt when I slept with Jenny.

Mornings, if I was the one to wake first, I watched her sleep; I propped myself on one elbow and peeled the covers back to reveal her small, exquisite breasts—I admired them, kissed them gently, touched them as lightly as a breath. When she awoke she stretched and sighed and smiled, I kissed the hollow under her arm, she drew me against her. "I think my breasts are shrinking," she would say. "I think I'm turning into a thirteen-year-old boy." "I can prove you're not," I would say—and did. We played, we pleased each other, we hardly ever talked about sex. Throughout, I was intensely aware of my erections as they rose and ebbed like desire's tides, but we never Did It. One evening after a dinner with wine, we slid from her couch to the floor of the apartment, Jenny naked under her skirt, my fingers inside her so long a time that the fingertips were shriveled from her wetness. Both of us were mindless with excitement; I was certain I would enter her. "I'm afraid," she said, her voice small and strained. "Don't worry," I told her, and let her see the condom whose sealed packet I was about to tear. At once she started thrashing under me, struggling to get free, her passion gone. Ever afterward, we necked sweetly, held hands at the movies, did nothing further about sex.

I didn't love her any the less for her being frightened of me—I was frightened of myself as well—and when she was sent back to the States at the end of her tour of duty, I felt lost. She went by ship—the *Berlin,* which docked regularly in Bremerhaven—and seeing her off was sad for me, even though we both tried to make a party of it, sitting in the tourist-class lounge in a mob of people, drinking seventy-pfennig Scotch and generally making idiots of ourselves. This was the fall of '55; I wasn't due for discharge until spring, which meant six months of letter writing and perhaps the extravagance of a transatlantic telephone call a time or two. Once the *Berlin* had sailed, I kept right on drinking, and I retain various memories from that wasted period of my life: stumbling in a bitter-cold rain at dawn through the gate at the Marine Barracks while my comrades hooted at me from the windows of the bus taking them to work at the operations building across the city; playing a dice game called "Horse" with Heinz, the bartender at the Constanze, and losing drink after drink to him; meeting Erika. I was desolate; desolation was my excuse for every excess. I said Jennifer's name to myself a hundred times a day; its syllables were like mental worry beads, or a Catholic's rosary. Without Webb's carnal wisdom to guide me—he would have said that "the only cure for a woman is another woman"—I began the adventure he would at the time have approved of.

Erika was blond, mid-thirtyish, tall, bilingual. She sat next to me one evening at the Constanze, and when I offered to buy her a beer she said, "Let me buy for *you.*" She wore bulky gold jewelry—bracelet and necklace and rings. She seemed to have ample money. We took turns buying rounds, Heinz raising an eyebrow each time he set new bottles before us, as if he were warning me. I paid no attention. I was learning that Erika was the wife of an American who worked for an oil company— Aramco—in Dhahran, Saudi Arabia. They had met in Frankfurt while he was on third-year leave from his job, and they had fallen in love. He had taken her to the States with him, to meet his parents in Cincinnati, and there they were married. Now he was back in Dhahran, making living arrangements for the two of them; he would send for her soon; she was very lonely without him. I told her about Jenny—that I too was very lonely. Having established that we were soul mates, Erika and I left the bar together.

What Webb remembers of my account of this first time I really slept with a woman is that in the morning Erika took money from me—that she wept and confessed it had been more than a month since she had heard from her husband, that she was running out of money and her rent was due, that she hoped I wouldn't think badly of her but could I help her out with "a small lend"? I left her eighty marks—something in the neighborhood of twenty dollars. Webb called it "an initiation fee" and thought it was funny. That I believed Erika's story Webb found even funnier.

What I most remember is not the sweaty pleasure of making love to a woman who wanted me—demanded me—over and over, and not the image of Erika's room the next morning: our strewn clothing, the shabby furnishings, a writing table under the window—on it a lamp and a vase of flowers, a few books, a half-written letter, a thick-barreled fountain pen uncapped, so you knew that if you tried to write with it the tip would be dried out—and not the one window opened slightly to let in the noise of children playing and a chilly trace of breeze that made the lamp shade teeter and the dying flower petals tremble. What I most remember is that I was wearing my air force blue uniform, that when I left Erika's room the sun was high and bright, and that as I walked the four or five blocks to the Haf-enstrasse where I could find a taxi, I was followed by a gang of young children who skipped and chanted and in general re-minded me how foreign I was, how guilty I felt, how I already knew without admitting it that I had only spent my first night of love with a prostitute.

I'M SITTING in the American Eagle gate area, drinking coffee out of a styrofoam cup, when Esther reappears and slumps into a seat beside me.

"They haven't called our flight," I say.

"I know," she says. "Have you seen any movie stars?"

"No. Have you?"

"Not yet." She opens a pocket of her backpack, finds a comb, and begins working at her long hair. "You probably think I'm super vain," she says. "Actually this is just a nervous habit."

"I'd rather think you were vain," I say.

She flips the hair back over her shoulder and puts the comb away. "Suit yourself," she says.

"Did you talk to your mother?"

"She wasn't home. I talked to her machine."

"I hate answering machines," I say.

Esther cocks her head at me. "You 'hate' lots of things. Why is that?"

"I didn't know it showed."

"Well, 'dislike' then. The answering machine, the freeways, crowds."

"Motels," I say.

"I don't remember that one, but that's consistent."

"You told me you hate California."

"That's right, I did." She fumbles in her pocket and produces a tattered package of chewing gum. She offers the package. "Gum?"

"No, thanks."

She unwraps a stick and folds it into her mouth. "I overstated my California hatred," she says. "I should have said that I *prefer* Massachusetts."

"Uh-huh," I say.

"Why are you looking at me like that?" she says.

"I hate to see pretty girls chewing gum."

"If you weren't so judgmental," Esther says, "you'd waste a lot less positive energy on negative things."

"You're probably right."

"So judgmental and *so* sexist," she adds.

"I'll try and watch it," I say.

Our flight is boarded, and I wonder as we cross the apron to the commuter plane at my dealings with Esther, if her flippancy has to be met with flippancy of my own, or if I should take some more sober tack. Then, as we take our seats on the plane with a dozen or so other passengers, another thought occurs to me: what must Esther's mother be like?

"I don't mean to be such a brat," Esther says.

"I didn't think you were."

"No, I am. I'm saying a whole bunch of bratty things. I think I must really be tired."

"Well, you're forgiven."

"It's after one o'clock in the morning in Massachusetts," she says. "That's the heart of the problem."

"In Maine, too," I say, thinking of Prudence and Mindy, a mother and daughter bereft, and realizing that I already miss them. In a curious way, by carrying out Webb's dying wish I'm running away from his death and from the problems the death has made for those who most cared for him.

But perhaps my life has come full circle; perhaps this is the "closure" my academic friends talk about when they discuss everything from television shows to the mystery of human relationships. I think I can hardly wait to see how Jenny has turned out, because at the same time I may finally see how my own life will turn out. Already I'm a different person—Webb has changed me by his abrupt departure—for after a long marriage, a lifetime connection to one woman, I have all at once become enmeshed with several: Pru, Mindy, Jenny, this child Esther. Perhaps this is my real legacy from Webster Hartley.

"Do you hate small airplanes?" Esther asks.

"Very much."

"I thought so," she says. "Are you afraid of them?"

"Maybe," I say.

She leans her head against the seat back. In a few minutes

she is dozing; by the time we are ready to land—we are in the air less than a half hour—she is asleep on my shoulder, her long hair already beginning to need attention, her face a picture of wonderful trust. I would like to memorize the lovely detail of that face, but I am increasingly farsighted and her features are no more to me than a dreamlike blur.

When we arrive at the Santa Barbara airport I go through all the rituals of renting a car—showing my driver's license and credit card, waiting for the printout, initialing this place and that place on the form, signing for the car, declining insurance, admitting liability. As I take up the rental folder and keys and leave the counter, I see Esther scowling at me from a bank of telephones. Having caught my eye, she waves and trots toward me, slinging the backpack up over one shoulder.

"My mother can't pick me up," she says. "She let Elmer Fudd drive her car home."

"Who?"

"This guy she knows. He calls me Polly—short for Poly-ester, which he thinks is funny."

"That's upsetting. That your mother can't come for you."

"She told me to take a taxi." Esther falls into step alongside me. "Why don't you come talk to me while I get my baggage?"

"Why not?" I say.

We walk together to the baggage claim, looking, I imagine, like father and daughter—an image that makes me self-conscious. Harriet and I had no children, though we tried, and I know she felt regret at never having been a mother. I suppose I felt a similar regret, though as time went on I persuaded my-self I would have been less and less apt as a parent. What would

I have done with children? What could we have talked about? God knows I've been indifferent enough as a teacher; sons and daughters would have been impossible. And yet—

I glance over at Esther. Her face is solemn, her stride purposeful; her knuckles are white from the force of holding the strap of the pack at her shoulder. I imagine that this is a daughter I could have comprehended; everything about her at this moment says *anger,* says *frustration.* And rightly so. What kind of mother is it who can't meet her daughter's flight? What good is a parent that isn't around when you need one? What kind of life is it that shuttles a girl back and forth between a mother on the West Coast and a father on the East, between Santa Barbara and Martha's Vineyard, like a perpetual, tedious soap opera? As we cross the terminal, I hope the other travelers, few as they are at this late hour, notice Esther and me; I hope they think we're related. What made me think I couldn't cope with a daughter? I wonder, whatever *it* is, if it is an unanticipated by-product of studying at a men's college. What if I had gone to the University of Maine, or Northeastern, or B.U.? What if I had never met Webb? What if I had married Jenny?

In the claim area, Esther says, "You know what you could do? You could give me a ride home in your rented car. That would save me taxi fare."

"I could do that."

"And my mother would put you up for the night. It's a big house. And you hate motels."

"That's true," I say. "But shouldn't you ask first?"

"Mother's always ready to entertain," she says. "You don't ever have to worry about that."

"You're sure?"

"It gives her a chance to prove how gracious she is. She's very heavily into graciousness." She hauls a piece of bright red plastic luggage off the platform, elbows me aside when I move to take it and carry it for her. "Unlike me," she says.

WHILE ESTHER DIRECTS ME out of the airport parking lot and into the traffic of Santa Barbara, I wonder what sort of woman her mother must be—how does one get "into" graciousness? Harriet was a gracious woman when she was healthy; she had a knack for putting strangers at ease when they first came to our home, brought out the better qualities of familiar people—colleagues of mine, sewing-circle friends of hers—so they rarely became tiresome, hardly ever boring in the repetitiveness of their stories. And Jennifer. Perhaps genuine graciousness is a quality reserved to women. Jenny had all the grace Webb and I lacked when the three of us lived together in Baltimore, and probably she arrived on the scene barely in time to save us from eviction, our parties—Webb's parties, really—having got progressively further out of hand until neighbors lost patience and we began to know several of the city's finest by their first names. The three of us would emerge from a grocery store not far from the apartment, and Jenny would say, "Did you see the strange look that policeman gave us when we walked by?" and Webb would say, "Oh, that's old Fred," and would explain the occasion for our meeting him—some night of loud music, some incident of a broken window or a shouted obscenity. Probably Jenny came back into my life just in time to save Webb and me from jail. Halcyon days. I wonder if Jenny thinks of them that way. I glance over at Esther.

"Is this downtown Santa Barbara?" I ask.

"This is Goleta," she says. "It's a kind of suburb."

"What's it like?"

"A lot of the university students live here. There's a joke about it. It goes: 'What's the difference between Goleta and yogurt?' "

"I give up."

"One of them has a live culture," she says.

"Cute."

"*I* didn't make it up," she says defensively.

"Do you know a place near here called the Zodiac Ranch?" I ask.

"I might," she says. "But you just keep your mind on the road."

I obey. For a brief time we're on the 101, a divided highway punctuated here and there by orange threats of Construction Ahead, though at this hour the threats are never carried out, and we're moving in light traffic below a hillside aglitter with lights. Presently we turn in the direction of the glitter and drive through what seems to be the city proper. Esther steers me right and left, right and left, always gaining altitude; the outlined rooftops of houses cascade down the hillside toward the highway and what I imagine is the ocean beyond and behind us now.

"You and your mother must have a terrific view from this height," I say. "Nothing like Massachusetts."

"Different," Esther says. "Sunsets instead of sunrises."

"Nothing more?"

"There's a sharp bend in the road just ahead," she says. "Try to take this one properly."

"What does that mean?"

"It means you're supposed to brake *before* you go into the curve, not *in* the curve."

"You don't even drive," I say. "Or so you told me."

"I didn't say I didn't know *how.*"

We enter the curve; a high stone wall on the left takes me by surprise as the headlights sweep over it, and I touch the brake reflexively. Esther slumps in her seat and says, "Christ" in a tone of disgust.

"You could have gotten a cab," I say.

"Don't remind me." She yawns. "You'd better slow down here. You have to take a really sharp right—see where that blue car is parked?—exactly there, and then you're going to go immediately left."

I swing to the right; the road pitches downward, and I go left onto gravel.

"There we are," Esther says. "You can pull into the driveway just this side of the mailbox."

I park and turn off the car. For a moment we sit in silence, as if we have come to this place to listen to the engine oil drip into the oil pan, the sound of metal contracting into coolness.

"I don't mean to be such a grouchy bitch," Esther says. "I'm truly wiped out."

"It's O.K."

"I seem to have to keep apologizing," she says. "It must be chromosomal."

She gets out, drags her pack out of the backseat. I open the trunk and reach in for her suitcase.

"Just bring your own," she says. "I can get my stuff tomorrow morning. It's only dirty laundry."

The driveway slopes steeply down to a single-car garage; alongside begins a series of flat stones that meander in the direction of a front door lit by carriage lamps. The house is brightly lighted from inside, its walls mostly glass. From where I'm standing in back of the car I can see a sofa and a cluster of soft chairs, a fireplace, an enormously tall sound-system speaker. Trees and shrubs and what appear in the shadows to be flower gardens are everywhere; even though I've already seen from the street the yard lights of scores of nearby houses, from here they're invisible and this house seems isolated. If I look up, the stars are plain to see. Landscaping. I wonder what view I'll have tomorrow when I look down the hill from the other side of Esther's mother's place.

"I'll set the scene for you," Esther says. She precedes me down the path to the front door, her pack dangling from her right hand, almost dragging on the ground. I straggle behind her with my softsider slung over my shoulder. "Mother won't open the door for us. It'll be unlatched, and when we go inside she'll be standing in the living room, looking surprised. She'll have a highball in one hand—a Scotch and water—and a cigarette in the other. The cigarette will look as if she's just this second finished lighting it—which she has—and she'll be facing the kitchen as if she was on her way to get fresh ice for her drink, only she stopped when she heard the door open."

"And have you written her lines for her?"

"That's harder to do. It depends on how many drinks she's had, and on whether or not she has her contacts in." She pauses at the door. "Ready?"

"Ready."

"It's possible she'll think you're the taxi driver," Esther says, "and she'll offer to pay you."

Then she pushes open the door and steps inside. I hear a woman's voice say, "Sweetie, you're home," and when I follow Esther into the house I hear, "You poor darling; I never dreamed you didn't have cab fare."

Esther says, "Mother, this is Alec. He's not skillful enough to be a taxi driver. He rode on the plane with me from Boston. Alec, this is Natalie Kramer, my mother."

THE SCENE is exactly as Esther has designed it. Her mother is an attractive, blond-haired, severe-looking woman dressed in black—a black sweater set, black slacks, black flat-heeled shoes; a wide gold necklace, a gold belt buckle—and she holds a drink in her left hand, a cigarette in her right. The drink needs freshening, the cigarette is hardly smoked.

I nod to the woman. "A pleasure," I say.

She returns my nod, gives me a shallow smile, and puts her drink on a counter—perhaps it's a bar; high stools are arranged in front of it—that runs between living room and kitchen. "Forgive my mistake," she says.

"Alec needs a place to sleep. I told him we have lots of room, and that you wouldn't mind."

"Not at all," Mrs. Kramer says. "Would he like something? There's Scotch or bourbon, and I think there's gin."

"Thank you," I say. "I'd better not."

"You won't mind if I drink in front of you?"

I am taking an immediate dislike to Esther's mother—to her mannerisms and her tone of voice, which are so effete and affected that I marvel at the daughter's genuineness—but I'd rather not offend Esther by letting my reaction show. I start to say, "Mrs. Kramer—"

"Natalie."

"Natalie—" I want to tell her that she needn't put herself out, that I'll be happy to find a motel even at this late hour. "If I'm imposing—"

"You're not," she says. "Essie was telling the truth. I live alone in this house, and there *is* plenty of room." She is at the refrigerator, half out of my sight, rummaging among ice cubes. In a moment she reappears. She crosses the room elegantly, as if she is balancing a book on her head, and sits on the edge of the brown sofa. "Why don't you put your bag down? And come sit with us."

"Thank you."

"Perhaps you'd prefer a cup of coffee? Or tea?"

Esther has gone to the kitchen, and now she bangs a cupboard door closed. "Perhaps he'd prefer milk and cookies," she says. "God, Mother, let *up* on the poor man."

"Essie, I'm only trying to be polite."

"Never mind 'polite.' Be human."

Natalie Kramer looks helplessly in my direction.

"Esther's already apologized to me twice for being bitchy," I tell her.

"The dreary journey from town has weakened me ever so," Esther says. Very British. She lifts the back of a hand to her forehead—in the other hand is a can of Diet Pepsi—and sinks down on the sofa beside her mother. She leans to kiss Natalie's cheek. "I fear my fatigue may be terminal. Sorry, Mater Dear." She concludes with an elaborate faint into the pillows.

"This is how she always come home from visiting her father," Natalie says. "Histrionics are his strong suit. Bitchiness is his secret talent."

"Mother's strong suit is reserve," Esther says. "If you could merge my mother and my father into one person, you'd have a single well-balanced human being."

"And that's why we had you, dear," her mother says.

Perhaps I might be able to learn to like Natalie; irony is not an easy commodity these days.

Esther sits straight, sips from the Pepsi, stands between us. "Well," she says, "back to the drawing board," and starts to leave.

"Wait, sweetie. Show your friend where he's going to sleep, before you go off and succumb to your terminal fatigue." She stubs out her cigarette and looks at me with a tired smile. "We can talk at breakfast," she says. "I expect Essie will sleep in."

"Don't you wish." Esther holds her free hand out to me. "Come," she says in a sepulchral voice, "I will take you to the haunted bedroom."

I AM ESCORTED to more than a mere bedroom. In fact, Esther leads me into a complete furnished apartment in the lower level of the house—a living room that features television and an inlaid chess table someone has set up between a pair of blond Breuer chairs, a kitchenette complete down to the disposal and trash compacter, a full bath with a shower as well as a sunken tub and Jacuzzi, and a bedroom with a floor-to-ceiling window that overlooks the twinkling lights of the city.

"This was Daddy's retreat, when Daddy lived with us," Esther says. "He built it with his own hands; he said it was therapy and escape all rolled into one."

"It still smells new," I say. It does: a lingering paint odor, a trace of plaster smell in the atmosphere. "Hardly lived in."

"He didn't stay here much," she admits, "and he didn't leave us very long ago."

"How long?"

"Ten or eleven months, I guess." She drains the Pepsi can and drops it into the compacter. "You like it?"

"It's homey," I say.

"You could probably stay as long as you want." She stands inside the bathroom and opens a cupboard door. "Here's a generous selection of fluffy towels," she says, "and spare toilet paper and stuff."

"I'm sure I'll have everything I need."

"Do you think you'll stay a while? Here, I mean."

"I doubt it."

"We wouldn't charge you rent or anything."

"Let's talk about it sometime when you aren't terminally worn-out." I'm tired myself; I don't feel up to a discussion about living arrangements.

"O.K.," Esther says. "I'll see you at breakfast."

"Fine."

"Oh." She pauses at the foot of the stairs. "I forgot: you're not used to our famous water problems."

"I know California is having a drought."

"So don't flush any more often than you absolutely have to. My dad used to say, 'If it's brown, flush it down; if it's yellow, let it mellow.' Isn't that gross?"

"What about bathing?"

"Well, you can shower, but you can't use the tub or the Jacuzzi. And there's a bucket inside the shower stall so you salvage as much water as you can; we use it on the plants."

"I'll do my best," I say.

She smiles and shakes her head as if I were a trying child. "That's hardly very encouraging," she says. She scowls as if she were trying to remember something. "Don't let the shower run while you're soaping," she says, and then she runs upstairs before I can think what I might have said to get back at her for her critical view of my abilities.

As I get ready for sleep, I try to imagine Natalie Kramer's husband doing the same, down here by himself, undressing and crawling into this empty bed—thinking about his beautiful wife upstairs in *her* empty bed—and I wonder was he ever tempted to leave his solitude, to say the hell with it and go to her, to be apologetic, remorseful; did he ever take her—make love to her—in her own bed as an act of contrition, a favor of forgiveness? Or did he always stay angry and remote, refusing to be haunted by her cold beauty, falling easily into dreamless sleep? That was more likely—both of them self-centered, brittle, walled-in: Natalie regal in black and gold, the husband—no one had told me his name—distracted by the business of money. I remember my own marriage distractions—none of them monetary, none concerned with tangibles—the preoccupation with students, classes, books neither of us had time to read but nevertheless found ways to discuss; coming home late in the day, ready to have a drink—sometimes one Martini, sometimes two—dozing through the television news, having an easy supper, perhaps with wine, falling asleep on the sofa. Harriet waking me to tell me to come to bed; after so many years of the bridal couch, nothing more between us, no touching, no desire. Do we succumb to cancer because our lives lose their zest and their intention? I think I should meet Mr. Kramer, talk about our women and their outcomes. We might talk about the different ways we have chosen solitude for ourselves, and why we did it. Priorities. Lives cleansed of emotional clutter.

THEY SAY men marry women that remind them of their mothers. If so, my choosing Harriet was an irony that proves the wisdom of our ignorance. My mother died of cancer, as had her mother before her—both of them in the same upstairs room of the Thompson homestead in Brunswick. Webb remembered the house well—and the occasion for his being inside it—because it was directly across the street from the campus, on the Bath-Rockland road. We passed it every day on our way to English class in Adams Hall. "My grandmother lives there," I told him, early in our first freshman semester. "She's dying." He looked startled at first, then he shrugged and sighed dramatically. "No more chocolate milk and cookies," he said. "No more holidays at grandmother's house."

By this time, my mother had moved up from Scoggin to take care of the dying woman, leaving my father to fend for himself. I wasn't a frequent visitor at the homestead, but I stopped in often enough, usually after my swimming class, so I could sit in the front parlor, reeking of chlorine, and let my hair dry while my mother and I talked in quiet voices about my college life and my future. Sometimes Webb was with me; my mother liked him—he was marvelously polite to her and played to her vanity—and thought he was a good influence. "That's a beautiful lady, that mother of yours," he said once. "You better not turn out to be a failure. It'd kill her." It was true that she was obsessed with my future; it was also true that I was an indifferent student, that her hopes for me were at that time maternal and unfounded.

Our conversations were quiet, of course, so as not to disturb the woman in bed above our heads, and I rarely went upstairs, rarely spoke to my grandmother, even though she had long been my favorite. As a child, I'd spent summers with her, and I still remember her as quirky, unpredictable—a woman ahead of her time, strong-willed, independent. Eventually she made a hobby of real estate, buying houses, living in them long enough to make improvements, then selling them at great profit. Even today I could drive to that college town and find a half-dozen houses that had been my grandmother's; I could describe their interiors without ever entering them. She raised canaries in one of them; it was a white bungalow whose living and dining rooms were always filled with birdsong and the small patter of bird feet on newspaper. In another, a rambling place on a wide lot that overlooked the river, she raised Irish Setters and I remember a summer of clumsy puppies, big-pawed and wet-nosed.

I suppose that by avoiding her as she lay dying, I imagined

I was avoiding death. Her room reeked of it, I thought—the air heavy with the smells of stale breath and sweat and the mustiness of closure that made me want to sneeze. When I did look in, I had nothing to say. "Hello, Grandma. How you doing?" She was aware of me, knew who I was, but never spoke. She was all thin hair and pale face and narrow shoulders in a pink bed jacket; there seemed to be almost nothing of her under the covers—only a rumpling of the bedspread in the contrived shape of a person's hips and legs.

I was not there for her death. Nor was I there for my own mother's death a dozen years later—a year after my marriage to Harriet—though I tried, flying from Chicago to Boston, renting a car, arriving at the homestead barely an hour after she died. "It's all right," the doctor said. "She wouldn't have known you." *But I'd have known her,* I wanted to say, but didn't. What I did do—after the services and the condolences and the well-wishes from people I hardly remembered from my youth—was come home to Harriet and curse whatever fates visit cancer on the women we love.

Understand: I knew nothing of what would happen soon enough to Harriet. I was simply selfish—angry at the early death of my mother, guilty all over again for the way I avoided the ordinary kindness of sitting at my grandmother's bedside, and, now, worried for myself. I went to our family doctor, anxious lest cancer strike next at me. He listened to my fears, weighed them, shook his head slowly. "Breast cancer," he said. "*You* carry it, genetically speaking, but the chances of your being stricken are slight. The studies would reassure you—a very slightly increased risk of prostate cancer, but nothing statistically significant." And then the corners of his mouth turned up, as if he were smiling. "If you should have a daughter," he said, "that would be another story. Those same statistics argue that *her* chances of dying from the same cancer that killed your mother and grandmother are almost certain." What a legacy, I thought then. What perverse good fortune, I think now, that poor Harriet could not conceive my doomed female children.

I TURN OUT the bedside lamp and lie awake for a while. A subtle illumination fills the room like an aura—a mix of sky glow and thin moon filtered through whatever trees surround this house. I can make out on the walls the shapes of pictures, but not their content; the outlines of furniture, but no color or texture. I suppose I'm too tired for sleep. I have Jenny to find, and by the time I find her, I hope I will know what to tell her about Webb—or, rather, *how* to tell her what I am expected to tell.

The days when all of us lived together in three rooms carved from the top floor of a Victorian house near Hopkins seem a thousand years in the past—so long ago that they have taken on the objective quality of history, or of some fiction you were made to read when you were younger but have mostly forgotten, so that when you try to retell it you leave a lot of it out. "It went *something* like that," you say.

They had unfolded over time, those days; they had a shape: a beginning, a middle, an end. Sometimes they progressed by accretion, like crystals on a thread submerged in sugar water. Sometimes they were linear and simple. First I lived there, doing my graduate work while Webb had his first real job, still in Yankee country, at a boys' prep school in New Hampshire. And then after a year he joined me in Baltimore—untuned piano and Brunswick couch clotheslined into the box of his pickup— and paid half the rent in whichever months the art school managed to issue checks to its staff.

And at long last Jenny arrived to complete us. I had kept in touch with her as closely as I could after she sailed away on the *Berlin*. She went first to live with her parents in Denver, then took a job with the university library in Salt Lake. For as long as I was in Germany, I wrote to her every week, sometimes every day, and once a month made the transatlantic telephone call whose expense I hoped would impress her, would emphasize how much I missed her. When I came home to the States and returned to my schooling, I wrote less often but no less passionately, and my letters were longer. Away from the boring and limited routines of the military, I had much to tell; I told her about my professors, the books I was reading both in and out of my courses, the differences between the freshman I'd once been and the upperclassman and veteran I had become— and I told her about Webb. Perhaps I told her too much about Webb. I must have made him sound both glamorous and mad; she always asked to be remembered to him when she wrote to me, and whenever Webb saw me writing a letter to Jenny, he insisted that I add a postscript from him. The postscripts were always silly; once he made me write:

Fir yew I pine.
Fir yew I balsam.

It was something we'd seen stitched onto a sofa pillow in a souvenir shop in Freeport, the pillow stuffed with fragrant evergreen spills. "Down East kitsch," Webb called it, and it wasn't until Jenny arrived to share the apartment with us that I learned he'd actually bought one of the pillows and sent it to her as a joke.

But even kitsch can be appropriate to an occasion, and during the year I lived alone I did indeed pine for Jenny. After Webb joined me he accused me of indulging myself in a "perpetual mope" and of driving away his muses. "I can't bring a girl within fifty feet of you," he'd say. "You take the curl out of her permanent and dry up her juices." And when Jennifer herself came to Baltimore to live with me, she claimed it was my continual whining that had made her give in at last—though she later admitted that Salt Lake City had gotten to her as well. "Not that I couldn't lead a normal life in that place," she said, "but that when I did, I felt guilty."

Seeing Jenny again—having her as part of my real life, and not simply as a daydream whose impalpability left me unhappy and irritable—revived me. She was prettier than I'd remembered her from Bremerhaven, and livelier, and far more self-confident. It had been four years; she'd been living by herself in big cities. "Worldly-wise," she said. "Uh-huh, that's me." Her hair was shorter, her face thinner, her behavior assured. We slept together the first night she moved in, taking the bedroom away from Webb, and I made love to Jenny— and she to me—for the first time ever. No more Everything But; no more chivalric restraint. Now when I woke up in the morning, the vision of Jenny's face on the pillow beside me first startled me, then gladdened my heart. I got out of bed willingly, made coffee for her, brought her orange juice, propped myself against the pillowed headboard to watch her dress. It was as if her every action were an entertainment devised for my selfish delight. I believe that those were the happiest months of my life.

It was Webb who was the gracious one then. He gave up the double bed—which he had occupied in the first place because he was unarguably the more sexually active of the two of us—and took over the daybed in the living room without a word of complaint. "Anything for peace in the family," he told me. Now when he had his involvements with women, his "orioles"—because this was Baltimore and Webb liked baseball—he stayed elsewhere, waking in various beds in strange neighborhoods, coming home with stories extravagantly embellished to amuse us. "Birdsongs," Jenny called them. "Give us the latest birdsong," she'd say when the three of us were at table together. Webb was her perverse Audubon, glorifying the creatures he brought to ground. Once, I wondered out loud where that persistent bird imagery of his came from; I talked about W. C. Fields and "my little chickadee"; I remembered the Russian diminutive endearment, *golubochka,* "my little pigeon." Jenny got impatient. "It's a man thing," she said. "It isn't just Webb here. You're all hunters, and we women are only game to be tracked down." "It can't be that simple," I said. "Why not?" she said. Webb watched and listened. It always pleased him to be the center of a discussion, and when Jenny and I talked, he was quiet and attentive—especially to her. At the time, I never thought that he was doing the mirror dance, falling measure by measure into Jenny's rhythm until one day the lead would pass naturally from her to him.

I WAKE WITH A HEADACHE. A digital clock on a table beside the bed tells me in spidery red numerals that it is 6:44 in the morning. I wonder if I can go back to sleep and, if I do, will the headache be gone the next time I open my eyes. The room is already light—the drapes are open and I can see a pale sky outside—but it is subdued; the window faces the Pacific, the sunset horizon. In Maine—in Scoggin—and in Evanston as well, it is crows that announce the morning, beginning their raucous noise at the first inkling of dawn, calling from tree to tree, the racket like the next-door barking of lapdogs. Here the day has begun in silence, as if the drought has dried up the sounds of waking life.

When I get out of bed and stand at the window, I see a hot tub covered by protective green canvas, and a patio with a blue-and-white umbrella furled above a round metal table. The tub is made of redwood and the few chairs arranged near the table have redwood-slat backs and seats in aluminum frames. I can't see the ocean; in the way are vines and shrubs and thin trees whose tops carry wisps of fog.

I decide I'll take my headache back to bed. I go first to the bathroom to relieve myself, and I'm already under the covers before I realize I've flushed the toilet—the thoughtless, automatic action of a man not intimate with drought. I imagine a confrontation with Esther, an I-told-you-so expression on her face, arms folded, one sneakered foot tapping. As I begin to doze off, sinking into the wonderful neither/nor of half-consciousness, I picture myself explaining, hear myself pleading geography and forgetfulness.

When I next drift up into wakefulness it is nearly eight o'clock and my head feels worse than before. What is it? I wonder. More symptoms of aging? Mere hunger? Some California disease I have no resistance to? And then, still somehow touching the fringes of sleep, I have a curious vision of Prudence Mackenzie at the table in her Scoggin kitchen and I know—simply *know*—that she's feeling as lousy as I am.

There's a phone behind the clock. I pick it up and dial Pru. When she answers, my "knowledge" is confirmed by the quality of her voice.

"Hi," I say, "it's Alec."

"Oh," she says. "My goodness."

"How are you?"

"Awful. I didn't sleep, I couldn't read, my head feels like somebody bopped me between the eyes."

"I knew it," I say. "I could feel your headache calling to my headache all the way across the continent."

"And across a bunch of time zones," she says. "What time is it there?"

"Not quite eight. What was it kept you awake?"

She is silent for so long, I think perhaps something has broken the connection. Then I hear voices in the background—cartoon voices—and picture Mindy in front of the television, playing solitaire while she watches.

"Is everything all right?" I say. "Talk to me."

"Everything's awful," she says. Her voice is strained, as if

it's about to break against something too harsh for her to handle.
"Webb's ashes arrived yesterday."

"Oh, Lord."

"You'd barely driven out of the yard when the UPS truck
pulled in."

"The ashes came by UPS?"

"Isn't that crazy?" She stops, gets control of her voice. "This
young woman in her brown coveralls hops out of the truck and
trots up to the porch with a package in one hand and her clip-
board in the other. I thought maybe it was something you'd
sent me as a gift, so I wouldn't miss having you under foot. Or
maybe it was supplies Webb had ordered—some new pastels
he'd said he needed. I thought the worst it could be was a
wedding present he'd ordered, the week before he died; I was
ready to cope with that—that intrusion—if I had to."

It's odd how mundane circumstances betray us. The few
days I had stayed on at the farmhouse, I watched Pru getting
stronger, lighter in her attitude toward the everyday. I'd con-
gratulated myself: that I was helping her forget her grief, that I
was a successful amateur therapist, that perhaps she was beginning to lean toward me and away from the sorrowful memory
of Webb's heart attack—as if my caring for her had become,
even for her, more than the attentiveness of a responsible friend.
Now all of that seems gone, erased in a moment by the simple
arrival of a delivery van, and I am listening to a young woman
struggling all over again to manage the death of love.

"When I was unwrapping the package," she says, "I didn't
have any idea what was in it. I got the paper off, and at first I
thought it was a coffee can painted black. But then I could see

that it was a different kind of canister—metal, squat, like something my mother would have used to pack peanut brittle. But it was heavy."

She stops. Her breathing is hoarse, her voice thin.

"I shook it." She gives a strange little laugh. "That's what we do to figure out what sort of gift is in boxes, isn't it? I shook it to listen for something rattling—and then I looked again at the wrapping paper and saw the return address of the funeral people."

"Jesus, Prudence," I say, "I'm so sorry." As if what had happened was my fault.

"Mindy opened it," she says. "Mindy got an old spoon out of the kitchen drawer and pried the lid off and looked inside. She told me it was dirt. 'Who would send us a box of dirt?' she said. Then she reached in. She took out a handful and let the stuff run between her fingers."

"Jesus Christ," I say again. It's as if I'm being told about Webb's death for the first time, and here I am saying the same words—the prayer, the supplication, whatever it is—and feeling stricken for the loss of a friend.

"I'd never seen them before—a person's ashes. Even in that tiny handful they were—I don't know. Horrible. Black and gray, and w'·h little chips of white. *Flesh and bone.* And I started crying. Mindy put the lid back on the canister. She touched my face to wipe the tears away. She said, 'It's Daddy, isn't it?' "

"Pru—" She was weeping, the way she had wept when I held her in the studio.

"When I looked in the bathroom mirror, later, the ash was smeared on my cheeks."

Silence. The hiss of it in the phone's earpiece. I can't think what to say.

"It was strange," Pru is saying. "Every so often I have this fantasy that Webb's still alive—that this has all been a practical joke, or an insurance scheme like the ones you see in the movies. That I'll be looking out the window one morning and he'll come up the driveway, laughing and waving."

"He wouldn't have thought of such a thing," I tell her. "It would have been too cruel."

"More cruel than ashes?"

"I suppose not."

"Dear God, Alec."

And then it is as if I'm talking to a different woman: the voice brightens and strengthens, the sorrow has evaporated, we're changing the subject.

"All right," Pru says. "That was yesterday. Mindy can't decide whether Webb belongs in the back garden under the rose-bushes, or in the pond with the herons and ducks. You'll have to help decide."

"I will."

"How was your trip?"

"Pleasant," I say. "I met a girl."

"Oh, my gosh," Pru says. "Webb sends you on an errand, and you pick up his bad habits."

"Calm yourself," I say. "She's only thirteen."

Pru is silent for a moment. "Curiouser and curiouser," she says.

"I'm staying at her mother's house, just for the day. I think she knows where Jenny's place is."

"You haven't talked to Jenny yet?"

"Not yet. What's Mindy up to this morning?"

"Mindy's being Mindy. Right now she's playing cards."

"Solitaire?"

"Whatever it was you guys played before you taught her cribbage."

"Say hello for me."

"I will." I hear her clear her throat, delicately. It's as if she's preparing to say an important thing, but again the line is hollow with her temporary silence and the distance of morning television. "What's the mother like?" she says.

"What mother?"

"You said you were staying with this thirteen-year-old girl's mother."

"Oh. She's very pleasant. Very nice."

"What's the father like?"

"He isn't here," I say. "He's in Massachusetts. They're divorced."

There is a moment of silence at Pru's end of the line. "Is she pretty?"

"She's quite attractive."

Another silence. "Did you sleep with her?"

"What ˙ nd of question is that?" It startles me. Even when I have wished Pru to bend to me—even when I have felt more than sympathy for her—it would not have occurred to me that she might be jealous of anyone else I met.

"I'm sorry," she said. "Does that mean you didn't?"

"That's what it means," I say. "I don't think it even crossed my mind."

"It would have crossed Webb's."

"Yes. But I'm not Webb."

"I'm sorry," Pru says again. "This is such a bad time, I can't think straight."

"It's all right," I say.

"It's none of my business if you do sleep with her," she says.

"That's probably true."

I hear her take a long, deep breath. Then she says, "I've been giving this a lot of thought since you left here yesterday: other men—most other men, I'll bet—would have questioned Webb's wanting you to go all the way to California to tell Jenny he's dead. They'd have thought, 'Why isn't a phone call just as good?' I don't think *that* even crossed your mind. You're really wonderful."

It's odd to be told I am wonderful by this unhappy young woman, when in fact self-interest is my deepest motive, when I am already half-certain that the messenger is more important than the message.

"But I expect you won't really know what's what until you've talked with Jennifer," she says. "We both know Webb: he's strange—*was* strange—but he has his reasons."

"Reasons that will always outlive him."

More silence—and I realize I've provoked it this time.

"Apparently," Pru says softly.

"I hope your headache goes away," I say.

"Yours too," she says. "What's the address where you're staying with this woman? Can I write to you?"

"I suppose you could write to General Delivery in Santa

Barbara, but I won't be here very long. Probably not long enough for a letter to come from Maine."

"Will you call me after you talk with Jennifer?"

"Either that or hop on the next plane and deliver my report face-to-face."

"Both," Pru says. "Do both. We have a lot of things to talk about." She pauses. "Did I say I'm giving up smoking? I am."

And then the line is only empty noise, a faint buzz suggesting that there was truly a connection between me and another, that the possibility of further connection across a continent is not truly dead. Pru's voice has conjured up for me the whole setting of the Scoggin place—the old house, the studio at the end of the ell, the lightning rods at each end of the roof that surely have no modern efficacy, the gnarled lilac beside the porch providing a screen across the kitchen windows. I imagine Mindy dancing naked through the low-ceilinged rooms; perhaps Prudence too has put off getting dressed—there are no men in the house, no strangers expected. How lovely Pru would be: her young skin, the curve of her shoulders and hips, the wondrous swell of the baby she carries. I'm not so pure-minded as I'd like her to think. Mindy understands. Why should beauty be hidden? Why *should* anyone have to be covered in this difficult world?

WHEN I EMERGE into the wider light of upstairs I feel a little like some ground animal scrabbling toward day, and there is a subtle change of temperature I feel on my face and the backs of my hands. The wall of the living room that faces the ocean is floor-to-ceiling glass, so that the oblique morning glow floods the room; the vinyl couches, the sling chairs, the glass coffee table all seem to have auras and to float on a sea of brown shag laid over parquet flooring. An aggressively abstract painting in colors of scarlet and orange and raw yellow hangs above the mantel of a sandstone fireplace. The wall away from the ocean is also glass; it looks up the hill Esther and I descended last night: a sharp slope of green lawn broken with waxy shrubs and islands of pink gravel, the flagstone walk bordering the driveway, the back end of my rented car—silver and black, with its unfamiliar California license plate. In the room's far corner is the mate to the tall, thin speaker I'd seen through the window when I arrived, and on a low table in front of the window is a complex of stereo equipment, all of it black and arrayed with knobs and switches and dials. In a corner are magazines and newspapers stacked carelessly; a selection of other magazines is disarranged on the coffee table in front of one of the couches.

Natalie Kramer is seated at a glass-topped table angled between the kitchen and living room, a newspaper open in front of her, a bright red coffee cup in a white saucer at her left hand, a lighted cigarette in her right. I walk behind her and stand at the oceanside window; I can see perhaps a hundred yards down the hillside before the fog begins its work of obscurity—a tumble of bushes and treetops and the carmine roofs of neighboring houses. This is a little like being on the coast of Maine, except that somewhere out there is the Pacific instead of the Atlantic.

"You must have quite a view when the fog lifts," I say to Natalie.

"There's coffee on the kitchen counter," she says. "Help yourself." She turns a page of the paper, sips from the coffee cup, takes a drag from the cigarette. She doesn't turn her head to look at me as I pass her on my way to the kitchen.

"Thanks," I say.

"How did you sleep?"

"Fine. Though I woke up with a bit of a headache."

The coffeemaker on the counter is very modern, white-enameled, European. I struggle a bit, sliding the pot out from under the filter receptacle, and fill the clean cup set beside the apparatus.

"You came from Boston?" Natalie says.

"Yes."

"Then you've slept too long; that's why the headache." She leans to read a clock on the wall above the refrigerator. "It's after noon where you came from."

"Probably."

"Do you need cream or sugar?"

"Sugar."

She lays the cigarette over the edge of the ashtray and comes to the kitchen. From a cupboard over the stove she brings down a white sugar bowl; in a narrow drawer near the sink she finds a teaspoon   d sets it beside the sugar. She is still wearing black, but this morning it is a black robe—chenille or terry or velour, something with a nap to it—wrapped tightly around her and held with a broad belt. She smells, as she passes me going and coming, of perfumed soap and toothpaste and a faint undercurrent of tobacco.

"Thank you," I say. I stir sugar into my cup and join her,

sitting at the other end of the table to face her. "Where's Esther?"

"Still sleeping. You mustn't ever take seriously her threats about early rising."

"I've never lived with a teenager."

Natalie looks at me; it's the first time she's deliberately turned her gaze in my direction. "Did you have children?" she asks.

"No," I say.

"Then you can't imagine." She goes back to her reading. "And Esther's twelve. If I knew how to keep her out of her teens—or if I knew how to vault her from here to the age of twenty—I'd be a happy woman."

"I've heard that girls are difficult."

"Different," Natalie says. "I've had both boys and girls; I don't know which is more 'difficult.'"

"Well—" I sip the hot coffee. "She's a charming child."

"You can try waking her, if you'd like." She gives me a smile I read as sardonic. "If you think you'd prefer her company to mine."

"I will if I get bored," I say.

The smile softens. "'Alec,' isn't it?"

"Yes."

"Just seeing what her room looks like would be an adventure for you. She has mounds of clothes heaped up all over the place. That might confuse you: one of the mounds might actually be Esther."

"I won't risk it."

"What brings you to Santa Barbara?" Natalie says after a

moment. "Essie didn't seem to know, except that you asked about the Zodiac Ranch."

"I have to look up an old friend there. Esther said she *might* have heard of the place, but I thought probably she was still being bitchy. Do you know where it is?"

"Everybody knows it. Esther takes riding lessons there, when she's not in school or visiting her father. English pleasure. I expect she'll resume—no, I'm *obliging* her to resume; I'd hate to think we bought all that tack for nothing."

She stubs out her cigarette and draws the lapels of her robe tighter together—whether because she is cold or out of some sudden modesty, I can't tell. Looking at her now, her face pretty even without makeup, her hair pulled back enough to hold it away from her face but not enough to keep stray wisps from straggling at her temples, I can imagine earlier breakfast scenes in this place. Natalie and her husband facing each other as we do this morning, the paper divided between them. *What's on the agenda for today, dear? Not much: Esther has her riding lesson at two; I thought I'd look for something nice for dinner.*

Webb would have admired Natalie, would have put her in the *desirable older woman* category, probably would have slept with her last night—somehow, on some plausible pretext, that being the way he was. I wonder what man has her car, and why.

"Zodiac," she says, "is about an hour and a half from us, on the other side of the mountains behind us. It's real horse country."

"I'll have to get directions from you."

"Why not come with us today? Esther enjoys you; that's clear—"

"She enjoys making fun of my incompetence."

"—and we'll have a lark. It's Esther's regular lesson day; I know a lovely restaurant where we can all have dinner. We'll give you a grand tour."

"I'd enjoy that," I say.

"But we'll have to take your rented car," she says. "I forgot I don't have mine."

"Esther can backseat-drive," I say. "She'll feel empowered."

Natalie smiles. "Let me heat up your coffee," she says. She takes my cup to the kitchen, empties it into the sink, refills it from the glass carafe. "A lot of sugar?"

"A half-teaspoon."

"You mustn't let Esther bother you," she says as she sets the coffee before me. "She's not so wise as she tries to seem. The young nowadays—" She sits across the table from me, lights a new cigarette. "—They're quick studies. They pick up the voices, the gestures, the nuances of the adults around them; they have a whole wardrobe of grownup *stuff,* but they're really just children dressed up."

"I'll try to remember that."

"How do you know Jenny Warner?"

I almost say, "Who?"—but of course Jenny would have re-married after Webb; why not? She had young children, no assurance of support from Webb; she was still young, attractive.

"We're old friends," I say.

"Esther thinks she's an old lover."

"So she told me—and naturally she's right."

Natalie smiles. "Sometimes she's her father's child."

I sip the sweetened coffee, Natalie Kramer a misty vision

across the oval image of the cup, her words an obscurity between us.

"It was an easy guess," I say.

And an easy end as well. I had come home in the rain from a night class at Hopkins, at a time of my life when I had never been happier. Jenny and I were already talking about marriage, where we should live in this world with its boundless geographies and its universities hungry for young professors, whether we would ever measure up to the clichés of mortgage, station wagon, two-and-a-half children. I was later than usual—as a Teaching Assistant I had advising duties, and a student had cornered me after class, demanding advice. The apartment was dark and silent, no light except the tiny bulb above the stove. I assumed Webb and Jenny had got tired of waiting for me, had gone out for a drink—a custom we had when I got home from this class—and were perhaps expecting me to drop my books and notes and join them around the corner. But I was tired, distracted by the thought of paperwork I had to do in the morning on behalf of the student who had delayed me. I went straight to the bedroom, wanting to get out of my wet clothes, wanting sleep—and blundered in on the two of them in each other's arms, tangled in the love knot. The room reeked of sex, the ozone produced by the electricity of passion. My best friend; my bride-to-be.

What could I have done except the obvious? I said not a word; I was numbed; I walked out. The next day I was in a place of my own in a different neighborhood.

"You seem distracted," Natalie Kramer says, and I realize that my coffee cup is poised at my lips and I'm staring not *at* her, but *through* her, as if something far beyond the attractiveness of her features has captured me, drawn me out of the moment and this morning occasion.

"Sorry," I say. "I think I've just had an insight into one of the reasons I'm in Santa Barbara." And I have: Webb wants me to forgive Jenny for that night in Baltimore and, through my forgiveness of her, to forgive him as well. Through all the years we kept in touch—reluctantly at first—then came grudgingly back together, became and stayed friends, we never discussed the betrayal; it is a loose end in Webb's life and he wants it tied off *in memoriam*. He must always have believed that Jenny could explain it—that I might never listen to him, but that surely I could not refuse her under this new circumstance.

"I thought you were looking up your old friend."

I put the cup down. "I just realized why. It has to do with a cliché: 'My friend stole my true love from me.' "

"Ah."

Then I explain to her about Webb's heart attack, and about Jennifer, and about the letter sending me to California, and about the distant, dreadful night in Baltimore that began it all. It is an odd sensation—an oddness that colors my tale even as I tell it—to be unburdening myself to this stranger, and odder still to realize that as I talk, she is being drawn in, she is rapt, she is sympathetic. Her eyes never leave my face, she doesn't even smoke, I seem to be the center of the world for her as we sit together in the morning brightness of this glass-walled space. "Oh," she says, "yes." She feels my pain as I describe it, shares my outrage. "God, yes, I can understand," she says, punctuating my words. She nods, she winces. When I finish, she is captivated; she is all mine. Is this Webb's secret? Now that he's dead, am I his mimic, trying out what he taught me over the breadth of forty years?

"Men," Natalie says, "*some* men, are like that. They operate under nobody's laws but their own when it comes to dealing with women. They take, and then they're shocked when the world gets upset by the taking. The fact that he wanted to be friends again, in spite of stealing your woman and in spite even of being in his grave—that says this Webster fellow was like that. Perfectly innocent: that's how he thought of himself."

"Or proud of being guilty and getting away with it."

"Or that. Yes." Now she smokes. "Kent is like that. Kent's my husband—my ex-husband. It hasn't been long enough for me to get used to the *ex*."

She gets up from the table and goes to the pile of newspapers and magazines in the corner of the living room, comes back with a slick-covered booklet. She puts it on the table in front of me and I see that it's a lingerie catalog, one of those full-color, fancy pieces featuring beautiful women and handsome men wearing next to nothing in bedroom situations. Flimsy underthings of net, of silks and satins. Teddies, tap pants, chemises, garter belts. The men in white-silk pajama bottoms. Once in a while such catalogs came in the mail to Harriet, and the two of us would read them together, bemused by their inappropriateness to our average lives.

"This came a couple of weeks ago," Natalie says. "I didn't pay much attention—there's so much fourth-class junk in the mails these days, you'd think the post office would raise those rates instead of pushing up the price of people's letters and newspapers. I glanced at it; I thought, *Well, maybe I'll have to buy some of this stuff so I can capture a new husband,* and then I tossed it in the corner.

"So about a week later Kent phoned. 'Did you get that underwear catalog I sent you?' I said yes. I said I hadn't realized he was the one who sent it." She takes a drag from her cigarette and looks away from me. "He asked me to get it, bring it to the phone. 'Look on page eleven,' he said. I did. It was a beach house scene, a man and a woman sitting on the deck, the man in pajama bottoms, the woman in a flimsy peignoir; you could see the shadow of her nipples, her pubic hair. 'That's my new girlfriend,' Kent said. 'Isn't she something?' "

"What a shit," I say.

Natalie smiles. "She looked twenty-four or -five. Long chestnut hair. Wise eyes. Ripe lower lip." She shrugs, looks at the cigarette tip. "A firm young body; I can't really blame him."

I want to say something to make her feel better—anything to lighten the expression on her face—but I remember my morning daydream of Pru, and again I can't think what. Natalie looks desolate, looks suddenly ten years older. She turns the pages of the catalog, slides it across the table to me. Page eleven confronts me, and the scene is exactly as she has described it. The slick paper smells of ink and fantasy-sex.

"I can't blame him," she says again. "I'm forty-four."

Esther appears beside the table, in denim jeans and jacket, barefoot, frowning.

"For God's sake," she says to her mother. "You're so tangential. I've coached you and coached you: you *never* tell men how old you are."

Natalie gives me a look that says *You see what I go through?* and stubs out her cigarette.

"I'd better give Bobby Mills a call and tell him I won't need my car back," she says.

"Elmer Fudd," Esther says, behind her mother's back.

ESTHER JOINS ME at the table, a glass of orange juice in one hand, a bagel slathered with cream cheese in the other, while her mother phones the man who for one reason or another took her car home last night.

"Who *is* Elmer Fudd," I ask, "and why do you call him that?"

"You'll see. He's this weird person who wuvs my muvver."

"I can hardly wait to meet him."

"I heard her telling you the story of Daddy and Summer," Esther says.

"Summer?"

"The woman here." She opens the catalog, which I had closed, to the cruel page. "I was there when Daddy made the call Mom was talking about." She chews thoughtfully. "So was Summer. It was a big joke; she was sort of all over him while he was bragging about her to Mom."

"That's pretty strange," I say.

"They didn't know I was just in the hall. They thought I was in the TV room."

"Still," I say.

"I know. But people in love are weird anyway, don't you think?"

For an instant, the image of Pru flashes into my mind—Pru being helped out of the car by the minister while I watch from the porch, Pru at one level or another in a state of shock, Pru holding the wilting bouquet of flowers against the swell of her abdomen.

"Sometimes," I say.

"Summer is," she says. "Not just weird. Really tangential."

"Whatever that means."

"And they're always making plans. Plans for the day, plans for the month, plans for next year. There's always a big pile of travel stuff, brochures and folders and tacky magazines, telling about Greece and the Caribbean and winter in New Zealand. Stuff like that."

"It must be nice."

"They won't do it," Esther says. "It's all fairy tales. They've got me planning the wedding, and when I tell them how much it's going to cost they say 'Too much' and I have to go cut something else out of the arrangements. I started them out with a four-piece jazz group for the reception, but they'll probably end up with some black street kid doing rap." She smiles at me and licks at the cream cheese on the bagel she's eating. "That's just an example. Plans are a thing with them."

"Will they really get married?"

She shrugs. "What difference does it make?"

"I suppose you're right. It doesn't matter."

"Actually, Summer's twenty-three," Esther says, "but she wears a ton of makeup. It makes you wonder what she's covering up." She chews bagel meditatively. "I think she's probably got acne. Or the heartache of psoriasis."

"Heart*break*," I say.

"Same thing," she says.

I know better than to try to explain to her how different they are, though it is clear to me: the distinction between what I felt when I found Jennifer in Webb's illicit bed and what I have often felt in the years since. Instead, I fall back on the conventional: "They say beauty isn't only what you see on the surface," I remind her.

"I know. I like her, really." She swallows, wipes her mouth with a paper napkin, crumples the napkin into Natalie's ashtray. "But I don't see her as adequate stepmother material."

She retrieves the catalog and studies its pages, pushing her long hair back over her shoulders with a graceful movement of her right hand, first over one shoulder, then the other. Behind her, outside the tall window, the fog is higher and thinner, the world of Santa Barbara becoming more and more real as housetops and trees materialize and solidify down the hillside.

Esther is absorbed in the catalog, captured by it, her lower lip caught meditatively under her perfect front teeth. She slides the booklet toward me. "Here," she says. "Summer is also on page twenty-five. She told me about the man in the picture—that he's gay. She said a lot of the male models she works with are gay, and she likes them because they respect her and don't threaten her. What do you think about that?"

HOW MUCH OF THIS conversation with Esther is an example of what Natalie has called "children dressed up"? And how much is real precociousness, the talk of a girl truly savvy beyond her years because she has been so long in the company of wise and sophisticated adults? How comfortably should I discuss a father's affair, an ex-husband's cruelty? I think even Webb would have no answers.

Yet he would have understood the questions. Once—it was in mid-July of one of our visits to Maine—the four of us were sitting in the kitchen of the Hartley camp on Square Pond when Webb started to tell about a wedding he and Jenny had attended only a month earlier. The sun was low behind the pine and spruce on the other side of the lake, the last motorboat had left the water, a loon had settled into the shadows of a cove on the opposite shore. I'm not sure I knew where the children were by then, but I'm certain that, so late in the evening, Webb and I were both tipsy from our afternoon overseeing their play. Harriet and Jenny were always patient with us, perhaps because Webb and I so rarely saw each other, but it couldn't have been easy. "I hope you appreciate Jenny's forbearance," Harriet said to me after one such evening. "She hates it when Webb has too much to drink. She thinks he sets a bad example for Amanda and Will."

"We went," Webb said, "even though I hate weddings almost as much as I hate funerals. By God, that's why I'm giving my body to science, so there'll be nothing to bury and no excuse for a depressing ritual."

"Maybe science won't want you, Webster," Jenny said mildly. "I hear they'd rather do their own pickling."

Harriet smiled. I waited for a reaction from Webb, but none came. Those were the days when I had no clue to any serious strain in Jenny's connection with Webb. I suppose I was enough occupied with my old fondness for her that I saw any tension in the Hartley marriage as an expression of my own ego, and prudently discounted it. I knew about Jenny's impatience with Webb's drinking habits, but that didn't seem a serious matter—he was no alcoholic. Anyway, at Jenny's little dig Webb simply gave a small shake of his head and went on with his story.

"But the Lowries were old friends—they live just a couple of miles down the road from the farm—and so I put my scruples aside and we went.

"It was O.K. The ceremony was mercifully short, the young couple hadn't written their own bad poetry, no bearded friend of the groom's appeared to play folk songs on the acoustic guitar, the minister didn't try to tell jokes or give a sermon on peace in Vietnam, which was our war at the time."

"And there was plenty to drink at the reception," Jenny said.

"Indeed there was," Webb said. "And there was a piano, which is a more important fact for the purposes of this tale I'm telling."

"Webb and his pianos," I said. I winked at Harriet.

"Can't resist them," he said. "This reception being no exception. Anyway, it's late in the day—the bride and groom are long gone, Jenny and Betty Lowrie are in the kitchen doing up the punch cups—and I'm at the piano, giving the surviving guests my repertoire."

Harriet was still smiling. I watched Jenny, who was not. As Webb's story went on—I remember it now as a longer tale than it needed to be—her lips got thinner and the skin around her mouth tightened into deeper and deeper disapproval.

"I was playing something sentimental," Webb said. "Maybe

'Moonlight in Vermont,' or 'I Cover the Waterfront,' when one of the Lowrie cousins shows up and sits next to me on the bench. This is a plump little brunette, cute face, freckles, maybe thirteen, fourteen years old, a little older than Amanda is now—" At this point, I remember, Jenny got up from the table and started running hot water over our dinner dishes, though her eyes and her obvious displeasure were still on Webb. "—And she's changed her clothes since the wedding hoopla. Now she's wearing a red t-shirt and cutoffs—you know those recycled blue jeans that are so short they make a girl look like she's all leg?"

"And they're always so tight," Harriet said. "You wonder about their mothers."

"Exactly," Webb said. "So anyway, she asks me if I know this song or that song—stuff on the charts these kids listened to—and I have to say I don't, that I closed out my repertoire in the middle nineteen-fifties. She thinks that's funny—I'm such an ancient—and then I notice how close to me she's sitting. She's got this bare thigh right up against me, and I think, 'What's this?' and I slide up the bench a couple of inches."

Jenny came back to the table and sat stiffly.

"What happens is that this nymphet does the same: half a minute later I feel her thigh against mine again. Then, the crazy thing, I start to get a little excited—not because I want to; I think it's just the physical pressure of that thigh, and the warmth, and I suppose a little bit the *idea* of it—"

"The idea of *what?*" Jenny said then.

"I don't know," Webb said. "Of something happening, of being seduced by this freckle-faced, long-legged, totally innocent—"

"Don't kid yourself," Jenny said. "She knew *exactly* what she was doing."

It was a stunning moment. Harriet and I talked about it later in the privacy of our guest-room bed.

"You saw the way Jenny looked at him," she said. "A dagger. A *sword*. Something's wrong there."

FORTUNATELY, Natalie's reappearance rescues me from having to decide what to think about Esther's sophistication.

"Bobby's bringing the car back in a half hour," she says. "And you," to Esther, "have a riding lesson at three."

"That's news," Esther says.

"Jenny knew you'd be back this week. She said she didn't know if you'd want to start today or a week from today, but she was kind enough to keep today open. She's hired a new instructor; I think she wants you to check him out—tell her if she chose wisely."

"Can't I have the week to recover from jet lag?"

"No," her mother says. To me she says, "More coffee?"

"Thanks."

"I hope you'll like Bobby," she says. "He's my confessor, my drinking partner, and my only male link to the future."

"A fragile reed," Esther says.

"That's enough," Natalie tells her. "Why don't you go get your laundry out of Alec's car before you forget it." It isn't a question, and Esther obeys. At the front door she pauses and looks back.

"Did you tell her I want Commodore?"

"Jenny told *me*," Natalie says. "Commodore has missed you."

This puts a smile on Esther's face, an expression that transforms her into the child she is supposed to be as she turns away.

"Sometimes I wonder," Natalie says as she sits at the table opposite me. She has changed clothes since we shared our cups of coffee, has put on a white skirt and blouse to go with white low-heeled shoes. Her legs are tanned and bare. A pale blue cardigan is draped around her shoulders, and she has tied a gold scarf loosely at her throat. "There are times when she acts her age, but those times are rare around me."

"She loves you," I say. "That's obvious."

"And that makes her difficult to break," she says, "if you don't mind a horse metaphor. I know the jokiness is just a daughterly stratagem, but her brothers handle that much more easily than I. Unfortunately, they're not very often around."

"What do they do?"

"Scott's in politics. He's the older of the two, and ended up in Sacramento, representative of someplace north—Occidental; I don't recall the district. Perry—" She hesitates, takes her lower lip momentarily under her teeth. "Perry's a college dropout; he still hasn't quite grown out of the surfer phase of his life. He hangs out—or hangs loose, or whatever they say now."

I smile. I can hear Webb explaining his secret ambition, one rainy weekend afternoon when we were living in Baltimore, sitting in a booth at a nearby tavern while Jenny was at the library. "Consider the animals," he was saying. "What do they do with their lives? I'll tell you: they just hang out." He took a swallow of beer. "If I ever make a lot of money," he said, "that's what I'm going to do. I'm going to hang out."

Not realizing it was an ambition he'd already satisfied.

"And I didn't mean to suggest Scott had really 'ended up' as a state assemblyman. He's young." Natalie lights a cigarette—very thin, orchid-colored, unlike the ordinary brand she has smoked until now. "Bobby says he'll end up running for President—although Bobby also says that's not so desirable as entering the House of Lords and eventually becoming Prime Minister."

B OBBY M ILLS ARRIVES just before noon in Natalie's car—a sporty red convertible with a vanity plate that reads TASHA—and bringing her a fresh loaf of caraway rye bread as "an offering of peace and gratitude." He is a short, round-faced man in his fifties, very British in accent, with a way of pronouncing his *S*'s and *R*'s that sounds to me like an impediment, some sort of lisp, but that a speech therapist friend in Evanston once told me was the mark in England of an upper-class education. That explains the nickname Esther has given him; when I look at her, she rolls her eyes. He calls Natalie "Tawi," and Esther "Powwy," and he hugs both women like a doting uncle. When Natalie introduces us, he puts out a hand that is as soft as my own, but much better manicured.

"Delighted," he says. "Any friend of this household is a dear friend of mine."

Bobby wears a white linen suit, white tennis shoes, white socks, a white sport shirt buttoned to the collar—but no tie—and a soft white hat that makes him look rakish, or like a tipsy golfer in a nightclub, in spite of his otherwise formal appearance. He is downright puppyish around Natalie, he clearly dotes on her, and it's equally clear that she's flattered by his attentiveness. He reminds me of a man Webb and I worked with our first summer in Ogunquit, a dishwasher named Vincent—Vinnie—who quickly became Webb's disciple. Vinnie admired Webb's calm in the face of the overwhelming stacks of dishes, Webb's speed and efficiency in rinsing them and feeding them into the machinery, his speed and care in stacking and shelving them when they were dry. Vinnie was twice our age, and slow both mentally and physically—"Why would a grown man take a job like this," Webb said, "unless he was retarded?"—but he lived to please Webb, and when Webb told him about benzedrine, how it would energize him both physically and mentally, Vinnie quickly got addicted. He was Webb's pet and pal; he fawned on him, and was truly hurt to be left out of any part of Webb's day.

"You absolutely saved my life, Talie," Bobby says to Natalie. *Tawi.* And, to Esther, "Your mother is a Samaritan of the first water." *Muvver. Samawitan.*

"Bobby's MG is in the shop," Natalie explains. "It broke down."

"And had to be towed," Bobby says. "A humiliating experience, I must confess. I rode up front with the tow driver, hoping none of my friends would see me. Or recognize the car. Powwy, don't you find it amusing that automobiles and people both have breakdowns?"

"Most amusing," Esther says, deadpan.

"Though God knows a good mechanic costs even more than a shrink," Bobby says.

"I wouldn't know," Esther says.

"You didn't get my message, Bobby," Natalie says. "You can keep the car another day."

"Smashing," Bobby says. "How did I manage that?"

"Alec has a rental."

"Talie," Bobby goes on, "that wonderful loaf of bread is to be eaten with honey. Mornings when you're in your counting-house."

Natalie is in the kitchen, sliding the round loaf into a bread-box on the counter to the right of the refrigerator. "It's a sweet present. We'll finish it in no time."

Bobby turns to me. "Bless you. Alec. I love to drive Talie's cabriolet."

"What model MG do you have?" I ask.

"It's an MGB, the GT model. Relatively rare, I think. Actually, I'm not the original owner." Bobby settles onto one of the stools and sits so he can speak to both kitchen and living room. "The car is reputed to have belonged to a well-known movie star. Possibly that's true. One of the first pieces of business I had to attend to was replacing the windscreen, which was so pitted—a thousand millions of tiny holes—" He stops and grins at me. "Do you know the song? 'Now they know how many holes it takes to fill the Albert Hall'? Well, that was my windscreen. Somebody told me that the celebrity in question only drove back and forth from Palm Springs to Studio City, obviously at high speed, and the desert sand had done the damage. If you drove into the sun, you simply couldn't see through the glass, the light was so refracted."

"A long time ago," I say, "a friend of mine owned an MG-TD."

"Oh, yes," Bobby says. "The classic machine. Very rare now. Very rare indeed."

"It was dark green. I remember that there wasn't a lot of legroom, and the lever to unlatch the door dug into the side of my knee."

"British Racing Green," Bobby says. "The phrase reminds one of the lost glories of Empire." He looks genuinely sad.

"Bobby," Natalie says, "do stay for lunch. Then Esther has a riding lesson."

"We can't do it tomorrow?" Esther says.

"Today's arranged, and I'm not about to cancel. Besides, Alec has to talk to Jenny."

"I'll be overjoyed to have lunch with you," Bobby says. "You and your new friend." He slides down from the stool and hugs Esther around the shoulders on his way to the table. "You're becoming such a beauty, Polly. You should be a model."

When he has let her go, Esther looks at me and wrinkles her nose.

AFTER LUNCH, I sit by myself at the glass table and gaze idly out across the rake and green of Santa Barbara, out over the water where it is just possible to see oil-rig platforms and the low blue shadow of islands. Natalie is outside—I can see her below the window, pondering the hillside garden. Esther is in her room, getting dressed for her lesson at Jenny's ranch.

I can imagine what Esther will look like in her riding habit. Harriet rode when I married her; the two of us spent a lot of time at the stables where she boarded Starface, her thoroughbred gelding—the horse an extravagance it took me a while to accept—and we traveled to various horse shows until she began to complain of fatigue. I remember it as a world where young women like Esther were a tribe, a society, an almost mythological universe of creatures that looked down from their altitude like female centaurs, long hair tucked up under hunt caps as if to disguise their gender. They wore white shirts tied at the throat in silken bowknots, tailored black jackets with velvet collars, flared jodhpurs that distorted the line of their hips and thighs, polished boots that fitted the leg so closely the riders needed help to remove them—bootjack or parent or friend, prying mightily to free the leg. Sometimes the young women wore spurs, but even if they did, the rowels were dull and you knew the spurs were only for appearance's sake. After their events, the young women rode from the ring and doffed their caps; the long hair—like Esther's, like Pru's—fell to their shoulders; they shook their heads and lifted their hands—left then right, moving the hunt cap from one hand to the other—to make the hair flow freely.

I described this gesture to Esther before she went to change, and she reacted by looking perplexed.

"It's amazing, don't you think," she said, "how boys— men—don't seem to outgrow it. I mean this fascination with a person's hair."

"It's part of a woman's beauty," I said.

"Apparently. At least you and Elmer would agree on that."

"You don't think it is?"

"It isn't so simple. I guess probably this would be an ugly world if everybody was bald." The idea amused her for a moment, but then she was serious again. "But it's spooky. I think I have quite nice hair, and I've always liked it to be long—except in truly beastly-hot weather, when it's a pain to have a sweaty neck all the time—but sometimes, especially as I get older, I think about getting it cut."

"I think that would be a shame," I said.

"Mother talks about getting it cut, too. At first I said 'no way' to her, but it does things—long hair, I mean. It *provokes* things. Boys. Men. It's Elmer, telling me I ought to be a model. You know how males look at you if you have long hair, if you're pretty." She shrugged. "Maybe you don't know, since you're one of them."

"I appreciate long hair," I said. "I don't think it 'provokes' me."

"Maybe it's something that goes away with old age," she says.

"What 'old age'?"

At that, she put on an expression of make-believe fear and backed her chair away from the table. "Nothing personal," she said. "Mother thinks you look 'remarkably young for your years.' I quote."

"I don't think of myself as old," I said. "And I don't have a hair fetish."

She stood up to go change.

"I think I know what 'fetish' means," she said. "But whatever hair does to a male person, it scares me a little. That's all I meant to say: that a girl with pretty hair gets to feeling like she's some kind of furry animal all the boys are on the hunt for."

Now, sitting alone, I wonder why I lied about women's hair. I remember Jenny's from more than twenty-five years ago—the length of it, the scent of it, the silken feel it had under my hands—and Pru's, how the light brings out the reddish tint in it and makes me forget the years that lie between us. "Of course a woman's hair attracts you," I can hear Webb argue. "Of course you want to see it, fanned out on your pillow and no one else's."

TO GET TO THE ZODIAC RANCH, Natalie drives us up into the hills north and west of Santa Barbara, toward a town called Santa Ynez. The road climbs steeply, drops unexpectedly, climbs again, and it winds as if we were in the heart of mountain country—and apparently we are. Every quarter-mile or so are turnoffs for slow-moving traffic, and as we pass each one I can look off to my right over a grassy valley dotted with junipers and oak trees—black oak and live oak, I learn later—and here and there the houses and barns and outbuildings that are horse ranches. They are built on the sides and crests of steep hills, and the entire valley is ruled off by miles of white rail fences.

"A lot of quarter-horses are raised in the Valley," Natalie tells me. "And thoroughbreds. Nobody raises Arabians anymore; there's no tax break for the breeding of pleasure horses. We're lucky Jenny is still interested in English pleasure; most of what riding instruction there is around here is strictly Western."

"Barrel-racing," Esther says. "What a waste."

"And there's more and more dressage," Natalie says. "The wave of the future."

We keep climbing through the dry air. I sit in the back seat; Esther is sitting beside her mother in the passenger seat, her belt buckled loosely so she can turn to me when she talks. Esther is dressed for her lesson somewhat less formally than I had pictured: white t-shirt, khaki riding breeches, high black boots. Her black hunt cap and a riding crop are on the seat beside me. En route, I can't resist holding the crop, examining it, trying it out a couple of times—thwack!—against my upper legs; it is a little more than a foot in length, made of some knobby hardwood, with an ivory head shaped like a bird's beak at one end, and a loop of worn brown leather at the other.

"Do you need this?" I ask Esther.

"Sometimes you have to get the horse's attention," she says. "They're a very willful animal."

"Does it make you feel like a British colonel?" I say.

She gives me a pitying look. "It's not a swagger stick," she says. "It's *functional*."

On both sides of the car stiff grasses ripple along our way, dry and golden with the season. On both horizons are mountains.

"Do the mountains have a name?" I ask Natalie.

"Off to the left, toward the coast: that's the Santa Ynez range. To the right—I can't remember the name, but beyond *them* is the beginning of the Sierra Nevadas."

"It's gorgeous country." I'm surprised by it. I must have been expecting high desert: cactus, tumbleweed, anonymous wildflowers. Surely not the tumbled mountainsides, the breathtaking declivities we have crossed to enter the Santa Ynez Valley.

"Wait till you see the Warner ranch," Esther says. "It beats television."

"I can hardly wait," I say.

True. I'm feeling an impatience tinged with apprehension. I'm pleased that Natalie has arranged so soon for Esther to recommence her riding lessons with Jennifer Warner—I'm beginning slowly to get used to the name of a second husband I haven't known about—but uneasy about the reunion. Natalie hasn't told Jenny I'm coming along. It's my idea that I should be a "surprise"; I'm half afraid Jenny would refuse to see me, even if she remembered me.

"Is there cactus in this valley? I sort of expected it."

"Not much," she says. "Some low stuff; I don't know what you call it."

"I know," Esther says. "Elephant ear."

"You used to call it beaver tail," Natalie says.

"But now I *know* what they are, Mother." Her voice carries the edge I noticed yesterday: a mild mother-daughter friction. In ten years will Pru and Mindy be like these two? "I was very young then."

"This is storybook country," I say.

We turn off the highway. At the end of a long, two-lane asphalt drive is a stand of trees with pale yellow leaves, perhaps mesquite, and beyond them is an iron gate, painted green, framed by brick-faced pillars and dark shrubbery Esther tells me is greasewood. Natalie stops the car at the gate, enters five numbers on a keypad set at window level; the gate slides slowly open and we drive through. When I look behind us, I see the gate already sliding shut.

The road winds higher. Ahead of us is a large white barn, and beyond it, at the very top of the hill, is the Warner ranch house—or a structure that looks as if it is becoming the Warner ranch house, a house framed and roofed and sided, but obviously unfinished, with high empty windows in wooden frames primed white, raw white eaves, a white cupola whose lights still carry the maker's labels. We pull into the driveway. The lawns are clipped and geometrically crisp, the greenery around the house neatly trimmed; the flagstones of the front walk are meticulously fitted, and the oak front door stands open as if to welcome us. What contradicts the neatness of the landscaping is the clutter of building materials piled everywhere—the gutters and downspouts, the random lengths of lumber, the rolls of tarpaper and the brown-paper-wrapped shingling. A table saw sits under a tree between the house and garage.

"Doesn't look as if it's ready to be lived in," I say.

Natalie nods. "They were building the new place when Jen's husband died. It was horrible for her. I don't think she's had any work done since."

I understand now why everyone has heard of the Zodiac.

There are no workmen; no sign of construction underway. Whatever is happening on the ranch is happening only in the neighborhood of the barn, with a single exception: a small pickup truck with a topper sits on an apron next to the garage, and in it I can see the heads of two dogs—shorthaired and tan. I can't tell the breed from where we park. The dogs watch us, but don't move or bark.

When Natalie turns off the engine and we all get out of the car, the light breeze is dry and cool and smells of horses. We walk down the slope from the silent house, past a smaller ranch-style house toward the barn. The barn has dark red trim, and two or three other wood-frame outbuildings, all of them painted white with the same dark red trim, are clustered around it. Two horse trailers, one longer than the other, are parked near the entrance to the barn.

"There's Mrs. Warner," Esther says. She gathers the hunt cap and riding crop from the backseat, and trots off in the direction of a fenced-in area where a gray-haired woman is working a horse at the end of a longe line. The horse is reddish-brown, circling through a sunlit aura of dust, impressively larger than the woman at the other end of the rope. I can't see the woman's face clearly, because of distance and dust, but I can hear her voice—its rise and fall, its profanity.

Natalie follows her daughter, but I hang back and lean against the sun-warm metal of a fender of one of the trailers. I haven't seen Jenny in more than fifteen years, and I'm not sure I'm ready for the reunion—especially not sure if *she* is. Whenever Harriet and I paid a visit to her after Webb moved out, she was never less than polite, but she was never *more* than polite, as if she had determined only to be socially correct in her behavior toward a former lover and his sick wife. The pattern of these visits—and there were only a few before Harriet died—was that Harriet and I amused ourselves during most of the day, and in the evenings after dinner we sat by ourselves, me sipping whiskey and Harriet reading by the fire, while Jenny bedded the children. When she joined us, the conversation was guarded. If she had a nightcap—and it was rare that she did— you could be sure she would say something bitter about Webb. "My God, what did he do to her?" Harriet would say after Jenny had gone upstairs to sleep and the two of us were getting ready for bed. "I think it must have something to do with the children," I would say, though there was never any clue from their behavior—Amanda withdrawn and bookish, Will boisterous and impatient with his sister—that suggested they were unusual siblings.

When Esther arrives at the paddock, Jenny stops working the horse. She goes to it to unfasten the line from its halter, releases it, then strolls toward the gate where Esther is waiting. There is an animated conversation, which Natalie joins, and after a few minutes Jenny points toward one of the outbuildings. In that direction I see a man in jodhpurs and boots and a yellow shirt. He is saddling a spindly-legged sorrel; I imagine this is Commodore, the horse Esther will ride for her lesson. She and her mother stroll toward the man, Natalie with her arm around Esther's shoulders, Esther already putting on the hunt cap and fastening the strap under her chin.

Now there is nothing between Jennifer Warner and me except a closable distance.

t h r e e

■

IF I WERE ASKED about the first time I actually met Jennifer Grant, I imagine I would tell a long and vague and inconclusive story, much the way an unprepared student might have written an essay exam of mine. ("During the now scarcely-remembered Korean Conflict, Special Services libraries were indeed *special* for our servicemen stationed at far-flung American bases from Tokyo to Timbuktu. . . .") We met in Germany—Bremerhaven—late in 1953, a few months after Webb and I had been shipped to our respective overseas assignments, but exactly when, and exactly where— That moment isn't vivid in my memory after forty years.

From the day I first met Jenny until that moment of knee-buckling clarity when I saw her by chance at the bus stop and knew with certainty I was in love with her, probably we talked a hundred times. I was a reader in those days, half-educated, lonely, barely into my twenties; except for summer jobs and the two years at Bowdoin, I'd lived at home my whole life. I was ripe for anything and everything—witness my Erika foolishness—but at the same time I was timid about what those things might be. Books seemed a likely way to get without risk some experience of life, to learn without paying a price, to travel without spending my money or losing my luggage. Jenny helped. She recommended titles, encouraged my enthusiasms, listened to me rave or complain. She was as important a teacher as I ever had in school or college.

And I was taught not only from the books she presided over. Those were the days of Senator Joseph McCarthy, and though his influence among those stationed in Europe was attenuated by distance and a general lack of interest in politics, the senator had a brief surrogate presence in Bremerhaven when two of his staff, Roy Cohn and David Schine, arrived to survey the holdings of American overseas libraries. Were there subversive books on the shelves, books by communists and pinkos and fellow travelers, these two would ferret them out, remove them and report back to the senator. While their publicized focus was on libraries run by the U.S. Information Services, there came one cold afternoon in October when Cohn and Schine—and an entourage of unsmiling aides—appeared, unannounced, in Jennifer Grant's Special Services library.

"They're dreadful men," Jenny told me that evening. "They pulled book after book off the shelves. Just let them fall onto the floor as if they were trash. Nazis—that's what they were. Little pompous Nazis."

"Did they take anything?"

"That's the worst of it. They took nothing—not so much as a single Howard Fast novel. I don't think they had a clue about what they were looking for." She showed me some of the aftermath: a scattering of books on the floor of the nonfiction section she had not had time to reshelve. She let me help her bring order out of the chaos.

But I remember the less-heightened times—the long sunless afternoons in winter, the rainy afternoons in spring—when I was on the graveyard trick and didn't leave for work until eleven at night, when it seemed as if I were the only patron of the Marine Barracks library. Jenny kept a pot of coffee on a burner behind the checkout desk, and I suppose I spent more time with her, talking about books and drinking coffee, than I did with my roommates.

Probably she was responsible—as responsible as anybody—for my becoming a literature professor; it would have been an easy enough influer e. I would be returning to my junior year at Bowdoin, had no particular notion of the future—I didn't even have a major picked out. She represented both literature and sex—the former rather more than the latter, at least early on—and once when we got into an argument about a new Philip Wylie novel, she persuaded me to join her on a fifteen-minute radio show that the Armed Forces Network broadcast once a week. It was the AFN's single gesture toward culture, its aim to give its listeners the lowdown on recent books. The book was *The Disappearance,* and because to my mind Wylie could do no wrong, I gave it a rave review. It was a futuristic novel; alas, I can no longer recall whether it was the women who disappeared, leaving the world in the hands of the men, or the other way around.

In any event, Jennifer and I had the advantage of what used to be called *propinquity*—a natural closeness that allows a man and a woman to come gradually to know each other, with no self-consciousness about what form the relationship should take. Nothing like Webb's deliberate process of seduction, nothing to do with conquest and consequence. Nothing tensely sexual. I see from the vantage of my sixty-odd years that Jenny and I were friends first, and later we became whatever else we were destined to be: lovers in Baltimore and then strangers, acquaintances again in Maine and then family friends, strangers again—by the circumstances of geography and time—until today.

There were already four Jennys in my memory. There was the Bremerhaven librarian in the blue uniform and the smart little blue cap and the taupe raincoat; the small-boned woman with the long hair worn conservatively in a bun or a French braid; the pretty girl-next-door who was nearly always smiling, whose dimples made pixie-ish whatever expression she wore.

Then there was the Jenny of our engagement, the relaxed, often wanton woman who loved me in Baltimore with a passion I would not have expected of her overseas persona; the hungry woman, face flushed and hair loosed, who tangled herself in me and spoke not in words but in animal sounds that excited me all the more; the playful, teasing woman who bowed over me, both of us naked, and let down her long fine hair, brushing me with it lightly and deliberately from face to thigh until I was crazy again for lovemaking.

And oh, there was the Jenny of betrayal, the Jenny sweat-drenched and disheveled from her copulation with Webb, the Jenny I despised in the rush of an instant, the woman I called next morning "bitch" and "whore" and "cunt"—words I regretted at the very moment I said them, though I would not have denied them.

Last of all was the Jenny of our foursome's friendship, all hatreds and hurts unmentioned if not quite forgotten, the Jenny of domesticity, of motherhood, of long patience and eventual disillusion with Webb. This was the Jenny I lost touch with fifteen years ago, when she divorced Webb and Harriet's cancer had begun its overt course and all our lives seemed to come unstrung; the Jenny nearest—if not clearest—in my mind today.

FOR A FEW MOMENTS I'm not quite able to match this gray-haired woman walking toward me with any of the Jennys of my past, but as she comes closer—and as a tentative smile plays around her mouth and eyes—my memory begins to do its job of connection, that knack the mind has of making forgotten faces familiar until you wonder how you could have missed the similarities in the first place. Her hair—alas—is cut short; her face and neck and arms are ruddy from exposure to the California sun, the lines around her eyes and mouth etched deeply, her hands looking large and competent and thick-veined. *Character, not age,* one says of such features. She is thinner than I remember her, but she's wiry, not skinny. This is a new Jenny, an outdoor Jenny, a Jenny whose strength and independence are obvious and impressive. She wears jeans, a denim shirt, a dark blue neckerchief, scuffed boots.

I stand away from the horse trailer and wait for her to give me her hand, but she doesn't offer to shake hands. Instead, she sets both fists against her hips, stops and surveys me. The smile is still on her face, not quite open yet, but not erased.

"Well," she says. She compresses her lips, shakes her head slowly. "I suppose it's a sign of the times that old acquaintances don't let anyone know they're coming to visit."

"I wasn't sure I'd be welcome," I say.

She tips her head slightly. The sun comes at us from an angle that makes her squint, but she is sizing me up—making her own mind do its memory work, fitting me into the man she once loved and then cheated on and later tolerated.

"Why ever not?" she says. And now she puts out her hand. I take it; our hands are clasped for all of two seconds. Her hand is tough and hot and dry, and I can feel the strength of it.

"You know," I say. "All the old reasons."

"Layers of them."

"Yes."

"We'll hash them all over, I'm sure," she says.

"Probably." I feel at an advantage, knowing Webb is dead.

"I'd have recognized you," she says. "You haven't changed all that much, hiding behind all the years. When was it that Harriet passed away?"

"Ten years ago."

"So it's more than that."

"More like fifteen."

We are a tableau, both standing, facing each other a yard or so apart, matching presents and pasts. Jenny looks pensive; I imagine I look uneasy and a little stupid.

"Come on, stranger," she says. "I have some work to finish up, and then I'll be gracious and make us a pot of coffee."

She turns and starts toward the barn where I first saw her—this woman I loved and wanted in the days when everything was a possibility—and I follow, catching up, letting her surprise me by taking my upper arm with both her hands, squeezing it as if she has decided to be a pleased old friend.

She looks up at me. "Amenities aside," she says, "I wasn't lying. You haven't changed to speak of."

"I'm sure my hair is a lot thinner. But—"

"But who wants fat hair?" she finishes, still remembering the kind of sophomoric humor I used to share with Webb. She falls into step alongside me. "God, we used to think we were so hilarious."

"You've cut yours," I say. "Your hair."

"I guess when you go gray, it becomes a question of how much reminder of age you can tolerate. It's not an attractive color—unless you pretend it's ash-blond—so I figured the less, the better." She puts her hand up to her forehead and pulls a lock forehead, as if to show me how short it really is. "Besides, it gets brittle. It falls and clogs the drains."

We walk. The ground is dry and feels loose under my feet. The white barn is just ahead of us; the smell of horses—a smell Harriet always called "healthy and clean"—the odor of manure and sweat and leather, is rich on the arid breeze.

"I think about Harriet more than you might imagine,"

Jenny says. "At the moment because all this hair talk reminds me of the wig she was wearing at the end. Not the very end, but the end I knew. The chemovanity. But in general she flashes into my mind at odd moments. Unexpected visions. You must miss her, even after all this time."

"I do." I don't say anything about Pru—how the week I spent with her sits at the front of my thoughts, sits like a screen between me and old memories of the dead. To tell Jenny not only that Webb is dead but that he was going to marry a woman barely thirty, and then to tell her that in some insidious and unpremeditated way I seem to be moving, or *want* to be moving, toward the same decision, the same young woman—that set of circumstances makes me uneasy.

"So tell," she says.

We're inside the shade of the barn now, stalls ranked along one side, horses' heads like busts of nobility watching our approach. The barn seems remarkably long, a narrow field open at the other end into sunlight.

"Tell?"

She takes down a length of rope and stops in front of one of the stalls, swings open its gate, takes hold of the halter of the horse inside. It is an enormous animal, almost mahogany-colored in the dark of the barn, its eyes slightly mad—or so I think—as they look down at me. Jenny clips one end of the rope to the halter, attaches the other end to a closed hook at the rear of the stall.

"Natalie let it slip," she says, "on the phone. You're not here by coincidence. Seeing me is the whole point of your trip out to California."

"Webb's dead," I say. So much for devising a best way to read her Webb's obituary: simply come out with it.

She crosses to the other side of the barn and takes down a second length of rope from a welter of hanging tack.

"I thought that might be it," she says. She is frowning, but I don't read the frown as some version of grief. Then I remind myself that Jenny's reaction is not part of my mission. What I'm after is more selfish than that, and has to do with reconciliation and a distant past.

"I'm sorry to be the messenger," I say, as if my news were bad.

She shapes the rope in her hands into a coil. "You remember what we used to say in Germany? Back in the days when you and I met?"

"I remember we said a lot of things."

"I don't mean anything personal. I mean what *everybody* used to say." She goes back into the stall and smacks her palm hard against the horse's neck in a gesture I take to be affectionate. "This is Lorca," she says. "A lovely gelding, but inclined to be flighty." She looks at me. *"Macht nichts,"* she says. "We used to shrug our shoulders and say, *'Macht mir nichts.'"*

"I remember," I admit. And if in those days one of us asked, *"Was ist los?"* there was always someone else who answered, *"Der Hund ist los."*

"What on earth made him think he had to send you on some kind of mission to announce his death to me? You could have clipped the death notice out of the paper, mailed it to me."

Jenny loops the second rope around the six-by-six at the end of the stall and makes it fast. The gelding dances backward, then forward, and resigns itself to the cross-tying.

"He was still living in Scoggin?"

"Yes."

She takes down a curry comb and runs it over the horse's flanks and rump, her teeth gritted half in concentration, half— or so I imagine—in the reawakening of old anger.

"You could have sent me the Scoggin *Tribune*," she says. "I'd have read it and done my jig and drunk an Irish, neat. 'In memoriam,' I'd have said. 'Thank you, God,' I'd have said."

I wonder how to respond. My last memory of Webb and Jennifer together is from all those years ago, at the lake house, and there was no such acrimony between the two of them at the time. Tension, yes—the incident of "the piano babe," as Jenny once called her—but not the kind of antagonism that outlasts divorce and death.

"I'd have burned the clipping in the sink," she says. "Ashes to ashes." She strains onto her toes to reach the gelding's back. "Down the fucking drain."

"Maybe the mission was for my benefit. Not yours."

She stands flatfooted and pushes the fringe of hair off her forehead with the back of the hand that holds the comb. She is out of breath, leaning against the stall. "Maybe," she says.

"Maybe it's that you're supposed to tell *me* something I need to understand." I know I'm fishing. I have no idea what Jenny might be able to tell me about Webb that would be useful in a world empty of him.

"Or maybe it's all for *his* benefit," she says. "Looking out for number one, even from beyond the grave."

"How so?"

"That he wants you to be friends with me. He wants you to forgive him his trespasses."

As she is saying the words, a small white terrier appears in the doorway of the barn. The horse is startled—does a noisy little waltz step and shies against the woman currying him.

"Shit," Jenny says. She shoves mightily at the horse. "Get off me, you ox."

I get behind the gelding and put my shoulder against his rump to help, but I can't seem to budge him. He's pinned Jenny against the side of the stall. She strains to make him move so she can get free, and her face is florid.

"Get the damned dog out of here." She sounds breathless, and then she says to the horse: "You fucking scaredy-cat."

I start after the dog, which runs away from me and sits in the dust of the barnyard, panting and wagging its stubby tail. When I go back into the barn, Jenny is free and sitting on the overturned grain bucket, wiping her face with a handkerchief.

"You O.K.?" I say.

She shakes her head, not to deny that she is all right, but to express disgust. "Thirteen hundred pounds," she says. "You don't realize what a big animal a horse is until it throws all that weight on top of you. You could break a rib or two."

"I was never much for horses," I say.

"And they're none too bright. Contrary to what the little girls who love them may think." The horse moves abruptly, its hooves making a terrible clatter on the barn floor; the terrier is inside again. Jenny throws the metal comb at the dog. "Get away, Snowball," she yells.

"Who's the dog belong to?" I say.

"He thinks he belongs to me. Somebody from town dumped him out on the road to fend for himself and he adopted me, hangs around the barn, gives mongrels in general a bad name." She pulls herself to her feet and proceeds to untie the horse. "That's all the attention you get for now," she tells Lorca.

She slaps it hard on the flank and the horse trots away, but then it stands between us and the doorway, an enormous silhouette blocking the daylight, as if it is waiting to be invited back into its stall.

"I can't bear to let dumb animals starve," Jenny says. "Even if they try to hurt me." She tucks the handkerchief into her back pocket and walks past the gelding toward the front of the barn. "Come on," she says. "I guess that means you, too."

THEY ARE TWO HOUSES that we walk toward. The one I have seen from the gateway, with its unfinished, almost skeletal profile against a bare sky, is the larger of the two. Downhill from it is the house Jenny seems actually to live in; it is modest but pleasant—ranch style with a sunporch that takes up most of the south side of the building and has a greenhouse at its east end. A profusion of green leaves and white and yellow blossoms glows behind the greenhouse glass; the individual panes carry small auras of moisture that cloud their corners. Given the climate, I wonder why anyone would build such a room into their home. All sorts of wild plants and flowers flourish here, even during drought.

"Jack had a passion for orchids—among others," Jenny says

when I ask. "He'd been in the marines during the war, and they'd stationed him on an island somewhere in the Pacific; Java, Borneo, Sumatra—I don't remember. I don't mean yours and Webster's war. I mean World War Two. Anyway, Jack used flowers to run away from the dying. He was a doctor."

"He was older than you," I say.

"A bit," she says. "Anyway, I do my best to keep the plants alive, even though I hardly ever know what I'm doing. I'm not noted for my green thumb—just for my knack with animals." She grins at me. "And my increasingly bad language."

"What about the construction up the hill—that big house?"

"Ambition," she says. "Jack decided he wanted elbow room in his old age, so off we plunged. It's like people who retire, and then die six months later. We poured the foundation, did the framing, got the roof up and some of the siding in place . . . then bango, Jack's gone."

She leads me inside and motions me to the kitchen table. I sit. It is late enough in the day that the sun is low in the sky and has taken on a rosy cast from the dust and fog to westward—though I have no sense at all that an ocean lies in that direction. Looking down past the barns I see Esther, astride the sorrel horse whose size dwarfs her, her instructor standing a few yards away from her with his bare arms folded. I picture Jenny's adventure with the gelding; frailer Esther would not have gotten off so lightly.

"I can give you that coffee—a little burned, I'm afraid, from sitting on the stove all day—or I can offer you a drink." Jenny pours coffee for herself and studies me from in front of the stove. "I don't approve of liquor so early, but this is an occasion, isn't it? My first lover, visiting me alone after more years than I care to count?"

"Not right now," I say.

A pale-orange cat, its tail only a stub that stands straight up from its rump, strolls into the kitchen and finds a place in the sun near the refrigerator. The cat's tail-less walk is odd, a trot like a puppy's.

Jenny notices me watching the cat. "It's not a Manx. Some animal took its tail," she says. "A coyote, most likely."

"Webb had an orange cat."

"Do tell." She sits across from me. My cat footnote has apparently annoyed her.

"Was your other husband a drinker?" I ask. "Is that why you don't approve of early liquor?"

She cradles the coffee cup and looks into its depths. "Jack Warner was many things, but he wasn't a drinker. It's simply that his prejudices became mine, I think. He had meticulous habits, iron routines. A brandy Manhattan just before dinner— that was his only drinking. Maybe a glass of wine with the meal. He's nothing like Webb, who'd swallow anything, any time it was offered."

I consider her words, her husbands. *Jennifer Grant Hartley Warner,* I think, as if she is only the sum of the names the men in her life have given her. I feel a twinge. Do I still wish my own name were on that list? The longer I am in her company, the more the face I remember from the far past comes clear in her present features. The longer I look at her, the more she is the woman I loved.

"Jack died four years ago," she says. "Kidney failure."

"How old was he?"

"He was in his seventies. Not quite seventy-two. 'Natural causes' is what the medical people called it—being a doctor himself, he probably would have concurred."

"You think it was something *un*natural?"

"Nothing sinister," she says. "I can't help thinking that something he caught in the War—the malaria, which he *did* have, or something more exotic—finally managed to do him in." She puts up her hand as if to foreclose any words of mine. "I know," she says. "Seventy-two is old enough. But he came from a long-lived family. A father who lived to be almost a hundred; uncles who persisted into their nineties. It's part of the reason I married him: I didn't want any more children, but I did want a man who'd live with me into my own old age."

"Probably you could still find another." What I'm thinking is that Jack Warner's ambitious retirement home has been sitting unfinished at least the four years since his death. Who will finish it? Or will it stand incomplete, until Jenny herself dies, like some sort of perverse monument?

She tips her head, compresses her lips, gives me a look that is almost unfriendly. "Maybe," she says, "but don't you dare imply that *you* might be coming on to me, that you're the late arrival to salvage me from my widowed state. Not after the way you acted in Baltimore."

"How should I have acted?"

"You could have stayed for an explanation. It might have changed all our lives."

"Or *you* could have explained later, when I swallowed my pride, when Harriet and I started visiting you and Webb."

She responds by pushing her chair back and taking her coffee cup to the sink. "What in holy hell would have been the point?" she says. "By then I was a practicing wife, a mother with two kids, a woman you hadn't loved in a thousand years."

A thousand years. "It only seemed that long," I say.

Jenny stands at the window, looking toward the riding ring.

"Excuse me," she says. "I have to go see what the new man thinks he's doing with Esther and that gelding."

I WATCH HER WALK down the shallow embankment toward the barn, her hands pushed into the back pockets of her jeans, the length of her stride suggesting anger or impatience. The man in charge of Esther and Commodore looks toward her, raises a hand to Esther in mid-trot, then opens both hands toward Jenny as if to say, *What have I done?*—a gesture that for a moment reminds me of Webb in his rare defensive moments. I think how different Jenny is, how strong. How much more profane. *How we change.*

Jennifer Grant is the only woman I have ever struck.

It was in Germany, not so terribly long after I'd met her, fallen for her. As one of the few American women in the Enclave—*young* American women—she was in demand among the unmarried officers, whether army, navy or air force. She was always invited to the Officers' Club parties, and while she was certainly free to decline the invitations, often she did not. "It's not as if I were being unfaithful to you," she would tell me. "It's just that it's boring for me to sit around the apartment alone, especially since most of your work is in the evenings."

There wasn't much I could say to that. It was true that during the hours of darkness I was frequently in the Operations building, doing my military duties in front of the gray faceplate of the Hammarlund receiver, searching the dials for Soviet military traffic, the image of slender-ankled Jenny a kind of mist that filtered in and around my immediate attentiveness to a possible enemy. Why should she not walk into the Officers' Club on the arm of some transient colonel or major—a handsome man on his way home to the States, or just arrived from there and waiting for transport to Wiesbaden or Frankfurt or occupied Berlin? What was so wrong about that?

But I was grudging in my acceptance of fact. At the library the following morning I would begin with the innocent question: "How was the Club?" And she would tell me, define the occasion—Lincoln's Birthday, Easter, some obscure Canadian or British or French holiday whose existence was an excuse for dance or drink—describe the man, his rank, his destination; summarize the menu, the music. She usually learned a good deal about the man—his wife, children, what he had done or would do as a civilian. I remember there was an endless stream of lawyers passing through, as if we had won not a war but a litigation managed by the Judge Advocate General's office.

Of course my objectivity waned and my jealousies grew. Age had something to do with it: these professional men, these older and settled types who knew their ambitions and looked forward to healthy incomes and comfortable families—they had *arrived*. They walked through the world with a confidence I could only imagine. I had college to go back to, and I had no notion of the shape my future might take: I could not then have dreamed of being a college professor and childless and an unexpected widower. All I knew on the nights when Jenny was dancing at the Officers' Club was that her partners swam in an aura of self-confidence that surely bathed Jenny in a confidence of her own—a trust that might persuade her to forget me and fall in love with *him*. On some nights, the rare ones when I was free and Jenny was on a "date"—"I *couldn't* say no; I was the only woman available"—I sat at the service club and brooded over my beer, inventing scenarios that inevitably led to the image of Jenny in the naked embrace of some smooth-talking, forty-year-old attorney.

On one such night I went to the apartment house where Jenny lived, and there, sitting on the front steps, I waited for her to come home from her party. I'd had too much to drink, sitting at the bar of the Constanze for a couple of hours, and my imagination that night was especially cruel to me. By the time the Mercedes taxi stopped at the curb, I was at the near side of helpless rage. Before the cab doors opened, I was already hidden behind the shrubbery at the front of the apartment house. I watched the two of them, Jenny and a tall, broad-shouldered army officer, come up the walk together and go in at the building's front door.

They didn't see me. For a few minutes I could hear their voices through the half-opened door, and then the man emerged. The front door clicked shut behind him as he walked to the taxi and got in. When the taxi drove away, I came out of my hiding place and went into the apartment building. It was my plan, I think, to climb to Jenny's apartment on the second floor, hammer on her door, confront her with my jealousy. Perhaps I intended to deliver some kind of ultimatum; I can't say, because what actually happened was so far from my intentions.

As I started up the stairs, Jenny was still on the second-floor landing, rummaging in her purse for her key. She was in uniform—the cap, the military raincoat, the black pumps—as she always was when she went to the Club. Halfway up the stairs I stopped; all my resolves were ebbing away. In the dim light of the hall I saw her surprised smile. "For heaven's sake," she said, "what are *you* doing here?" "I just took a chance you'd be home," I said. She unlocked her door, pushed it open. "It's awfully late," she said. "I really can't ask you in."

By this time I was standing one step below her, so that I was nearly at eye level with her. "That's all right," I said. "I just wanted to see you." "That's flattering," she said. Then: "How was the evening?" I asked her. "Very nice," she said. "I saw the guy you were with," I confessed. "He was just leaving when I came around the corner." "That was Major Swift; he's quite a marvelous dancer." "Did you let him kiss you good night?"

That was a question I had never asked before, and naturally I regretted it. Jenny raised one eyebrow at me. "Yes," she said, "I did."

I slapped her, hard, the flat of my hand catching her across the mouth as she was turning her head away from me. A jealous reflex. She looked not hurt, but amazed at what I had done.

So was I amazed. I felt terrible—stupid and guilty and bereft in the knowledge I had done something I could never atone for. "Oh, God, I'm sorry," I said, and I reached out to put my arms around her, as if by holding her against me I could undo what I had done.

She backed away from me into her apartment. "You'd better go," she said. The door closed between us.

A few years later, in Baltimore, I told her how vividly I remembered that night. The three of us had been sitting around the kitchen table, planning the month's budget, drinking gin and tonic because it was August and hot, and I suppose the drink had made me melancholy and ripe for confession.

"That's the worst thing I've ever done to you," I said, and I know my eyes were moist. "Or to anybody." Fresh remorse.

Jenny looked perplexed. "I don't remember any of that," she said. "Are you sure it was me?"

So today, when she returns from the riding lesson, resuming her seat in this different kitchen under these far different circumstances, I ask her if now she remembers being slapped.

"I don't," she says. "I remember your telling the story, and I've sometimes thought it had something to do with your not raising your hand to me on a worse occasion—but I still think you must have made the whole thing up."

I shake my head; Jennifer smiles.

"I do remember Webster's reaction," she says. "He laughed at you, and he said, 'All those years of guilt. All that anguish wasted.' "

"I'M SURE I haven't forgotten anything that happened in Baltimore," Jenny says. "I never could."

"I remember Baltimore too."

She looks pitying. "You can't remember what you never knew."

"I've told you I regretted that. Everything I called you."

"Which doesn't excuse it." She shakes her head slowly, her gaze somewhere between my solemn face and the arena where Esther rides. "You can't imagine how many times I think of that rainy night—that cold, that relentless rain on my face. What I picture . . ."

She stops.

"Not the bedroom scene," she warns.

"That's *my* picture," I say.

"But there were so many questions you never asked," Jenny says. "You never knew all that happened."

"I only know what I saw," I say. "That was enough."

"Do you really *remember* that night?" She puts her coffee cup aside and leans her elbows on the table. Her eyes are fixed on mine; her look is serious—angry, I think.

"It was raining," I say, lamely. I call up my recollection of that night—locking the office I shared with three other graduate assistants, shrugging into my raincoat, tucking a folder of undergrad essays under the coat so they wouldn't get wet and smeared. I see myself stepping out into the parking lot, crossing it to the street, trudging home. "You're right: it was a cold rain."

"And there was sleet," Jenny says, "and a bitter wind."

"Yes," I agree.

"It was as if winter had changed its mind, and stopped in its tracks, and was turning back on Baltimore to teach it some kind of lesson about trusting spring."

"Well," I say, "at least the rain was cold." Over the years I'd almost forgotten Jenny's literary mode.

"I was the last person to leave the library that night," she says. She folds her hands in front of her, looks down at them as if she is gathering herself to remember something unpleasant, returns her gaze to me. "It was just after ten o'clock. The sleet had stopped and there was only that rain—the wind drove it straight at me when I opened the front door. I had three or four books I'd put in a brown paper bag to bring home—for all of us to read. It was a struggle: hanging on to that bag of books, trying to be hunched up against the weather, fumbling with my keys to lock up the library for the night. God, I was chilled to the bone in no time—ice water down the back of my neck, the wind freezing my legs."

"It was bad." An hour later I had been shivering in the same wind, the same wet, turning onto our street, seeing the vestibule light of the apartment house and looking forward to sitting down with Jenny and Webb over a brandy, maybe bundling up warm and going out again to a bar.

"When I'd locked the door," Jenny says, "I put my head down and turned around to face the wind. There's a broad entrance to the library building—you remember? A kind of red brick terrace you have to cross after you come up the steps?"

"Yes."

"I was halfway across that space, my head down so the wind wouldn't sting my face, taking a quick squinty look ahead every couple of steps." She stops. "Jesus," she says, "I can feel that cold; I can see that man."

"What man?"

"Just at the top of the steps, half on the terrace, half sprawled on the stairway, was this man. Lying there. I almost fell over him. At first—that first instant—I thought I was imagining him. I hadn't seen him there, but of course I'd only taken quick looks and then ducked my head again. I wasn't expecting anybody to be out in that weather, at that time of night."

She pushes her chair back from the table, stands. She's pale now, and she seems suddenly nervous. I realize she's right: I haven't ever known much about that night; there were a lot of questions I didn't ask. Webb knew that, of course; he had to have. I wonder why he never brought it up.

"Are you O.K.?" I say.

She shakes her head—not to say that she isn't all right, but as if she isn't able to believe the old images from a rainy night in Baltimore.

"God," she says. "That I can still get the shivers from it." She is standing by the window, looking out across the valley, the wonderful beauty of that view toward the mountains. "Are you sure you don't want a drink? I'm going to have one after all, early as it is."

She goes to a cupboard over the sink and takes down a bottle. "I know you drink Irish," she says. "It works in coffee." She splashes some of the whiskey into her cup, offers the bottle to me. Jameson's, Webb's brand.

"No, thank you." I couldn't explain why I've refused. Something to do with getting things straight, not fuzzing them up.

"The man was on his back. There was enough light from the street lamp at the foot of the steps for me to see that he was lying face up—his eyes were wide open. One of his hands looked tucked under him—for warmth, I thought, because his other hand was stretched out and I could see he wasn't wearing any gloves. You have to remember how unusual this was—how it was long before the age of the homeless persons that are everywhere you go nowadays. I spoke to him. I said, 'Are you all right? Do you need help?' "

She replaces the bottle, sits down and leans on the table, her hands around the coffee cup.

"I don't know if I finished saying that. 'Do you need help?' I knelt down beside him, this wet paper bag of books slowly disintegrating against my chest and the wind blowing my hair in my eyes, and I saw the blood. A whole lot of blood."

I can tell she is seeing the blood now, as she talks about this man on the library steps. Her eyes are strange, tears glistening in them. She sips the spiked coffee, sets the cup down again. Her movements are mechanical, too quick.

"His throat was cut." She takes a long breath. "You know how you hear about people having their throats slit 'from ear to ear'? Well, that's what someone had done to this man: cut his throat from ear to ear. The blood had just poured out of the cut and you could see it like a waterfall down the steps to the street, the rain pushing it down. I think by the time I found him, he wasn't bleeding anymore. He was damned sure dead."

"What did you do?"

"I ran," Jenny says. "Maybe I screamed first, but I do know I ran—down the steps and up the street toward home. I remember stepping over the stream of blood where it was washing into the gutter, wanting it not to get on my boots. I ran all the way to the apartment. I was sick, I was dizzy from running, I was scared stiff that whoever killed that poor man would chase me and cut my throat too. You know the horror movies. If you're a witness the murderer has to get you too, so you can't tell anyone. When I had to stop at a cross-street because the light was red, I was sure I could hear the killer's footsteps gaining on me. By the time I'd gotten inside our door and up the stairs to the apartment, I was in a state. I was damned near hysterical." She shuts her eyes. "No," she says. "I *was* hysterical."

"Did you call the police?"

The question seems almost to amuse her. "Oh, Alec," she says. "What the hell is the matter with you?"

I shrug. "That's what I'd have done."

"I *know* it is," she says. "That's one difference between you and Webster. If you'd been home when I came in all out of breath and weeping and scared out of my wits, you'd have told me to call the police. You'd have been concerned for law and order and getting the body picked up and taken away. Be neat. Unclutter the landscape."

"Webb made it an excuse to seduce you," I say. It's startling, but I feel my own anger and wounded pride almost as strongly now as when I walked in all those years ago and found Jenny and Webb in bed together.

"You don't understand," Jenny says. "You didn't have a clue then, and you haven't put it together since then. Or maybe you haven't even thought about it."

"I've thought about it."

"But all you see is the sex part of it."

"I knew Webb," I say. "I knew his knack for getting women into his bed."

Jenny takes another drink of the coffee and whiskey. This time her movements are relaxed, her expression is calm. "God knows," she says, "there were a thousand things I despised about Webster Hartley, and while I was his wife, what you call his 'knack' with sex betrayed me over and over again. I was never so happy or so unburdened as when I finally threw him out of my house and divorced him. But that night—"

I wait for her to finish the sentence. She looks as if she is thinking of Webb, of the years between them, between us. It's curious that in Jenny sitting across from me now I keep seeing more clearly the Jenny I met in Germany in the 1950s, the arrestingly lovely Special Services librarian I wanted dearly to marry. The lines there now are like embellishment, little accents to call attention to the finer points of her features; her gray hair is as attractive as her blond hair was when she was young; she's older, *old,* but she wears age without self-consciousness. I suppose it's because I can conjure the Jenny who was unfaithful to me with Webb that I feel an echo of the emotions I felt then.

"I don't think Webster ever *intended* to take me to bed," she says. "You were his closest friend. He wouldn't have wanted to do that to you."

I don't say anything; I don't want to be sarcastic.

"I told it all to him. All the blood. The terror. He calmed me down, soothed me. He held me and patted me, and then he wanted to put me to bed, give me a pill, get me to sleep. I wouldn't let him leave me alone—I was still scared, all the things I was thinking. Would the murderer always be looking for me? Could I ever go out that front door again, ever go to work knowing I might be the next person stabbed—by some maniac, some crazy who didn't like books. God, I was a case. I hung on to Webster, I made him get into bed with me. I practically raped him."

"And that was what I saw."

" 'Said the blind man.' " She leans on her elbows. " 'Who couldn't see at all.' Webster knew I was hurt, and he saw how deeply, and I think he realized I needed something—some action—strong enough to match the hurt, to counter it, to erase it. He let me do what I did. But I didn't think about that at the time. I only knew that in a funny way it recaptured my sanity for me. Afterward I thought it was a little bit marvelous— that yes, he was certainly fond of sex, but he knew it could be healing."

"You're rationalizing," I say.

"No," Jenny says. "That's where you're wrong. That's what you've never understood all this time."

"It didn't take you long to decide to marry him," I say. "You never came to me—to explain, to ask me to forgive you, to say you still wanted to marry me."

"Poor you," Jenny says. "Would you have given me the chance? You cursed me and called me terrible things. You walked out and never came back. You dropped me—as they used to say—summarily."

"Later on, after you were married and we all got to be friends, you could have explained."

"To remind Harriet that she was second choice? Is that what you thought I should do?"

"I didn't mean it like that." But perhaps I did, and I feel ashamed of myself for the possibility. It's as if I've needed the satisfaction of being holier than Jenny, morally superior to her, and I wonder if Webb while he was alive saw, but never had the temerity to tell me about my smallness.

"And I didn't agree to marry Webster Hartley until after I realized I was pregnant." She puts her hands flat on the table. "I don't think you even knew *that,*" she says.

I didn't. I didn't know—or care—about the man who had his throat cut. I didn't know—or care—if the killer was ever found. "I didn't know much of anything," I say.

"IT WASN'T A GREAT MARRIAGE," Jenny says, "whatever you may want to think. Not only because of what you call Webb's 'knack,' or what it pleases some people to call his 'roving eye,' but because in general we were a bad match. Physically, I mean. Biologically."

I sit across from this woman I was once so terribly in love with, and I wonder if I want to hear any of her life with Webb. My time with her still seems vivid, clear, *right;* what happened in Baltimore—whether Webb or Jennifer was chief betrayer seems irrelevant at this remove—is as fresh and wounding as a cut I might have given myself in Natalie Kramer's kitchen this morning. But then I think: why have I come to her, if not to learn *everything?*

"We were always somehow out of sync," Jenny is saying. "If I was in the mood to make love, he'd manage to be involved in a new painting, and when I was late for my job and trying desperately to leave the house, he'd be around me like some horny high-school kid. More and more, we were out of step with each other."

She looks at me almost shyly. The intimate details of her dead marriage—she surely needn't share them with me, of all people.

"Whenever we did make love," she says, "and after he'd carried out what seemed to him the obligatory affectionate gestures and said the necessary affectionate words, he'd always go to the bathroom. I could hear him urinating, flushing the john, washing his hands and face. It was a ritual; it bothered me that he'd leave the bed so quickly, as if it was a performance the curtain immediately came down on—*show's over, on to the next thing in life*. Once I made the mistake of asking him about it—and you know what he said?"

"I can guess."

"He said it was something he'd learned when he was in the air force, that they'd had a sex lecture once, warning the troops about venereal disease, and one of the things they were told to do was to urinate right after intercourse as one way of avoiding the clap."

She sits back from the table and gives me a look that is probably as offended as her original response to what Webb told her.

"Not that he thought I'd infect him—he insisted it was only habit—but how do you think it made me feel?" she says. "Not very damned loved, I'll tell you. Tainted. Alien." She drinks some coffee, folds her arms, shakes her head in a sort of wonder at Webb, at men.

"Maybe I'll have some of that whiskey now," I say.

"You side with him," Jenny says. "I can tell."

"I heard the same lecture," I say.

"And the so-called *ritual?* Remember: Harriet and I were close."

"Well—" I want to hedge, but can't, quite. "Sometimes the coincidence makes me think about the warning."

She fetches a tumbler, pours me an inch of Irish. "You were two of a kind, you know—you and Webster."

"Not so."

"Don't deny it," she says. "I know you both too well. And you only have to look at the way you both treated me." She runs both hands through her short hair and rubs the back of her neck as if her muscles ache. "Thank the good Lord, *you* weren't a painter."

"I'LL TELL YOU the last straw," Jenny says. "Never mind the women or the way he dealt with the children or the insults in the bedroom." She is at the cupboard as she talks, and this time she brings the bottle and sets it in the middle of the table. "You've seen the witch painting?"

"Yes."

"You remember how ugly she is."

"Gorgeously ugly," I say.

"Well," Jenny says, "that 'gorgeously ugly' person was me. I was the model for the witch. I was so fucking flattered when he asked me to pose—it was maybe three years into the marriage, and I thought at last we were going to integrate our lives, make them complementary—" She shakes her head, as if at some foolish innocence. "That *shit*. You know what he said to me when the painting was finished and I was looking at it and feeling sick about it? He told me he'd tried to imagine what I'd look like when I was seventy, and that was how he'd painted me! How's that for beauty in the eye of the beholder? How's that for a husbandly vision?"

"He never told me it was you," I say. "He had a different story—something about a local character."

"A shit and a liar to boot," Jenny says.

I wonder if this is why Webb has brought me to California— to understand how deep was the mutual rage in his marriage with Jenny, so I might somehow excuse him for being a rival, so I might see he had made a mistake. Is this supposed to make me the best man after all?

I can see that painting in my mind's eye; it was one of the many Webb showed me, the same day he lectured me on my inadequacies as art critic, and it was horrific—an archetypal crone of a witch, hooded in black, her features bleached and palette-knife-thickened to a caricature of age. The crowning horror was a bright gobbet of blood that flowed from one of the sleeves of the witch's cape and puddled on the brown earth at her feet. In the left background, almost invisible against a storm-tossed sky, was the image of a cat, its eyes a vivid mix of yellow and harsh ﾉrange. On the other side of the canvas, upper right corner, was what seemed to be the skeletal silhouette of a house, sketched in white. I hadn't liked the picture; I'd thought it too melodramatic to be appreciated. I certainly hadn't seen anything of Jenny in the figure of the witch.

"There's a story behind this," Webb had told me, "a local folk legend I heard when I was a kid."

The story existed in various versions, he said, depending on who was doing the telling, but in all the versions there was a witch, a cat—usually black—and a sawmill. I assumed it was the sawmill that was represented in the upper right corner of Webb's painting.

"It's a couple of stories, actually," Webb had said. "First, there's a sawmill on the Scoggin River, and there's a black cat that turns up every day at the mill. It's a kind of mascot. The men at the mill make a pet of it, give it milk and scraps, and the cat in return entertains the men with the usual cat stuff— chasing its tail, pouncing on imaginary mice in the sawdust piles—and its best trick is riding the logs down this long trough that leads to the buzz saw, and leaping out of the way of the saw's teeth just in the nick of time. A really daring cat.

"That's story one. Story two is the old crone who lives on the road that leads from Scoggin over to the Kennebunks. No one knows her name, but she's lived in this ramshackle house— windows broken out, yard full of rusty junk and wildflowers— forever, and the kids who live out that way say she's a witch. You know kids; when they've got nothing better to do, they follow her around and make fun of her, call her names—that whole cruel side of children at a certain age. You'd see her out along the county roads all dressed in black, scavenging for tonic bottles and beer bottles, which she turns in to the nearest grocery store for two cents apiece. Nowadays she'd get a dime, and she could collect cans too.

"Anyway, you see where the two stories are headed. One day at the mill the black cat rides a log too close to the blade, and before you can say it, the cat's lost a forepaw. Let's say it's the left one. So the next day the children see the witch collecting her bottles as usual, but this time she turns on them and raises her left arm as if she was shaking her fist at them—only the children see that the hand is missing. What she's shaking at them is just a stump, and it's still bloody."

"A pretty story," I remember saying.

"COME," Jenny says. "At least I can show you the dream house."

As we leave the kitchen by the back door we entered through, she takes my hand. I feel a peculiar thrill of familiarity, as if across all our years and loves a connection has been restored—that small, cool hand in mine, scarcely different now from forty years ago in Bremerhaven when the two of us walked along the Hafenstrasse, looking into store windows some afternoons, drifting between bars on nights when no merchant ships were in port to pollute the dark. If I close my eyes I can imagine both of us as we were, with promises before us instead of past.

"Or I probably ought to call it the nightmare house," she says as we trudge up the hill, "except that Jack and I had so much pleasure in the designing of it, and Jack especially was like a kid when he was picking out the appliances and furniture."

"Will you ever finish it?"

"I don't know. I think not." She lets go my hand to unlock the now-closed front door—an overwide oak portal with narrow lights alongside and a half-circle of stained glass above. The pickup with its dogs is gone from the driveway. "Probably I'll just die and leave it to the children. Let Amanda and Will tailor it to their own families or put it on the market."

The door swings inward into a hall I can only call majestic—high-ceilinged with a chandelier like crystal icicles and a staircase that rises to a landing and bends leftward to the second floor; there is no banister. The walls are open, so the rooms behind and beside the entrance hall are visible through the upright two-by-fours awaiting wallboard. From inside, the house is all skeleton.

"We got everything enclosed," Jenny says, "except the guest quarters at the rear—those are the open roof trusses you can see from outside."

I follow her through the hallway into a large room with a picture window. The outer walls are sheathed but unpainted. The ceiling is plastered; there are cutouts for light fixtures, but no fixtures. The floors are wood, unvarnished and covered with plaster dust. Cardboard cartons are scattered about.

"This is a sort of living room and library combined. We were going to build in that far wall with bookshelves, and there was supposed to be wainscoting—everything dark-trimmed. Mahogany or teak—we hadn't decided."

"What's in the boxes?"

"Stereo components. The whole house is wired for sound and video—speakers and television outlets in every room." She hugs herself. "Talk about the cart before the horse—but Jack liked the notion of *all at once*. If you'd convinced him there was really a universe parallel to this one, he would've tried to live in them both."

She leads me into an adjoining room.

"Den," she says, "for television or checkers or naps on Sunday afternoons." She points to an enormous carton, the word SONY prominent on its sides. "He'd already picked out the TV— a 32-inch monster."

"Even if you don't finish the house," I say, "you could sell the electronic stuff."

"If I needed the money, I suppose I'd do that. And all the kitchen stuff too."

Now we're in the kitchen—wide counters, an island with one cutout for a sink, another for a stovetop. More cartons with logos for Jenn-Air, KitchenAid, Kohler. In a small room roughed in just beyond the kitchen, a toilet and sink gather dust in boxes half-opened. It's an enterprise that seems to me both ambitious and horrifying. The idea of so complete a dream turned into the mere props of the dream.

"My God, Jen," I say.

"I know. You don't have to tell me what I think of when I walk through this house alone. Waste. Loss. Insanity, sometimes."

"Maybe it's just a little bit sentimental to leave it this way," I say.

She cocks an eyebrow at me. "Look who's talking." Then: "Let's get out of here," she says.

As we walk downhill toward the ranch house, and around it, along a path that leads through a garden with a trickling fountain in its center, Jenny sighs and takes my hand again.

"There was a time—a moment, a split second—right after Jack's funeral, when I thought I might try to get in touch with Webster. I had the idea that he and I might make some sort of arrangement—not a marriage, not a love nest, but a kind of accommodation to each other. He could help me complete the dream house; I'd let him live in the ranch. He could paint, or help out with the horse business. He could even screw the little girls if he was so inclined—two kinds of riding lessons—so long as he didn't wreck the business." She squeezes my hand again. "You see how crazy Jack's dying made me."

"Webb was about to get married when he had the heart attack," I tell her. "He might have been interested in a new place to work."

"How fate steps in," she says. "Who was he marrying?"

"Her name is Prudence."

Jenny stops abruptly and releases my hand. We are at the foot of the hill, midway between the ranch house and the riding ring where Esther and her instructor are working in the failing sunlight.

"That son of a bitch," Jenny says. "Was he living with this woman?"

"Yes."

"Jesus," she says. "So he really did it."

"Did what?"

"Went to bed with Amanda." We walk toward the ring. "How long were they together?"

I'm confused, and the confusion must be manifest, for Jennifer sits me down on a bench just outside the fencing and pats me—almost maternal—on my knee.

"How long?" she repeats.

"About four years. Maybe five. Are you saying—?"

"Prudence Amanda Hartley," she says. "Yes. That's what I'm saying."

"But her name is Mackenzie."

"The guitar player. Yes, I remember it didn't last."

And now I'm sure: This is what I was sent to California for, this is why I sought out Jennifer Grant Hartley Warner at Webb's posthumous insistence—to unravel the relationship between and among us all. For Webb to confess—no, to *brag* about his incest.

" 'Prudence' was the name of a maiden aunt of mine," Jenny says. "I liked the old-fashioned sound of it; Webb didn't. We always called her Amanda." Jenny smiles. "You never got that story?"

"Never." I flash suddenly on the first day I met Webb's Prudence, helping him unload her car, a luggage monogram: **PHA**.

"You should see your face."

"Jennifer— My God." My confusion is complete, my judgment of Webb scrambled, my composure certainly damaged. How can I go back to Maine? What shall I say to Pru? I think of the child she was when Webb and I drank by the lake, watching his children at play. I think of his attentiveness to her, her playfulness with him, the kisses. "She's given him one child. She's pregnant with h second."

"It's something married people do," Jen says. "They have children." Almost instantly she realizes what she's said. She puts out her hand to take mine. "God, Alec, forgive me. I'd forgot."

"No, it's all right," I say.

"So Webster wanted me to tell you the truth about his bride. Your mission was as simple as that."

"He wanted to shock me," I admit. "He wanted me to know he was going to marry his own daughter."

Jen laughs.

"Poor you," she says. "You've only got half the truth. Amanda was never *his* daughter. Amanda is *yours*."

"ALL THE TIMES you and I made love in Baltimore," she says, "with and without protection— Did you really think we'd go unscathed forever?"

"You never said." Back in the kitchen, my cup of old coffee spiked to a fare-thee-well, I feel buffeted, blindsided. That very morning, on the phone to Pru, I'd begun genuinely to believe that my attraction to her would grow into love, that there was no more age disparity between her and me than there had been between her and Webb, and why shouldn't I be allowed to look at her as a lover looks at the love object? But now what? All the similarities of speech and gesture between Webb and Pru that I had put down to their being constantly together—an illustration of how one person's particularities rub off on another—I was just for an instant poised to ascribe to their shared genetic code . . . and now, almost in the same instant, Jenny had taken that away from me. "How can you be sure?"

"There's no question," she says. "By the time I got confirmation, I was two months along. That meant it had to be yours."

"Why didn't you tell me then?" I say.

"Would you have listened? You were stupid with rage." She covers my hand with hers, cocks her head at me. "Glad you came to California?"

"Did Webb know?"

"Never from me. He'd have resisted—he would have wanted to keep her as *his* baby. Whether or not he found out from Amanda—I've no clue, but common sense says she'd have told him."

Some friend. The idea that Webb might have been aware of my relation to Prudence, that he was in effect parading her before me and—possibly—delighting in my ignorance, makes me helplessly angry.

"And look at Will," Jenny is saying. "Weren't you men ever struck by how different sister and brother were? Their features? Their temperaments?"

"I didn't pay that much attention. Will was sort of always in the background. On the fringes. Webb gave his attentions to Amanda. To Prudence." *Can I get used to this?*

"He did go overboard for her." Jenny sighs and leans back in her chair. "Even in public. It got so that they were never father and daughter; they were boy and girl on a date."

"Yes." Harriet and I would watch them together, Webb so solicitous of Amanda, forever treating her as an adult, even when she was eleven, twelve. He took her shopping, dressed her the way a sugar daddy dresses a mistress. Harriet would say, *I don't know what I think about that.* "You're really sure she's mine?"

"I'm not a frivolous person, Alec."

"And he didn't know?"

"Alec." She shakes her head. "What's important is that Amanda didn't know. Not then. Besides, as far as Webster was concerned, would it have mattered?"

"Perhaps the knowledge would have made him feel . . . *licensed,*" I say.

"I don't know. I don't know what made him tick," Jenny says. "I just know that what he felt for the girl, and how he showed his feelings, was upsetting—if not just plain sordid."

She hugs herself, her rough hands clutching and unclutching her upper arms, so that with each flexing I see the white outline of her fingers impressed on the darker skin.

"What he felt," she says again. "I used to ask myself what a stranger—a bystander, a looker-on—would have imagined."

I think about that. Without making excuses for Webb, I wonder if perhaps it was truly love he felt, and if he did not differentiate the various kinds of love a man is capable of feeling—if his love for women simply overflowed into the place one is expected to reserve for one's children, if here were the two kinds of love swimming together in Webb, indistinguishable from one another.

Jenny reads my confusion. "I could tell you stories," she says.

I nod. I think: *So could I.*

"In the end," Jenny says, "I drove him away and finally got a divorce from him. You know what happens to girls who fall for father figures—so-called; you read about it all the time in the papers. Then the shame stays with them; it lies in their bellies like a poison at the bottom of the sea, and one day it comes to the top and wrecks them. I didn't want Amanda to be one of those women who makes herself famously infamous with the public confession, and I certainly didn't want her to be a woman who'd kill herself, thinking she was acting out some kind of atonement."

"Of course not."

"The touching—the *unnecessary* touching—the hugging and kissing that were perfectly all right when she was eight and nine and ten, but then, when she was in her teens . . . I used to cringe when they kissed good night."

"But eventually you told her. Explained to her."

"After the divorce. She was what—fourteen? It unsettled her. I don't think she ever saw anything wrong with Webster's behavior. I think she believed that's how all fathers behaved toward their daughters."

But to find him and marry him, a dozen years later. I don't say it—for the simple reason that I can't now be objective. I'm a jilted suitor, a jealous man who wants to crawl off, sit in a corner, ruminate.

"Then you licensed *her,*" I say. "By telling her."

"Oh, Christ," she says. "You're *accusing* me. You think I've robbed you of something. You really wanted to step into Webster's shoes, didn't you?" She looks contemptuous. "People used to call that 'sloppy seconds.'"

"No," I say. "Don't insult me."

"And don't let me stop you," Jenny says. "Do your goddamnedest and out-Webb Webster."

WEBB HAD ALWAYS WANTED to be someone else, different from and *above* the rest, had wanted one way or another to escape his name and the self formed by nature and family and the wider world's conventions. It explained the pleasure he took from painting and the extent to which his canvases *became* himself—why it was that to criticize one of them, as I had sometimes done, was to provoke him to real anger. It accounted for the energy he put into his study of the Chinese language in the air force—an energy drained away from nearly all other needs and actions, so that in the end he had to be hospitalized and put through an intense program of therapy, finally coming home with a medical discharge. It may even have had something to do with his pursuit of women—his study of them, his use of them—as if they were the ideal *other* that canceled the shortcomings of himself.

And certainly he wanted to be beyond the ordinary—beyond the rules, the morality, the laws governing the rest of us. Why shouldn't he covet his own daughter? Why shouldn't he expect society to let him do things his way? Not that he was selfish about it. He'd have wanted everyone to live the same way—not selfish, but responsible for self; not egocentric, but self-assured. Authority might have existed, but it had scarcely anything to say to Webb.

When we were freshmen at Bowdoin he had persuaded me to commit a crime with him. Those were the days of draft boards and all their attendant bureaucracy. Every male was registered and classified on his eighteenth birthday, and the draft card was a common item used as proof of age in the bars of downtown Brunswick. We all wanted to be twenty-one, but few of us were. Webb's plan was to break into the campus draft office, steal a quantity of blank draft cards, and sell them to our fellow students. I was to be his partner in the deed.

"If you don't have the courage for this humanitarian adventure," Webb told me, "you aren't worthy to go to war for your country and your flag." He was persuasive. I'd known

Webster Hartley for a couple of years by then, and I'd never met anyone like him.

The office was a corner suite on the ground floor of Winthrop Hall, the college's oldest dormitory—Hawthorne and Longfellow had both lived there; there were plaques attesting to the fact—and I was to be his lookout. At three o'clock one Monday morning, Webb forced a window, climbed inside and closed the window after him. I waited in the hallway, nervous, sure we would be caught, obsessed with the knowledge that this "adventure" was more than a prank.

But we weren't caught. Ten minutes after he went in, carrying a flashlight and the putty knife he'd slipped the window latch with, Webb left the draft office by way of its front door and the two of us ran, giggling like children, down the center hall of Winthrop, across to Appleton Hall, where we lived, and up to the rooms we shared on the second floor. Webb laid out the loot on his study desk: a two-inch stack of draft registration cards, a rubber stamp and stamp pad, and an oversized chromed stapler.

"I thought you were only after the cards," I said.

He gave me a scornful look. "This is a signature stamp," he said. "It's what makes the card official."

"What about the stapler?"

"I've always wanted one," he said.

We made up our own false identifications on the spot. I still remember carefully typing my name on the portable Remington I owned in those days, subtracting three years from the year of my birth so that I was not only a Depression child, but an infant witness to the '29 stock market crash. When I added the stamped signature of the campus draft board director, I felt truly guilty; my hands were sweating, my stomach churned the way it had when I was ten and broke a neighbor's cellar window with a snowball packed around a rock.

Webb inspected my work.

"I'm disappointed in you, Alec," was what he said. "Here I thought you were a young man of talent and imagination, and this is all you can come up with?" He put his new draft card next to mine. "Compare," he said.

Like me, he had changed his birthdate to make himself 21. But he had also changed his identity. The name on the card read: *Hart Webber.*

A week later the two of us hitchhiked into Portland, went to the Social Security office there, and applied for Social Security numbers under assumed names. Webb was again *Hart Webber,* and I—Webb prompting me while I had filled out a second draft card—had transformed myself into *Allen Hoover,* because Webb remembered that Hoover was president the year we had decided to be reborn. The Social Security application required us also to make up the names of our parents. Mine were Jack and Mary; Webb's were Fred and Portland.

"Maybe it was provident that he died before the ceremony," I find myself saying. "Maybe it was the only way."

"*There's* a silver lining," Jenny says.

"Thanks."

"Perhaps you should stay around and let me sharpen my sarcasm."

We sit in silence for what seems a long time. My mission—if that's what it is—is accomplished, my past and future have been nicely skewed. What I dread now is returning to Maine, asking Pru the questions I have to ask, and doing it without seeming to be disappointed or horrified or, simply, baffled.

Jenny finally breaks in.

"Well," she says, "I can't say this hasn't been a *nice* reunion. It has, in some ways—but it's been upsetting in others."

"For me," I say, "especially."

After the talk—after the past that's been revived and relived in my mind during this hour and a half—I've turned moody and moodier. I've set aside the coffee cup and allowed Jenny to serve my whiskey neat, in an old-fashioned glass. A couple of times I've added whiskey to the glass; once I got up to add ice cubes from Jenny's freezer.

"I'm sorry," she says, "that I haven't had any genuinely sentimental things to say to you about us—the old 'us,' you and me."

"Too many marriages intervened."

That's one way for me to dodge the past. There's a song I used to know, a kind of Russian folk song, though I think it's modern, an imitation, written-down lyric. It begins:

Kogdá ya pyan, i pyan vsyegdá ya,
Ya chástoh vspomináyu vas. . . .

Which means: When I am drunk—and I'm always drunk—I often think of you. . . .

"I don't even know what you *do* now," Jenny is saying.

"Even when Webster and I were married, and you and Harriet came visiting in the summer, all I knew was that you were a professor—of literature?—"

"Comp lit."

"—And that you were underpaid."

"Always," I say. "And now things will never get any better; I'm retired."

"You make it sound as if your life is over."

"I hope not."

"Well," Jenny says, "I hope not too. You have your good points. You should use your retirement to hone them."

"I'll try."

I force myself to push my glass aside. Out the window that overlooks the barn and the riding ring I can see Natalie and Esther's instructor in conversation, Natalie rummaging in her purse, currency changing hands. Esther is trotting toward the house. I stand up from the table.

"Here's my ride," I say.

"And how will you treat Amanda, a.k.a. Prudence?" Jenny tilts her head, gives me a one-sided smile. "Will you stay in love with her, now that you know what you know?"

"I'm not sure *what* I know," I say.

She turns away from me. "Of course," she says. "You learned that much from Webb."

"Learned what?"

"That pretending ignorance gives you an excuse to resist the truth." She walks me to the door, opens it for me. "I wish I *had* remembered that slap you claim you gave me. I might be able to return the favor."

Talk about *last words*.

I TELL NATALIE most of what the day has revealed. Not in the car during the drive back to Santa Barbara—precocious though she is, I've no desire to share the day's surprises with Esther—but late that evening when Esther is in bed and we adults are at the dining room table over brandy and strong coffee.

"Was she trying to make you feel guilty?" Natalie says.

"I'm not sure. Probably not—she was never like that, never trying to get the emotional upper hand." I sip the coffee, which by my standards is far too strong.

"What a terrible face," Natalie says. "You're not obliged to drink it, you know."

I put the cup and saucer aside.

"Perhaps you should pour the brandy into the coffee," she says. "A perfect solution."

I shake my head *no*. Anyway, Jenny preoccupies me.

"I think she just wanted everything finished," I say. "Tied up. I was an anticipated arrival. She'd hung on to the facts—and now she's got rid of them by delivering them to me."

"Which means *closure* between the two of *you*."

"I guess so." That word, so comforting to literary scholars.

She purses her lips and looks down at the brandy glass she's turning between her hands. "Men are strange about that, aren't they," she says. "They don't want things to end. You've kept Jenny alive all these years by remembering how she hurt you and how you hurt her—and it kills you she doesn't remember your bad action."

"And is that universal? All men act this way?"

"Women can be sexist too," she says. "My examples are Kent, and now you, and Billy."

"Billy too?"

"Billy's gay—bi, actually—but he's male. Get him tight and he turns maudlin over some fellow named Timothy, who jilted him when he was twenty. He doesn't keep in touch with Tim, but he keeps track of him, knows where he is and who he's with. When Tim dies—and he'll die young, I'm sure—Billy will fall apart, just as if the love affair were current."

"And women?"

"Women have the happy ability to let go, get on about their lives. I know you think I'm an exception, carrying on so about Kent, but that's only because we share Esther, and because he makes such a point of reminding me he's still out there. He sends me his mistress's catalogs to keep our connection alive. He doesn't care if I'm jealous; he only wants me to go on being aware of him."

"Does he still love you?"

"Kent loves only if it's convenient."

She lights a cigarette, inhales the smoke in that way some people have of letting it drift to their nostrils and disappear. I've always considered it *sultry,* that gesture. The smoke is thick, focused, is drawn in lazily. It suggests something *wanton.* What does it say about Natalie? What does it say about me, unless my preoccupation with it simply emphasizes the loving that's *convenient?*

"Something more about that catalog," Natalie says, "the most recent one, full of the mistress of current choice . . ."

"Esther has met her, by the way," I put in.

She grimaces. "I know that."

I see that I've overstepped. "Sorry," I say.

"I think I have to *show* you what I want to say."

She lays the cigarette in the ashtray—she has a marvelously graceful way of handling smoking, as if she has studied its possibilities—and goes to the stack of magazines at the end of the couch. She returns with the catalog she showed me yesterday, opens it to Summer's page.

"You see," she says, "how the bra and panties aren't enticing enough by themselves. You see how she has this white material, something sheer, gauzy, wrapped around her—like a long scarf, looped around the right wrist, then behind her back, then around the left wrist and trailing away into the background."

"Yes." The pose is arresting; Summer leans into the camera, her arms out from her sides, her wrists braceleted by the white fabric.

"The scarf is everything," Natalie says. "I don't mean that it's what sells the underwear—though maybe it helps—but it's what sells the *sex*."

"It's attractive," I admit. "Provocative."

"Ah." She retrieves her cigarette, draws on it. "And it's the scarf that provokes. So clever, so almost subtle. *Oblique*. The implication of handcuffs, yes? Bondage? Or, looking at it another way, the suggestion that she's caught in the act of undressing—the cloth at her wrists the slipping-off of her blouse . . ."

Her voice trails off. She turns the catalog so it is right side up to her, looks at it thoughtfully.

"And here," she says. "The hand slipped inside the panties' waistband at the hip, as if she's in the act of taking them off."

"Mmm."

She closes the catalog. "Am I making too much of all this?" she says.

What can I answer? "Probably," I tell her. I'm not paying terribly close attention. I'm wondering if any of us ever fall *out* of love.

WE ARE IN THIS meditative posture, the two of us, when the doorbell rings and is followed by a tapping at the window alongside Natalie's front door. She looks up and squints.

"It's Billy," she says. "Speaking of the devil."

The door opens and Billy glides in, grinning. He's wearing a polo shirt, blue jeans and white deck shoes, the sleeves of a white sweater knotted loosely around his neck. Even though it's after dark, he looks as if he has just trotted off the tennis court.

"Are you talking about me?" he says. "I was passing, and my ears were burning."

He sees the catalog between us and puts a finger to his lips while he opens it and studies the pictures.

"Or maybe we two were talking about someone else?" He turns away and sprawls with a deep sigh on Natalie's sofa. "My God," he says, "I've been run ragged all day long."

"Tell us everything," Natalie says. She gives me a look that implies that of course there could be no stopping him from telling everything.

"Where to begin? I've brought your car back, undamaged and freshly washed, with its gas tank full. Professional courtesy. My mechanic called me this afternoon, actually, but I knew you weren't here. Now I do need a ride home." He rubs the palms of both hands over his brush cut. "My head is splitting."

"I have aspirin," Natalie says.

"Is that cognac? Might I have a cognac instead?"

She starts to get up.

"No, no," Billy says. "I know where it's kept."

He bustles about the kitchen, taking down a snifter, pouring himself the drink. It takes time, and I turn my chair so I can watch as he lays the glass on its side and carefully fills it to its lip.

"This is fussy but exact," he says as he joins us at the table. He turns the catalog and frowns at it. "So. Are we savaging The Other Woman?"

"We were discussing seductiveness," Natalie says. "How sex sells women's underclothes."

"Or vice versa," Billy says. "I'm always sensitive to the versa of vice."

"I was telling Alec that I think they're trying to make us think of bondage when they show a model's wrists draped like this."

"Maybe," Billy says. "Is this the one?"

"Yes."

He goes on. "I must say I've often been struck by the poses these women strike—one hip jutted out, the legs parted just so, the blouse pulled up or the waistband pulled down to reveal the navel."

"The romance of the belly button," Natalie says.

"You look at the navel," Billy says, "but you think lower down." He winks at me. "That's a pun," he says. "Down. *Down.*"

"Or consider the spiritual dimension," I say. "The omphalos, the chanting of *Om*." I'm not sure I can keep up with Billy's playfulness, but I feel I ought to try—something to do with *when in Rome. . . .*"

"That's very good, Alec," he says. "Insightful." He cradles the brandy in the palm of his hand, swirls it slowly, watching the gesture as if he intends to perfect it. "Climbing a ladder of lingerie to Nirvana."

"A gossamer ladder," I add.

"Esther's school is anti belly button," Natalie says. "She got caught once for revealing it—'displaying it,' the principal told me. Esther says her navel showed because she raised her hand to volunteer an answer, and the shirt rode up. They gave her detention."

"That's indefensible," Billy says. "They're discouraging class participation in the name of a foolish principle."

"Yes," Natalie says. "I thought he was a foolish principal."

Billy leans over and pats her on the head. "That's very good, dear. We both appreciate your cleverness."

He rolls his eyes at me.

"Billy loves to patronize me," Natalie says.

He finishes his brandy, pushes back from the table. "You always get even," he tells her, "but I do need a ride home. I have company waiting."

"All right." To me she says, "Do you mind? I'll be back in a half hour."

"I'll be fine."

As the two of them go out the front door I hear Natalie: "You have to promise to keep your hands to yourself."

The door closes before Billy can respond.

———

I POUR A LITTLE MORE COGNAC into my glass and flip a couple of catalog pages. It's an idle action; I'm not looking for Summer, not researching subliminal sex. Killing time.

Esther emerges from the back hall. She is wearing running clothes—a gray top and navy sweatpants—that I take to be her version of pajamas. She gives me a small wave as she passes into the kitchen, where she pours herself a glass of orange juice. She comes back and sits across the table.

"Can't sleep?" I say.

"Too early." She takes a long swallow of juice and sets down the half-empty glass. "I usually read until ten-thirty or eleven."

"Even on school nights?"

"Even," she says. She tilts her head and studies me in a way that obliges me to close the catalog. "Are you going to sleep with my mother?"

A shocking question that I don't—or can't—answer.

"You could, you know," Esther says. "She likes you."

"We just met," I say, my voice cracking. "We don't know each other at all."

"And she needs it. She's been alone a long time, and Billy's no help." She frowns. "Obviously."

"I don't think this is a proper topic of discussion," I tell Esther. "Not at your age. And not at mine either."

"I just like people to be happy," she says. She stands, picks up her juice, bends over me and gives me a light kiss on the forehead. "I guess that's the best you'll do," she says. "Good night." And she's gone.

I'm left to contemplate the improper topic that had never seriously crossed my mind before Esther's naïve question. I'm no saint—though I'm not as catholic as Webb in the matter of

seduction—and certainly Natalie is an attractive woman. I wonder if in some perverse way Esther is conveying a proposition
on her mother's behalf, if the offhandedness of the daughter
was rehearsed by the mother. And then I catch myself: *What in
the world makes me think I am a desirable object?*

With that, I gather up my drink, pick out a magazine from
the rack beside the fireplace and descend to my private apartment below stairs.

Of course I lie awake for a time. Natalie arrives home; I
hear her heels tapping over my head, wonder if she will come
down to me, perhaps on the innocent pretext of saying good
night or offering me a blanket or asking me the favor of a chat
while she smokes a last cigarette of the day. At first, when she
doesn't appear, I imagine she is in Esther's room, and that Esther
is urging her to approach me. Finally I understand that she has
gone to her own bedroom to sleep; all my wakefulness is mere
self-indulgence, a simple teasing of possibilities such as only an
emeritus could enjoy.

THE NEXT MORNING, very early—the sun barely risen and
the shadow of the house suppressing whatever vegetable color
slopes away from my windows—my private telephone rings.
It's Pru, and her voice is frantic, her words so clearly driven by
genuine fear that I don't even begin to think of all the questions
I want to ask her, all the explanations I intend to demand of
her.

"Alec—"

I sit straighter. I feel a chill of apprehension at the base of my spine. Never mind what Jenny has told me. Part of my mind thinks: *We are joined, Pru and I; some inexplicable bridge reaches from Scoggin to Santa Barbara, and whatever is happening to Pru is about to happen to me.* I believe this. I wonder if I'm in love with Pru, or if it is only anxiety I feel. Over the connection between us I hear a rush like wind in the pines behind her house and I wait for her voice to silence the rush, to tell me what I'm afraid to hear. Before me, the Pacific fog is beginning to lift, the Channel Islands are shadows low in the morning-pale water, the black of trees and shrubs is turning slowly back to green.

"Oh, Alec," she says. "Oh, dear God, Alec. I can't find Mindy anywhere. I think she's run away."

f o u r

■

WHEN HARRIET WAS ALIVE, but after we had learned the reason for her barrenness and the treatments had begun, and already she was resigned to the long slow downhill slide past mortality into whatever exists on the other side of it, I used to sit by myself in the front parlor of our home in Evanston, pretending to meditate. I would think: *Good cheer.* There is cancer in both our families, and we have sat, the two of us, at the twilit ends of our respective days, waiting without talking about them for those twin legacies to come into our own generation. Now one of them has declared itself; now I may give my devotion to my own curse, and wait alone, and imagine how it will taint my so-far-lucky life, how it will arrive, how I will know it.

I used to suppose that it would come like the postman on magazine mornings—that it would crack open the storm door with the noise of swelled wood stuck in the jamb, and it would slap down to the sill of my fears, heavy and final, a bulk to be stumbled over. Or that it would arrive like the insurance man, who always used the knocker as if the bell were out of order and then stood in the open doorway, shuffling with embarrassment and holding out a scribbled receipt for premiums paid; *blood scribbles,* I would tell myself, *nerve scribbles.* Or perhaps, I thought, it would not announce itself at all, but would be like the reappearing stranger who parked in front of the house and drew me over and over to the window so I could grumble about his blocking the walkway, or fret about his memorizing our habits—Harriet's and mine—so he could at some future time break in and enter our lives.

That was the tenor of some of my meditation: dreaming up metaphors for the disease that stalked us, that had already pounced on Harriet. Other times I sat at the desk in my study, letting student papers go unread while I maligned my parents and Harriet's, damning them for the dark reasons of health and hygiene, despairing of the tainted blood that throbbed in our veins. Time had tried to teach me the inviolability of *family*—its importance, the dependencies we are expected to nurture, relative upon relative.

It was of course impossible. Others in the family had children, and the children ran outside to play in their neighborhoods while the adults hovered in the arch of tied-back curtains to watch, to see in these young the long tunnel into the future, a future carrying the family name into—one fondly hoped—posterity. We had no children, Harriet and I. Instead we had cousins, and that was not the same. We complained about them. They grew and married and produced children of their own, and we never knew any of them. We sent them—on appropriate holidays, birthdays, christenings and anniversaries—the knitted caps and booties and best wishes. And, perverse geography: they were always on another coast or in another country.

I watched my wife die, and I am haunted by it. I was witness to her doctor's vigil, and in this second-handedness I imagined I would be untainted by Harriet's malignancy. If I am haunted now by her ghost as I hurry toward what may prove to be another, younger loss, it is that I seem to hear in the corridors of mind her voice from the sickroom. She did not know what to do, she said. Though she trusted the mercies of God, she could not read his intentions for her. *I am helpless,* she said to me.

As was I. She died on the first morning of the autumn semester, a chilling wind off Lake Michigan, the campus maples extravagantly orange, the streets wet with a cold drizzle. Coming home from my opening classes, meeting the doctor in the hallway, I caught my image in the mirror behind him, expectant for news, as blank as any page of wish or regret. *She's gone,* he said, and though I was not relieved for her, I could still hear the Harriet who did not trust God—the woman half sensible, half mad, pawing at my sleeve, murmuring: *Kill me; be kind to me.* Her voice was decayed leaves running ahead of the mortal wind. Now the kindness had been accomplished: I could read that much knowledge on my face in the glass, and that was a sort of relief. Death had eaten all but sixty pounds of her at its leisure; life had given up her narcotic flesh and the sorry heap of her bones. The memory of her pathetic outline under the quilt still from time to time informs my remorse; the odor of the death room can still fill my nostrils. And now, according to some perverse genetic code unique to my ancestry, I have introduced the chance of that scene into another woman's life. The distant short story Webb and I were assigned at Bowdoin told, it turns out, more truth than I care for about the death we live in the midst of.

OCTOBER IN MAINE is startlingly different from September, and the day I come back to Webb's farmhouse. I am met by a bite in the air nothing like the weather when I arrived only a month ago. The leaves have changed away from their various greens, so that only the pines and spruces and firs show dark, summery along the narrow roadways. "Webster used to say he'd gotten all spruced up for me." Jenny's almost-forgotten words are like a voice from the woods as I drive up the Turnpike and make my turn toward Scoggin. That he had always *wanted* Jenny—that all the while the three of us lived together in Baltimore he had quietly loved her but scrupulously kept his own counsel—had not come as a surprise to me. I know I am not supposed to think this way; Jenny has expressly foreclosed my jealousy. But it was no different from knowing, as of course I always had, that Webb desired practically every woman he encountered. That latter was an unfocused desire—a kind of amoral and free-floating lust after strangers, as pervasive as fog and as innocent—but the inclination toward Jenny was deliberate, purposeful, a thing I had turned over in my mind more than once on the flight from LAX to Logan. Except for the accident of murder on the steps of the library, probably it would have remained covert; some tramp had his throat cut, and my life changed forever. It was almost literary. My students would have been scornful of such a coincidence, such a contrivance.

As for my becoming a father—at my late age and overnight, as it were—that was something else again. A stunning *reversal*, as one says in talking about plot in literature—a change in the direction of one's ideas and fancies. I might have brought the subject up during Pru's—Amanda's—last phone call, except for the announcement of Mindy's vanishing. Now I would be helpless and mute; you cannot cross-examine a grieving mother. There was no way of knowing how consciously Pru pursued the man who had raised her, or how much she believed when Jenny told her the truth about her real, her *natural* father. About me. And was any of that important? Suppose she had simply followed her heart, plunged ahead, loved Webb without weighing consequence. Then what? In my dull universe it was impossible, all of it, madly impossible.

By evening I am back at Webb's house. The pickup truck is in its place, the old Chevy beside it; I see no special evidence in the gathering dusk that this is a house in crisis. By the time I've left the rented car, Pru is outside on the porch, a sweater over her shoulders. She hugs me, gives me a kiss that I find unsettling—knowing what I know, still clinging to what I must surely let go of—and the coolness of the tears on her cheeks touches my own face, makes me sharer of her worry.

"Robert and Terry are here. They drove up from Springfield this afternoon. They're staying at the Bar-H."

We sit on the shabby parlor couch while she tells me what she thinks has happened, and I listen without saying more than "It's O.K. It'll be all right. Shh, shh, don't worry, she'll be fine." Her tears turn hot and then cool and then hot against my throat; her voice is now clear, now muffled between my face and the throw pillow under our heads. Mindy was playing in the yard, she tells me; the last time Pru looked she was dancing with the orange cat—"That's what she always calls it: *dancing*"—and when Pru went out to call her in for lunch, only the cat was there.

"I was in a wonderfully good mood," Pru says. She hugs me, bows her head in the hollow under my jaw so that I feel the silk of her hair on my skin like a caress. "I remember I said to the cat, 'Did you eat up my Mindy? You bad cat.' "

I feel her shoulders shake. "It's O.K.," I tell her. "Mindy's clever. We'll find her."

"I called all over the place. I went down to the brook behind the old green barn and followed it to the pond—God, Alec, my heart was in my throat. I kept telling myself she couldn't possibly be drowned, wouldn't have been so foolish as to fall into that cold water and breathe it." She sits up, wipes at her eyes with the back of one wrist. "You know how smart she is. What a relief that there was no sign she'd been anywhere near the place—no little footprints on the bankside, no bent grasses or broken twigs.

"Then I went to the far meadow, where Webb and I used to have little picnics for her and there's an old apple tree—I don't think it's produced in decades—that Mindy promised us she was going to climb to the top of when she was big enough. And then I walked back along the sand road where we found blueberries in July as big as marbles. Mindy was ecstatic; she said they were blue pearls and when we got home she borrowed my sewing basket and squished a whole lot of them by trying to thread them into a bracelet."

I'm holding her, watching her face as she remembers where she's looked for her daughter. I think how we have to turn to the past when we lose something in the present. I did the same after Harriet's death, brooding over her absence, so many of the things we'd shared seeming as vivid as ever—but Harriet was dead, and Mindy is not. Pru's eyes are set on the past, watching Mindy's geographies, hoping to find her child alive in that past; it's how we used to look at complicated pictures whose captions teased us to find the face hidden in them.

"I didn't know where else to look," Pru says, "so I came home, and then you arrived. And here we are." She gets up from the couch. "Would you like me to make coffee? Have you had anything to eat?"

"I had a snack, so-called, on the plane," I say. I stand too. Both of us are going to make a show of sociability, I see. "But coffee would be good."

"I finally called the police," Pru says. She gets the coffee can from the freezer, loads coffee into the filter of the Chemex, pours water through it from a teakettle already hot. "That was the first thing after I'd looked every place I could think of. They were funny about it."

"How so?"

"I don't know what was the matter at first. The man I spoke to—a Sergeant somebody—kept asking questions that didn't have anything to do with Mindy being gone. Was I married? Where was the father? Was Mindy an only child, or did she have brothers and sisters? Would I spell my last name again?" She sets two empty cups on the table and I take a seat. "I think he was looking on his computer to see if I had a criminal record or something. Then he wanted to know if it had been twenty-four hours since I'd last seen Mindy. My God."

She returns the coffee can to the refrigerator. For a moment or two before she sets it on a shelf she holds it at chest level and ponders it, thinking, I'm certain, of the can that brought Webb's ashes to her. I wonder where she has put *that* can—that leftover of Webb's living.

Now she puts the coffee away and closes the refrigerator door. "My God," she says again and sits across from me.

"You have to make allowances for the bureaucratic mind," I say. "It's like the military: procedure is very important, and to real humans it seems to have become more important than the problem it's supposed to help solve."

Pru folds her hands and brings them under her chin as if she were going to rest on them. "Anyway," she says, "people were already looking, covering the same places I'd already been to. The volunteer fire department was all over the place—" She stops and separates her hands, holding them toward me. "Hear that?"

I hear—and feel—the pulsing and knocking of an engine, a helicopter, coming closer to the house. Through the window I can see the spreading beam of the helicopter's searchlight as it dances through the trees.

"State Police," Pru says. "They said they'd try for a while after it got dark, but the officer in charge told me not to expect any news until daylight. He was the pessimistic one. 'Frost tonight.' That's what he said."

"What was Mindy wearing?"

"Underpants."

"Jesus," is all I say.

"I know," Pru says. "But it was a warm morning—Indian Summer. Why should I have expected anything bad?"

By now the helicopter is directly overhead and we stop talking until it moves away and eventually disappears into the silent distance.

"They'll find her," I say. "Mindy's an amazing child."

We sit silently as the room darkens. Probably we are both defining the ways in which Mindy is amazing, both thinking of her conversations with Webb across the fence between life and death. Finally, Pru gets up to turn on a light—the hanging lamp over the table—and adds more water to the carafe. She waits for the coffee to be ready.

"Not quite so amazing," Pru says.

"How so?"

"You're thinking of her genius with the Ouija board—her funny little dialogues with Webb 'on the other side,' as they euphemistically put it."

"I suppose I am."

"Well, things have changed."

"What things?"

She turns a helpless look toward me. "I'm not exactly sure. I only know Mindy's lost her—her contact, whatever you call it."

"Bakkar? Her intermediary?"

"That's the word. Mindy says he won't answer her."

"So she's not able to talk with Webb?" As if she ever really *could,* my sensible self objects. "That's sad," I say.

Pru brings the carafe to the table and pours coffee for both of us. "It's just as well," she says. "She was spending all her time with him, telling him how much he's missed, wondering if he has any toys where he is—stuff like that. Once he was out of touch with her, at least I could get her to play like a normal little girl."

She starts to lift the coffee cup to her lips, hesitates, sets the cup down. Her mouth tightens, and she turns her head away from me, as if I'm not to watch her as she begins to cry. She raises a hand to cover her face.

"Oh, my god, Alec, what have I done? Where is she? What am I being punished for?"

I TRY NOT TO PRESUME what Pru is being punished for. Instead, I hold her all the night long, not in her bed, for that would be unbearable now, but on the parlor couch: me—her friend, her would-have-been suitor—not quite lying but leaning against one armrest with my heels on the floor, and Pru, asleep, soft in my arms, full-length on the sofa, her head in the angle of neck and shoulder so that her hair is feathers on my skin and her breath a slow breeze blowing them, the rise and fall of her breathing like an ebb and flow of tide. A thin blanket protects us from the autumn-night chilliness of the room. My shirt collar is damp from her tears, my back aches from the awkwardness of my position, my right arm is numb; I want to move, but can't. Won't.

But my mind is moving—whirling, dancing with frustration. I wish I could wake her, confront her, ask her the questions Jenny has presented me with. *Did he know?* I want to say. *Pru, did he know who you were from the beginning? How could he have been so deliberate, so conscious, so brazen? And did you encourage him?* Now I feel her stir, turn, her forehead against my cheek, and I think that perhaps she is waking up, that I can start asking. But I know better: she is possessed by Mindy, she can't answer anything until Mindy is found.

Slivers of daylight are coming into the room through the drawn drapes, the openings between them and the threadbare places in the fabric like smudged fingerprints of morning. A rumbling sound accompanies the light. The State Police are awake; their helicopter is airborne; its blades clatter over the house and recede into a near silence. Pru is awake, sighing, turning, wordless. For a short time, a matter of ten minutes or so, she lies with her eyes open, staring at the ceiling. Then a car pulls into the farmyard, doors slam, men's voices come near.

Pru sits up and pushes herself away from me. She yawns, musses her hair, looks at me and smiles wanly.

"Another day," she says.

"This is the day we find her," I say.

"Oh, God," she says, and her shoulders slump, as if in sleep her daughter's disappearance had slid from fact into a desirable dreamworld, and by mentioning Mindy I've made a nightmare real. *Conjure.*

Pru stands, finds and puts on her shoes, folds the blanket into a neat square that she puts over the arm of the couch. The men are at the kitchen door and she goes to open it. I raise myself, stamp my feet and rub my sleeping arm. I hope Pru will make fresh coffee.

In the kitchen are two men—a state trooper in his pale blue uniform with the darker accents of pocket flaps and epaulets; another, taller man in a suit and tie.

"This is Sergeant Jackson," Pru says, "and the sheriff—Sheriff Greenwood."

I put my hand forward.

"Alec was my husband's oldest friend."

The sheriff shakes my hand. "Fred," he says. The trooper touches his hat. "Sir," he says.

"I wanted to be sure you were awake," Greenwood tells Pru. "We're going over to pick up Allie."

"As you see," says Pru, her voice false and bright. "We're up and at 'em. Bright-eyed and bushy-tailed."

The trooper smiles. Greenwood bows to Pru and gives me a small salute of his hand. "We'll be back in about a half hour." And they are gone. The car—looking out a window I see that it has the Maine State Police logo on its driver's-side door—leaves the driveway.

"Who's Allie?" I hear myself ask.

Pru is taking down coffee from the cupboard over the stove,

putting a new filter in the Chemex, spooning the coffee into it. She puts away the can, fills a teakettle with water from the tap and sets it on a front burner. The gas when she turns the knob hisses and puffs itself into flame.

"There's a woman who lives south of town," she says, "out on Cat Mousam Road—that's the blacktop that runs from South Scoggin to Kennebunk. Webb must have told you about her. He liked her, or the idea of her. He said she was a witch."

"I remember a witch story. He'd painted her."

"Yes. He said he'd paid her five dollars to sit for him. Long before I came here to live with him."

"It's a surreal thing—an old woman and a black cat. Lots of blood color." I want badly to tell her about Jenny, her version of the painting, how much she disliked what she claimed Webb had done to her. I wonder if that particular painting is still among those stacked in the studio. "What about this old woman—this Allie?"

"She's also known as 'the lady who finds things.' "

My mind does a little stumble.

"A psychic," I say. "I hear they're much in vogue nowadays."

She makes a fist of her right hand and lifts it between us. "Don't make fun of me," she says. "All I've done is tell the sheriff. I want to ask her where Mindy is."

I don't believe in psychics—who does?—but I know what it's like to be desperate, to grasp for any hope, to try *anything* rather than give in to the awful purity of despair. I went through it with Harriet. I was almost ready to fly her to the Philippines and put her in the hands of a witch doctor who would part her flesh with his bare hands and pluck out the cancer that was murdering her—never mind that I knew, *knew* that such cures were the cruelest kind of fakery. What must I have thought? That a fake who gave me hope was better than a civilized medical doctor who denied hope entirely. It was that simple.

"What did the sheriff say when you asked him?"

"He's gone to fetch her, hasn't he?" She opens the fist and lays the hand on top of one of mine. "Please, Alec. What can it hurt?"

I'm afraid that next she will say, "*Maybe the magic has passed from Mindy to—*" but I catch myself. "And her name is Allie?"

"Her real name is Alluria. Alluria Ferris." She frowns. "I know. With a name like "Alluria," you'll expect her to be a raving beauty, something in the mold of Morgan la Fay."

"Kim Novak, at least," I say. I'm thinking of a movie Harriet liked, a movie romantic and full of cats. *Maybe the magic has passed from Mindy to Alluria.*

"I hear she's quite old." She gets up and starts pouring water through the filter. "The stories about her are weird. Amazing, some of them."

"Such as?"

"A student over at U.N.H. lost his father's allowance check and he got desperate. He phoned Alluria. She found it for him over the telephone, under a blotter in his dorm room."

Trivial stuff, I think. "Then why does she have to come here? If these people can work from distances—over the phone. Maybe by mail, even."

"She says she has to be in the place where Mindy was last seen," Pru says.

The telephone rings. Prudence leaps at it, holds it to her ear with both hands. Now she looks disappointed. "Yes," she says, and "yes" again.

She lowers the phone into its cradle. "It's only Robert. He and Theresa are driving over from the motel."

"To help us wait."

"Something like that." She looks grim—I suppose because of Theresa, not Robert.

"Emanations," I say, thinking of what we were talking about when the phone rang.

"What?"

"The psychic. She probably has to feel the emanations of Mindy's presence—or from what's left of her aura—so she can do her bloodhound act." Where do those words—*emanations, aura*—come from? Perhaps I'm remembering some pitiful student genre writing, or the careless reading of my own remote childhood.

Pru turns away. "You don't have to be mean," she says.

THE OTHER HARTLEYS ARRIVE. Robert looks glad to see me, pumps my hand, covers both our right hands with his left. Lawyerly sincerity, I suppose.

"It's a damned shame we always meet under negative circumstances," he says. "You remember Terry."

"Yes, indeed," I say. Theresa puts out her hand and lets me press it.

"No new news, I take it," Robert says. "Nothing either good or bad."

"Just nothing," Pru says.

"She's a small kid," he says. "She could fit almost any-where."

"Have you been part of the search?" I ask.

"A little. We pulled in yesterday morning. Late. Grabbed a bite and came out here. Covered that overgrown meadow, back and forth for an hour or so."

"Not a sign of her," Theresa says.

"Saw a red fox," says Robert. He measures a foot or so of air with the forefingers of both hands. "Brush this long. Beau-tiful."

"Something to hang from your antenna," I say.

He pulls out a chair and sits at the table. "You still don't think much of me."

"It's what you were saying," I tell him. "I probably associate you with the negative events."

"It's not as if I *create* them."

"Just that you have a negative imagination."

"Maybe it's my legal mind. A kid disappears—I think of the possibilities. Murder. Drowning. Kidnapping."

"Oh, Bobby, dear heaven," Theresa says.

"You can't rule out kidnapping," Robert says. "I'm sure the police haven't."

"Nobody's said anything to me about that," Pru says. Cer-tainly the idea frightens her; it shows in her expression, in a nervous twitch of one pale eyelid. "This road is hardly used."

"These things don't have much to do with traffic. Anything could happen, spur of the moment. Woman takes a wrong turn, drives by your place, sees Melinda." He glances at me, then at

Theresa. "Turns out she's lost a child—maybe even a daughter. Auto accident. Birth defect. Whatever. Sees nobody's about, stops the car, bundles the girl into the front seat."

"Mindy would bite her, kick her, jump out." Prudence snaps at her brother-in-law. She'd probably like to kick him and bite him herself.

"Ah," Robert says. "We all like to believe in our self-sufficiency, our ability to take care of ourselves. If that were a true reading, who'd need police?"

"Who'd need lawyers?" I say.

"For Christ's sake, Bobby." Theresa seems genuinely upset with him. "A little consideration for Prudence. A mother is worried sick, and you're inventing her worst-case scenarios."

Robert looks sheepish. "Sorry," he says. "When is this crystal ball gazer of yours supposed to show up?"

NEARLY AN HOUR HAS PASSED since Greenwood and Sergeant Jackson left. We drink coffee, and I let Pru pour an inch of Irish into my half-empty cup. It's how Webb would have waited, grumbling a little, letting Pru and anyone else within earshot know in what low regard he held psychics. All right for Art, but not for Reality. "Charlatans," he'd have said. "Meddlers in other people's tragedy. Misfortune-tellers." But he'd have been fiercely concerned for Mindy, and the concern—because helpless—would have excused a bit of drink.

In fact, I'm at the kitchen window, adding whiskey to a fresh half-cup when Alluria Ferris arrives, sitting primly in the back-seat of the sheriff's car. Never mind my own mistrust of "psychics"; the Ferris woman, when she steps from the car, is striking—I'm tempted to say bewitching. Now I can believe that Jenny, or almost anyone else, was Webb's model, the armature over which he laid a picture from his angry imagination. Alluria Ferris is nothing like the painting he once showed me— that crone with the bloodied hand, the black cat glaring malevolently out of the foreground of the canvas with its shattered yellow eyes. Instead she is as tall as the sheriff, erect, her hair pure white and cropped short, a black cape over her shoulders and fastened at the throat. She is somewhere between sixty and seventy, has high cheekbones, a generous mouth, eyes almost black—in the light of the kitchen, when the pupils shrink, the irises are brown, like chocolate or coffee or the burnt sienna Webb sometimes used as the solemn background out of which his subjects emerged.

She takes us all in, her gaze sweeping the room only for an instant. Theresa stands and offers a chair; Alluria Ferris sits, unclasps the fastening of the cape at her throat and drapes it behind her over the chair back. Her two hands are large, long-fingered, competent the way a craftsman's hands are—strength and skill implicit.

Robert jumps right in. "I don't mean to be a skeptic," he says, "but maybe you could tell us what you think you can accomplish here. My understanding is that a couple of dozen people, and dogs and a helicopter, have been searching for the kid more than two days, and they haven't found a clue. What can you do that they can't?"

"Robert, damn it—" Theresa begins.

But Alluria Ferris raises her hand and stops her. "I am not offended," she says. "This is expected."

The accent is slightly French-Canadian. I wonder if she has

married a Ferris, or if her surname is an anglicized version of something like *Frechette*—a gesture toward New England assimilation.

"I have no explanation," she tells Robert. "I have an ability, a power, that comes I know not from where. And I am not perfect. Sometimes the information that comes to me is strong, sometimes not. If I have an object belonging to the lost child, or from someone close to the child, it is possible I will discover a knowledge I never knew I possessed."

"So you don't know how it works," Robert says.

"Why would I need to know?"

"I think it must have something to do with auras," Theresa puts in. "People's auras rub off on things—objects—important to them."

Robert looks to Alluria.

"We all wear auras," Alluria says. "In many different colors—and not only the colors we see in the everyday world, but more bright, more subtle. Only someone like myself, or an artist, can relate them to this world."

Robert catches my eye, taps the side of his head significantly with a forefinger. *Crazy.* The woman notices, I'm sure, but she goes on as if nothing has happened.

"Mindy's father was an artist. Yes?" Now she turns to Robert. "Her father would have understood color, the importance of color for locating *the heart's place.* That is good for our quest, yes?"

"I'm sure," Robert says. I fancy he is trying to look away from her, but that her gaze is in some way holding him. "All right, I'll be optimistic," he says. Finally, Alluria Ferris turns her attention elsewhere; Robert looks down at his hands.

"Webster's ashes," Theresa says.

"What?" Prudence.

"Maybe she could use the ashes to find Mindy."

"Those of the girl's father?" Alluria says. "Get them."

Prudence goes to the parlor. We wait—Greenwood and Sergeant Jackson, the Hartleys, me—nobody with anything to talk about. When Pru returns, she is rubbing her forehead as if she has a headache.

"I don't know where I put them," she says. "I've been so upset, so spaced out. . . ."

"It's O.K.," Robert says. "Maybe this lady can locate them, sort of as a preliminary to the main event."

"The ashes aren't lost," this lady says.

"It was just a thought," says Theresa. "Shut up, Bobby."

"Only tell me," Alluria says to Prudence. "Where was the little girl when you saw her last, what was she doing, what was she wearing?"

Pru tells her story again: the Indian summer day, the white underpants, the orange cat, the dancing.

"And the cat?" Alluria asks. "It is also lost?"

"No, no," Pru says. "It's here somewhere."

Alluria fixes her gaze on me. "Bring me the cat," she says—no, more than *says:* she commands.

I look at Pru, at Robert and Theresa, at the sheriff and the sergeant. Their faces, all of them, show anticipation. They are depending on me. "I'll try and find it," I tell them, and I leave the room.

As I step into the farmyard I'm trying to remember where I last saw the cat. My mind surveys all my visions of it, all my sightings not only from the day of Webb's death when I waited alone on the porch steps with the crippled dog, but from years ago—earlier visits when everyone was alive and happy. Even Jenny's orange cat, with its stump of coyote-shortened tail, comes in and out of my thoughts. Where did I see Webb's cat? Cats sleep seventeen hours a day; where might this one be sleeping now? And how do I call it to me? What is its name, and even if I knew it, would the cat respond?

I circle the house. The day around me—late morning but still patchy with fog—itself has an aura, an orangey gold cast of light as if my mind's cat images have tinctured the very air. There is a gentle breeze from the west, warmer than last night's, and it smells of rain. More weather to fret about for Mindy's sake.

I scout the farmyard—behind rocks, under bushes, around the parked cars and the old truck. I widen my circle to touch the edges of meadow behind the outbuildings, where I gaze across the vistas of gold and brown grasses to catch a subtle coarser shading of striped orange; I narrow it again and consider all the furniture on the porch and lawn that no one has bothered to store. No orange cat. I feel a peculiar pressure to find the cat, as if to go back to the kitchen empty-handed will mark me as a failure—a serious failure. I think I genuinely believe that Mindy's life depends on the successful completion of my mission: "Bring me the cat." *Bring me the head of Jokaanen! Bring me my arrows of desire! Bring me my fiddlers three!* The importance of not being able to discover the cat is making me downright certifiable.

I sit on the porch steps—to think, or to outthink the cat. The little brown-and-white dog limps up to me, tail frantic, and

I pet his small head because we are old friends at a difficult time. It's then that I notice the door to Webb's studio is partly open. If I were a cat . . .

I leave the dog and stand inside the studio door, calling: "Here, Kitty. Here, Kitty-Kitty," feeling like a fool. "Talk to me," as if I'd understand *meow*.

But I do hear a noise, a rustle, something slight that could very well be cat, and so I go cautiously through the entryway into the studio, on my toes, not wishing to make so much racket that the cat will suddenly appear and streak past me into the outdoors where I will lose it all over again. The old odors seem fresher, stronger—the harshness of turpentine, the sweeter scent of cut wood, the mustiness of a space disused.

"Kitty?" I stop in the center of the room where the brightness from the skylight makes a rectangle on the floor. "Come here, Kitty."

Again the rustling sound, coming from a corner of the open room, behind sheets of Masonite leaning upright under a dusty-paned window. *Finally,* I think—though it might be a raccoon, come back after all this time to reclaim the place Webb evicted its parents or grandparents from. I walk quietly to the corner, kneel, put my head slowly around the edges of the boards into the shadowy triangular space they form, and she is there— Mindy, alive and mostly naked, and staring at me with eyes wider than any possible cat's. She is sitting cross-legged on the Ouija board; the can painted its dismal flat black is on the floor in front of her. Her face, her hair, her hands and arms, the white underpants—everything is streaked and smeared with the black stuff that must be Webb's ashes.

The child says nothing. She allows me to reach for her, to slide her out of her hiding place, to lift her in my arms and carry her outside. By the time I reach the kitchen door, I've been seen and the door opens for us. Prudence and Theresa are weeping and shrieking with joy, the men are smiling, Alluria is stern. As I give Mindy into her mother's arms I see that the ashes streaking her skin are also on her mouth and tongue, and my mind gives a little hitch: she was eating her father's ashes.

"Poor dear baby," Pru says, hugging and kissing the child. "You scared us so."

"How did she get so filthy?" Robert says.

"Ashes," I tell him.

Robert absorbs this news. "Oh, my Jesus," he says.

"We're off to the bathtub," Pru says. "I'll be damned if I care about the details." Theresa follows her; I hear their happy voices up the front stairs.

I turn to Alluria Ferris, who has lent her psychic presence to this happy discovery. I had half expected her to look at Mindy and say to me, "This is *not* a cat." Instead, she tells me, for everyone's benefit, "I knew what the gentleman would find," and shrugging the cape over her shoulders she lets herself be escorted grandly to the waiting police car.

The three of us sit quietly for a few moments, and then Robert swivels his chair toward me.

"Where was she?" he says.

"In Webb's studio, hidden in a corner behind some stuff."

"Probably there all the time," he says. "Stole the ashes, then while the world went nuts around her, she went to ground."

"She's not a fox," I say.

"What?"

"And I don't think 'steal' is the right verb when a child embraces her dead father's ashes."

"Well ex*cuse* me," Robert says.

The silence hangs between us only for a moment.

"You carry a real chip on your shoulder," Robert says.

"I don't mean to."

"But you do. I understand that you and my brother go way back. Best buddies and all that. But this proprietary attitude of yours toward Prudence—it gets a bit much."

Proprietary. It's not quite *fatherly,* but the word is more apt than Robert knows.

"I'm sorry," I say.

Robert reaches over to pat me on the shoulder. "It's O.K.," he says.

From upstairs comes the sound of water running, of Pru and Theresa chattering and laughing. I imagine Mindy's bath water swirling into gray, into black.

"I didn't want to mention this while Mindy was still missing," Robert says. "You know: all that stress, *Sturm und Drang,* et cetera."

I've no idea what he's about to tell me—or *reveal* to me, this being a time of revelations fit for the Old Testament.

"A while back—Webster was still alive and kicking—Pru came to me to ask what she called 'a favor.' She wanted me to find a buyer for the kid she's carrying."

"A buyer?"

"Well—" Robert lifts a hand, as if ransacking the air for a different, better word. "I don't know how to put it more succinctly than that. She doesn't want to keep the baby; at least she didn't want it when she spoke to me. I don't know if she feels differently, now that the father's passed away."

"And you can't find out how she feels until the whole trauma of Mindy's disappearance is behind her."

"Exactly. She hasn't brought it up. *I* haven't brought it up." Robert leans across the table, drops his voice. "You know what I wonder? I wonder if the baby's not Webb's."

"I can't imagine that," I say. But it's as if the world is conspiring to take all of Webb's children away from him—first Prudence Amanda, now the nameless fetus she carries.

"The hell you can't," Robert says. "Old man always chasing after other women, wife sits home with a three-year-old and does housework. Wife gets a part-time job in town, decides to get even. Sauce for the goose. Yes?"

"I'd rather not believe it."

"I know," he says, "you've got a crush on her yourself. You want to do something noble: take care of Webb's wife and his unborn heir. Two birds, one stone."

I want to say that it's not so simple as that, but what's the point?

"Anyway," Robert says with some finality, "that's between you and Prudence." He drums his fingers on the table. "I suppose Queen Psychic will be sending you guys a bill," he says. "Take my advice. Don't pay it."

"I WONDER what would have happened if I hadn't thought I heard the cat in Webb's studio."

I'm sprawled on the battered couch in the parlor, drinking a glass of red wine left over from lunch, talking with Theresa, who made the lunch. Pru is upstairs sleeping with Mindy, both of them exhausted from fear and fancy. Robert has taken his car into Scoggin to buy gas and today's *Globe*.

"She'd have appeared eventually," Theresa says. "Three-year-olds get hungry. They can't live on ashes."

And that remark sends us both into silence, both of us probably contemplating the meaning of what Mindy has done. Certainly I am—trying to think in some "literary" way of my discovery, wanting to milk metaphor as if I were not in fact retired but planning tomorrow's lecture.

"I hadn't seen his ashes before," she says. "Pru showed me that ugly tin can they arrived in, but you can bet I didn't peek inside." She finds a cigarette in her purse, lights it, drags in smoke. I watch the tip glow and fade. *Ash,* I think. *Ashes,* we both think. "I had a friend in college—sorority sister—died in a car crash. Her mother had a memorial service."

She holds the cigarette above her empty wineglass and taps it with a forefinger. "You know," she says. "The body, the face, too destroyed for the decency of a casket. Or the expense of it—the mother wasn't rich."

Maybe Terry and Robert are a better match than I'd thought. Or she is tired and her guard is down and she is drifting into a past when she was a different woman: snobbish, thoughtless.

"Anyway, we were required—we sisters—to hold a handful of Marilyn's ashes. My God. *Marilyn.* I haven't remembered her name in years."

I nod—*how understanding I am*—and sip my wine.

"They were gray," Theresa says. "Her ashes. Webb's were black on Mindy's face and hands."

"They were moist," I say. *Understanding and also helpful.*

"Yes."

"Or they could have added something to the fire—something that burned black. I read somewhere that they use an accelerant to make the flames hotter."

She stares at me. I suppose she can't choose between being horrified or amused by me, by my worrying of the facts of ashes.

"What shook me—" and she rubs the burning cigarette against the bowl of the glass until it falls "—was that I felt Webb's dying, his heart attack, hit me all over again. A trigger."

Synecdoche, I would tell my students. The part for the whole. Webb conjured out of the ashes on his child's face and hands. *Will this be on the final?*

"I still remember how awful it was," Theresa says. "That wedding day. We'd got there early, to help. Webster was already tipsy. Not drunk—you know what he's like when he's drunk, and this was way short of that—and he was clowning around. Mostly for Pru's benefit." She pauses; her forehead shows troubled lines for a moment. "Partly for mine, I like to think."

"Webb would clown for any woman," I say, and at once I realize I've said a cruel thing to Theresa. She wants to be set apart, to be special, even if it's only posthumously special. I see a glistening in her eyes that must be tears, and it dawns on me—I think how obtuse I am in the wake of this knot Webb tied all of us in—that Theresa too had been one of Webb's lovers. "It's past," I say. "We can't keep anything from it."

"Screw you," she says. "I'll keep what I want."

"I'm sorry. Really."

She finds a small folded handkerchief in her purse and dabs at the corners of her eyes. "It's all right."

"I meant—"

She stops me, low voiced but furious. "I said it's all right."

We sit for a long time in silence—a man who was once Webb's closest friend, another woman who loved him—until the silence takes on a weight that neither of us can bear, and Theresa begins again to turn over the memory she is keeping of Webb's death.

"Pru and I were putting out the refreshments. Everything was covered, wrapped, so the bugs wouldn't get at it. Webb would follow us around and sneak his hand under the shrink wrap—the Saran, the aluminum foil—and Pru and I would flap dish towels at him to drive him away. Robert wasn't much better; both of them started in on the beer early, though Robert's a slower drinker than Webster."

I remember how Webb, the rare times he drank beer, could drink it—chugalug it, tipping the bottle to the vertical, his head back, the bottle and his throat making a straight path on the way to his stomach.

It was a woman taught him that—at the Cliff House when we were in our teens, in our first jobs away from home. It was a waitress named Sheila; she was from New York, was twenty-one and worldly. Webb fell for her, although Sheila was probably the first woman of his life who avoided his bed.

One night as we came back to the hotel from an evening of bowling, we met Sheila and Marian—another Cliff House waitress—stumbling down the hotel's long driveway toward us.

Both of them were drinking, were drunk, and both of them carried bottles of beer. It was Sheila who drank so efficiently, the bottle vertical, the beer flowing by gravity, no swallowing necessary. "How do you do that?" was what Webb wanted to know.

I watched her teach him—she had bottles stored in all the pockets, inner and outer, of the denim jacket she wore—and the two of them guzzled until the beer was gone and they were both helpless. I was the one who finally steered him to bed.

"I was in a mood," Theresa is saying. "We'd been close, Webb and I—" She lifts her eyes to meet mine, sees what I've finally figured out. "We'd been together in Boston this spring—the second time, the last time—and we'd agreed it was a bad idea and we wouldn't meet like that again. I was the guilty one anyway; you can't blame *him*. Robert knew that."

"He knew?"

"I told him, after the first time." She shrugs. "It's remarkable: what a reasonable man Robert can be."

I nod. Is it that he is a lawyer and therefore sees consequences the rest of us overlook? His own brother, his wife, the domestic chaos exposed in a courtroom battle: better to forgive and forget, he must have decided.

"I envied Pru," Theresa is saying. "Still do—in a perverse kind of way."

Upstairs, a door clicks shut; the floor creaks, and I picture Pru going down the hall to her own bed, one hand gliding along the wall for support. Theresa erases the picture:

"I kept watching Webb, devouring him, wanting him, wishing someone would appear out of the blue and stop the wedding. Don't ask me why I was hanging on so. Maybe if I hadn't been hovering. Maybe if he hadn't been afraid I'd give us away to Pru . . ." She looks away from me. "I saw the instant, the very instant, he felt death. Saw his eyes go blank. Saw the glass fall. Saw his legs buckle."

She shudders.

"Those things happened in the same split second—all of them." She looks back at me; her eyes are brimming. "Everybody came running. Robert ran to his car, drove it right up on the lawn. He and I and Pru carried Webb and got him into the backseat; he wasn't even moaning, wasn't breathing. I knew he was dead. I knew anything the hospital did would be for show."

She stubs out her cigarette.

"Fuck it," she says. "We had our moment. What more can a woman ask?"

IT ISN'T UNTIL THE NEXT EVENING that I'm able at last to talk with Pru. Robert and Terry have left—around noon, to be precise—after a great deal of discussion about whether or not we should all drive into Greater Scoggin—the "Greater" is a Hartley irony aimed at the rusticity of the town—for lunch at the Hotel Belmont. I saw them to their car, shook Robert's hand, brushed Theresa's cheek with my lips, gestures that convey nothing but civility, all feeling subdued.

The rest of the day I spend reading. Pru doesn't come downstairs until it's time for supper. She settles Mindy into her highchair, feeds her instant oatmeal. I sit across the table from the child with a glass of wine. Pru has wine too; she sips it while she makes sandwiches.

"I hope you don't mind," she says. "Bread and cold cuts are

about all I ate while Mindy was out and about and the police and sheriff's people were coming and going."

"That's fine," I say.

"This is the last of the roast beef. I'll go to the store to-morrow."

We eat more or less in silence, Pru attending to Mindy—wiping the girl's mouth when she's finished the cereal, offering more apple juice.

We adjourn to the parlor with the dregs of our wine, Mindy looking sleepy, the floor lamp flickering, darkness surrounding the room.

"Jenny told me she's your mother," I say as I take one end of the couch. This is what's called "blurting it out," with small regard for whether this is the time or place to treat vital issues.

Pru chooses the rocker and settles Mindy against her shoulder. The child's white nightgown is stark in this artificial light, against Pru's dark green sweater, and she nuzzles her mother's neck, thumb half lost on her mouth. Mindy looks like any ordinary three-year-old on her mother's lap, drowsy and ready for bed, nestled against an unborn sibling—a brother, if she and Pru have their way. The reddish highlights in Pru's hair are echoed in Mindy's, only paler. I wonder if the new child will have hair whose color is a blend of these two.

"Is she?" I insist. I want to be stern, to hear Pru's side of all of this in unvarnished form, but looking at her, admiring the shorter haircut she has chosen in my absence, I feel at a disadvantage. I'm more vulnerable than she is; I know less than she does.

"Yes," she says.

"And she says I'm your father."

The focus of her green eyes—the color is strikingly plain, even in the lamplight—is on me, her level gaze not in the least flinching. "It's possible," she says. "Didn't she say it that way? That it's *possible* you're my father?"

"No. She said it was me. *Is* me."

"Does that change things between us?" she wants to know.

"I'm not sure. I think so. Don't you think it has to?"

She holds Mindy tighter. "I'm sorry for that," she says. "I really am."

"Did you always know it?"

"Not always. She was funny about it: she let the information out in bits and pieces, the way politicians confess their sins. It was after she and Webb separated that she told me he wasn't my father—but she didn't tell me who was. Not then."

"When did you find out?"

"After the divorce was final. When she knew you and Harriet wouldn't be such frequent visitors." She smooths Mindy's hair. "When you did come, she would spirit me away. Once she'd told me you were Daddy, she was afraid I'd pull some melodramatic stunt: fling myself into your arms, weeping."

"That would have devastated Harriet," I say. How betrayed she'd have felt; how disloyal of me to have had a child by someone else.

Pru is shaking her head sadly. "Poor Harriet," she says. "I think I was fourteen. I didn't know what to think about Webb. I had no idea what I was supposed to feel. How I was expected to change gears."

She shifts sleeping Mindy to her other shoulder and gets up

from the rocking chair. "Let me put this creature to bed," she says. "Mindy's had a scary couple of days. I don't think she needs to have this discussion incorporated into her dreams."

She leaves me alone, talking to myself. I think it was bad enough from the distance of Santa Barbara to rehearse this remarkable connection between father and daughter—to have heard Jenny's anger as she told me her reasons for cutting herself free from Webb, and to square her story with what I knew of Webb and Pru. In California it was like fiction—remote, a scarcely credible soap opera. Here, in this house where the sequel has played itself out, it is terribly unsettling. And what do I feel for Pru now? She isn't acting like a victim. She seems willful, calculating, a young woman of purpose—even though the purpose is still obscure to me. On principle, I would rather not credit Robert's information that she wants to give up the child she carries.

While I wait, the lamp flickers again, then goes out. I fiddle with the plug at the wall outlet; the light comes back on. If I stay here in Scoggin, I'll begin by repairing this lamp. Making myself useful.

I go back to the kitchen and open the cupboard where Webb keeps the whiskey. It isn't as well stocked as I remember it, which means that Pru hasn't adopted Webb's habit of making trips across the New Hampshire line to replenish the liquor supply, but here is a fifth of Jameson's, two-thirds full, standing among smaller bottles of tonic and bitters and a couple of liqueurs like a chess king among pawns. I take down the whiskey and pour some into a tumbler that has been sitting in the dish drainer. Then I fish a handful of ice cubes out of the freezer and slide them carefully into the whiskey. Plop. Clink. I can hear Pru upstairs, talking to Mindy. Precocious Mindy. Yet I've been struck by how ordinary—how dependent—Mindy has seemed since I got back from the West. It is as if she needed Webb alive, to feed her mind with his energy and his intense interest in her, to shape her temperament by his erratic and excessive talent with females.

It is a long time before Pru comes downstairs. I sit in the parlor, brooding over my drink, imagining that she stays with Mindy—washing her face and hands, tucking her into bed, lying beside her to invent a new chapter of the epic fairy tale she has made up for the thousand-and-one nights of their sisterhood—because she wants to put off for as long as she can the unpleasantness of my curiosity. She thinks I'll judge her; probably she's right.

Finally she appears. She has changed her clothes, has put off the day clothes she was wearing in the kitchen and now she is in the white terry robe she wears when she comes down in the morning to put the coffee on. The robe is belted above the prominence of the child she carries, and the way she walks makes me consider how a woman's center of gravity is so profoundly altered by pregnancy.

She stands for a moment at the foot of the stairs, a small frown on her face; she takes in my drink, the way I must be looking at her, the conversation we're in the middle of.

"Let's sit in the kitchen," she says.

I get up and follow her. Webb would say, "She wants an

equality between you. She wants to sit at the table so the belly full of child doesn't show, doesn't distract you, doesn't make you soft on her." *O.K., Webb,* I think. *You can shut up now.*

Pru gets a glass of her own and splashes a little of the Jameson's into it. She sits at the kitchen table with the whiskey, neat, in front of her.

"Why all the questions?" she says. "Are you looking for someone to blame for something?"

"I'm only trying to understand." I sit across from her. The overhead light casts unflattering shadows under her eyes; the color of her pupils is lost in this setting.

"You're entitled," she says. "Probably you always were."

I wait for her story, wait to secure my long-delayed "entitlement."

"I knew who he was from the beginning," she says. "Webster hadn't changed much in only a dozen years. And he knew who I was; after all, he'd come looking for me."

"How did that happen?"

"He'd been in touch with Will, who's out in Montana, teaching at one of the state universities. Something to do with an art-appreciation course Will was putting together, and Will wanted slides of a couple of things of Webb's he remembered from the pre-divorce era. Webb asked about me; Will told him I was living in Somerville."

"And he drove right over," I say. From the edge of sarcasm in my voice—I seem unable to control it—you'd think Jenny had never told me the family secret.

"It's barely an hour's drive," she says. "Why make it into a quest? And why use that tone of voice with me?"

"Sorry."

"I thought it was nice of him. To seek me out, to want to catch up on all the years since Mom kicked him out. I'd always, always had a funny sort of crush on him—"

"I remember."

"—and after I was told he wasn't my real father, I daydreamed about someday getting back into his life." She hugs herself as if the room has gone cold for her. "You don't really want to hear all this, do you?"

"I have to," I say. *I have to make sense of my own feelings*—but I don't tell her that.

"How we ended up in bed together . . ."

It's as if she's gathering herself for an effort. Perhaps all of this is unnecessary; perhaps there's too much of the confessional in this scene, with me as an unqualified—because too-involved—and literal father-confessor.

"One night he'd picked me up at the Coop. We'd had dinner, gone to a movie in Harvard Square. We were sitting in my little efficiency, side by side on the couch. I think I'd poured him a liqueur—Drambuie, Cointreau . . . something sweetish and unmasculine—and I think we were reminiscing about my precocious childhood. Anyway, we were laughing together, and I leaned over and kissed him. No, don't ask me why; just that in the moment, in that instant of so much liking him, so much enjoying whatever memory we were sharing, he was irresistible and perfectly lovable. It was a daughterly thing. There wasn't any sexual intent, but still, I shouldn't have. I knew it, I knew it, I knew the instant he kissed me back."

"And one thing led to another." What am I thinking as she

tells me about this crucial event? I'm thinking of what Jenny said about Webb's sympathetic responses to emotional gestures from women. Probably I look as disapproving as I sound, for Pru scowls at me.

"Not like that. Nothing happened the way you seem to think, because in the next split second Webb froze, backed away from me. It was like: *My God, this is my daughter I'm coming on to. This is not done.*"

"He didn't know?"

"Nobody ever told him. And I didn't either—not that night. We both sort of leaned away from each other and wallowed in the awkwardness of the moment. He made his excuses and got up to go. I walked him to the door. We didn't even shake hands."

She sits back, looks off into that famous middle distance that says a person is focusing on the screen of memory—a memory still resonating.

"And later?" I prompt.

"Webb stayed away for a time. Three or four weeks. You know the reason: it was the absence of a man who wants something he's not entitled to, but he's afraid he'll grab for it just the same. He wanted me. He didn't want to break a taboo."

"So you told him."

"He finally broke down, came back and took me to a movie. 'A fresh start' was what he said he wanted. We didn't have dinner first because the atmosphere of a nice restaurant and good food and wine and attentive service would soften him up. That's how he put it: 'You and the decor would soften me up and I'd forget who you are.'"

She reaches out to put her hand on mine.

"Is this fair?" she says. "Should I not tell you all this? Or should we do it some other time?"

"It's all right," I say. "Really." I find myself thinking of Natalie's ex-husband, burdening her with stories and pictures of young, blond, half-dressed Summer. But he was punishing, taunting. This isn't Pru's motive; she's only reciting history. It's Webb who did the punishing.

"He brought me home, walked me to my door. I think he was planning to pat me on the top of the head, father-like, and stroll away. But I spoiled the plan. I put up my face for a kiss, and I guess—also father-like—he couldn't disappoint me. He gave me just the lightest possible peck on the cheek, and I threw my arms around his neck and kissed him so hard I could taste salt in my mouth. He couldn't *not* kiss back, and in no time we had our hands all over each other—even though he was saying *no, no, no, no,* over and over."

She brings both hands to her mouth and makes one odd sobbing sound that's neither laugh or cry.

"So I broke the news, and that was because I wanted him to make love to me. God, did I want that. I suppose I should be ashamed, should have been ashamed at the time. He was my father, blood or no blood. It was inappropriate, going to bed with him. It may even have been a mistake. To sleep across that huge difference in our ages. But none of that mattered. Time has nothing to do with anything. We weren't related, really. We weren't going to produce cretins, or add to the list of Jukes and Kalikaks."

She stops. "Look," she says, "I loved him and I don't make any bones about it. No excuses. No regrets."

"Except that he's gone," I say.

Pru nods. "Except that he's gone." Then she grins. *Girlish.*
"He didn't believe me. Not at first. I told him the whole story,
pretty much the way Mom had told it to me, only more connected. I tried to make him remember his Baltimore days—I
was dredging up everything I'd heard from him and from Mom
and from you when I was growing up. I told him if he didn't
think I was telling the truth, he could call Jennifer in California
and ask *her.*"

"Did he?"

"No. Later on, when I asked him why not, you know what
he said? He said he was afraid she would confirm his suspicion
that I was lying, and that for the rest of his life he'd regret not
having taken advantage of me before he called her."

I don't wonder at that, for I sense the same sort of oppor-
tunism in myself, that sense that overrides convention and
reason—yes, and common decency—and permits a man to be
entirely selfish. Wanting to replace Webb in the woman's life,
perhaps I'm becoming him.

Pru reads my mind. "I'm sorry about you and me," she says.
"I could never think of you as my father; that knowledge, that
fact, isn't the same as wisdom. Liking someone, being comfortable with them. But as a friend . . . always."

"You don't have to smooth my feathers," I say.

"I'm not trying to."

"What did he say to you?" I ask. I have to. "That first time
you woke up in bed together?"

"What difference does it make, what he said, or what I said?
By then we were already in love."

"It makes a difference to me," I say. "Don't ask me why. I
couldn't tell you."

Which is the truth. It's as if this is some sort of showdown—as if by drawing the facts, the details, the *confession,* from Prudence, I am cleansing her. *Of what?* I ask myself, as if I believed in sin, like a proper New Englander.

This time she puts the tip of her little finger into the Irish, then touches the finger with her tongue.

"Much gentler," she says. "I was always amazed at how Webb could put this stuff away. Appetite—he had great appetite."

I wait a long time, eons, for the answer I'm sure she is framing—or remembering—while she temporizes with whiskey and the taste she doesn't share with Webb.

" 'The circle closed' is what he said, the first time we went to bed. He'd known, really, just as I'd known, really. That first time he held me, kissed me, I was twelve again, thirteen, his Mandy. I was the child whose mother took her aside and told her to be wary. 'It isn't right for your father to be kissing you on the mouth like that.' *Like that.* That made no sense to me then. My father loved me, we kiss those 've love, my father kissed me. I lived in a reasonable world; I thought my mother did not."

"You fought?"

"*They* fought. I was in the middle."

"Tug of war," I say, prompting.

Pru tips the small glass toward me, a pale brown eye between her thin hands. "I think now how silly it all was. There was nothing sexual in those family kisses, nothing sexual in the way he touched my shoulder, my face, the way he put his arm around my waist. I'm speaking for myself—not him. I don't know what he felt. What I think is that from the time Mother criticized us, warned us, his attitude changed toward me. It was as if he'd just then got the idea that I could *be* a sexual creature. By making our relationship adult, she'd thrown us out of the Garden, like God banishing Adam and Eve."

She pushes the whiskey glass toward me.

"I don't want this after all," she says.

I pour it into my own glass, though I don't especially want more to drink.

"Everything changed," Pru says. "No more kisses; no more casual touching; no more lovely 'dates' in the nice restaurants he used to take me to. No more showing me off, I suppose."

"He was trying to reassure Jenny."

"Yes and no. What happened was that he took me into his head. I'm sure of it. He'd *look* at me—not saying anything—as if he was weighing me, turning me over and over in his mind like an object that fascinated him, that he wanted to see all sides of. It scared me a little, and of course none of it was lost on my mother."

"So they fought some more," I say. It was this change between Webb and his young daughter that Jenny fretted about, the expulsion from the Garden whose aftermath Harriet and I were witness to in those days before the Hartleys divorced.

"Endlessly." She gets up from the table, abruptly, almost angrily, pushing the chair so hard it teeters on its back legs. "Jesus," she says. "Can't we ever let him be dead?"

"He sent me out to California," I remind her. "He kept himself alive."

She slides the chair into its place at the table.

"Let's talk in the parlor," she says.

———

"IT WAS A RELIEF to begin living with him," Pru is saying. "After being so tentative in Boston, always balancing on the edge of guiltiness."

We're sitting at opposite ends of the old couch I had shared earlier with Theresa. The windows are opaque with evening; delicate corners of frost have begun to form in the corners of the lower panes. With a kitchen table no longer between us, the swell of the child is evident under her robe, and she has drawn her legs up, cradling. The bareness of one thigh is a shadow under the hem of chenille; I try not to lower my gaze to it.

"At first I didn't realize how much a relief it was. At first I didn't care much for this place—not simply the remoteness, but the clutter of it, the squalor. You know. All this divorced man's furniture—indifferent stuff left over from old wives, or picked up at garage sales, or bought from cheap furniture stores with no payments till next year. Never mind that the day I arrived you and Webb were in the middle of your argument over aesthetics or whatever. I'd never seen his temper, you know. But of course I got used to it: the place, having to drive a dozen miles to buy groceries, Webb's moods.

"After he'd introduced me to you, after we'd had those two or three social evenings together, after you'd left to go wherever it was you were going—back to your classes, I suppose—I got the full taste of making a life with him."

"I don't imagine it was easy," I say.

"It wasn't so bad. Right off, I was pregnant with Mindy.

That made him extra attentive and considerate, and when she was born he was happy to have, really, finally, a daughter of his own." She shows an inward smile. "What took getting used to were his bad habits. I know that if you live alone, you do what you want and take for granted that it's the right way. But Webb— If he could devise a method for avoiding housework, like doing dishes, he'd make a rule about it. He'd use the same coffee cup day after day—just rinse it the next morning and let the new coffee absorb the dried-on from yesterday. He'd reuse dishes if there was nothing caked on. It took me weeks to persuade him I didn't mind doing up the dishes, that we could start clean at every meal."

"You probably don't remember," I say, "but when Harriet and I used to visit, and Webb *did* do dishes, he never got them washed properly. Too busy talking."

Pru laughs. "I guess I was too young to notice," she says, "but I can picture it."

She fumbles at the magazine rack beside the couch and finds a Salem pack. She taps out a cigarette, lights it with a match from the book tucked behind the cellophane—all this with a wary eye on me.

"I know," she says. "You don't have to chide me."

"As long as you know."

She takes a long drag, exhales, balances the cigarette in a ceramic ashtray.

"Since Webb died," she says, "I've begun to remember more and more about the time when he was my father. How do you say that? My *alleged* father?"

"Maybe your *ostensible* father," I suggest.

"Not so much the teenage stuff. That's odd, isn't it? But the early things. I remember when I was little, I'd wake up in the morning—this was even before Will was born; I was still an only child—I'd get up and go into my parents' room and climb into bed with them. My *ostensible* parents. I don't know how old I was when I started that. Obviously, I was walking—or at least I was climbing. But it was a ritual; I think it's something all children do, I don't think there was anything unusual about it, so you needn't look grim and act as if I'd done something I'm going to go to Hell for."

"I wasn't looking grim." But possibly I am. I believe I'm affected not so much by what Pru is telling me as by what I'm thinking of her as she talks, the undeniable attraction I still feel. I can't help it. It's a kind of jealousy, I imagine. Sitting here with her, watching in this insufficient light the shape of her face, the way her mouth forms language, the gestures she uses to illustrate the book of her memory, I resent Webb. He is an intrusion between Prudence and me; he has somehow spoiled her for me. She is a desirable object he had no right to take to himself; having had the pleasure of being her father, how dare he also appropriate the pleasure of being her lover?

I realize how far I've come toward loving Prudence, how what began as sympathy for her loss of a husband became now an affection, now an ache, now an intention—to bring her into my own bed, to care for her, to treat her children as mine, as the children my own marriage never brought me. Even now, as much as I am angry at Webb and frustrated by Pru, my mind turns over and over the ways and means, the obscure strategies I might use to erase whatever she has done that she ought not to have done. Never mind the erasing of the fact of the blood we share—though certainly I don't want either one of us to go to Hell.

"I don't know what there is about people in bed," she says, "the wonderful warmth of them, the sleep-smell of them, the comfort of them. Is it a womb thing?"

"I don't know," I say. "But I know what you mean."

"Maybe it isn't a womb thing. Maybe it's just that I'm pregnant and I have wombs on the brain. Anyway, I loved the mornings, snuggled between Mom and Daddy. So-called. It was the safest feeling I've ever had. All of us were naked; I was hidden away in a secret cave, and everything was warmth and textures of bedclothes and skin." She hesitates. Then she says, "Webb told me once that his mother seduced him when he was thirteen."

"He told *me* that too. I never believed him." I wonder now if I simply didn't want to accept such a thing, that I buried it so as not to consider it, that I simply subtracted it from the formula that created Webb Hartley.

"You have to believe it," Pru says. "He had too much detail to be lying—and besides, why would he want to lie about such a thing?"

"To give you a precedent," I say. "To make it all right for you to sleep with him."

She laughs, a short, humorless syllable. "Make up your mind," she says. "You want to turn him into an ogre, but you want to throw out the useful evidence."

I remember Webb's story well—how when he was thirteen, he and his father and his mother all shared the same bed. He lay between his parents; they never made love, he was never asked to leave the bed so they could. One night his mother embraced him, kissed him, roused him with her hands, guided him into her. "Then it was almost every night," he told me. "Sometimes my father was asleep, sometimes he wasn't. He never said anything when it was happening, never referred to it afterward. I didn't think I was doing anything wrong. I gave my mother pleasure; I gave myself pleasure. It was delicious. It was a way of showing how much we loved each other by putting our bodies together." When he was fifteen, it all stopped. He never again had intercourse with his mother. "It was tacit. She never mentioned it; I never mentioned it. Sometimes I would look over at my father when a car went past on our street and the headlights washed across the room—how his eyes were wide-open, staring at the ceiling. I'd remember the softness of my mother's breasts, the dampness of her thighs, the amazing heat of her when she took me into her. Or I'd remember her whispering into my ear: 'Oh, Bibbie; dear, dearest Bibbie.' 'Bibbie.' That was her nickname for me. After the first year of it, I remember thinking when I was inside her that this was the place where I'd come from, into the world, the light, the life she'd intended for me from the time I was conceived. I thought she and I were making a special kind of magic. It never occurred to me that the other guys I hung around with weren't doing the same thing to *their* mothers. 'Motherfucker.' I decided it was a super-dirty word you called people, to accuse them of doing it after they were supposed to have outgrown it."

When did he tell me this story? I think it was on the same

visit when we argued about his painting, the very week before Prudence Mackenzie came to live with him. Webb was telling me one terrible, oblique truth to illuminate another more direct, and—Pru is right about my being naïve—I hadn't the slightest idea what was really *true*.

"Just one selfish question," I say now. It's a question that has nagged at me ever since California, the Zodiac, Jenny's revelations. "Did Webb know *everything*?"

"Did he know it was you? That you were my real father?"

"Yes."

Pru shakes her head as if she's somehow sorry for me. "Poor Alec," she says. "Who else in the world could it have been?"

MY DAYS WITH PRU AND MINDY gradually settle into an easy pattern, though I can't say the pattern ever becomes entirely comfortable for me. In the downstairs guest room I have a narrow bed under a small-paned window, a maple dresser, a couple of straight-back caned chairs; a low bookcase is filled with broken-spined paperback novels. I read myself to sleep with them. They are mostly mystery novels: John Macdonald, Rex Stout, a couple of ragged Erle Stanley Gardners. I'm intimate now with Travis and Nero and Perry; they are new friends to take my mind off the loss of the old. It is probably the first time in my life that reading a book is a mindless action.

My days go like this: the orange cat wakes me before anyone else, to be let out. I dress, sit by the window at the back of the kitchen and watch the mist rise from the surface of the oval pond; the brown-and-white dog lies beside my chair, confident

of my tacit loyalty. Later on, Mindy joins me, feeds herself juice
and cereal and milk, keeps a solemn eye on me—as if we are
two chemicals whose inadvertent mixing will make a bad smell
or a loud noise. Then Pru herself appears, apologizing for not
getting up first to have coffee ready. She pours me my juice:
orange or tomato or apple, depending on what Mindy has badg-
ered her to open the night before; she brings me English muffins
and coffee stronger than I'm used to.

After breakfast, Mindy sits before the television. I watch Pru
move about the kitchen—washing dishes, baking cookies or pie
for the night's dessert, loading clothes into the washer in the
narrow pantry—and I think how young she is, how old Webb
was, how little difference age makes now that he is dead. Pru
seems to me now slighter than when she was with Webb, her
pregnancy—is it six months now?—a modest rounding under
her robes and dresses, a generosity of waist when she wears her
Levi's. She is invariably cheerful, bright eyed indeed, bushy
tailed if it were possible. ("Remember when we all had tails?"
Webb said one long night in Baltimore.) *She is,* I remind myself,
my daughter. Webb's daughter is my granddaughter, and—dear
God—Webster Hartley would have been my son-in-law. Shades
of Arthur Godfrey!

Later in the day, I might go to the store with Pru and Mindy.
Or I might stay home with Mindy while Pru shops alone.
Sometimes when Mindy naps, I nap as well. Sometimes Pru lies
beside me, a narrow space separating us, and we both sleep.

Other mornings, even if there is no cat to prod me I might
rise and slip into the kitchen to do the coffee chore, partly for
myself, partly to have it brewed for Pru when she is ready to

face the day. Or I might get up because I hear the television, which tells me that Mindy is already watching *Winnie the Pooh,* a cartoon movie she plays over and over again. The story and pictures seem always fresh to her; she laughs every time at the same scenes, the same actions. I see nothing of the strange child, almost mystical, who worked the Ouija board in Webb's studio, carrying on her playful dialogue with the dead. It's as if I've witnessed Wordsworth speeded up, Plato on fast forward. She is shy with me now, looks at me only with a corner glance. Except when we play cards. Then she is her old, nefarious self.

However each day commences, I see how much time and effort will be required to change my feelings for Pru—to make myself repress the old emotions I was beginning to bank on. Now there is blood between us, and yet more than a few times since the adventure of Mindy-lost was resolved I've caught myself looking at Pru like a man speculating, a lover longing. I can't stay here indefinitely, so close to her. But whenever I consider the prospect of packing up and leaving, something in me balks. *Not yet,* I think. Then Mindy perhaps tugs at my sleeve and I am brought from my reveries to the gaming table.

The house begins to seem less strange without Webb; he is the one who begins to seem like the visitor, who stayed around for a while, then left to attend to other business. Nothing untoward takes place between Prudence and me—nothing that would bother Theresa or perplex Mindy—and I'm becoming genuinely comfortable with her. One morning from the porch I see a heron standing at the edge of the pond, one leg raised, one eye set warily in my direction. I tell Pru I think it's really the stork, casing the place, planning his arrival time. She is less amused than I would have expected.

―――――――

ON MY NEXT-TO-LAST DAY in Scoggin, I invite Pru to
have a farewell lunch with me in Portland, at a restaurant I
know on the water looking across the harbor to the city proper.
It's a half-hour drive up the Turnpike, across on the Fore River
Bridge, along a winding two-lane blacktop into a graveled parking lot. No trouble finding a table in this place of polished wood
floors and tables and sills, precious few customers spaced like
train passengers against the dull noon light. At this time of year
only a couple of boats are moored under the restaurant windows: *Nautigal, Sally Ann, Polo II.* I remember others from earlier, summertime visits—*Solitude, Schnapps,* their harbors
identified parenthetically in smaller letters beneath their names.
Those boats and a hundred others I imagine drawn ashore at
Falmouth, Yarmouth, Freeport, a dozen other small towns
down the coast, out of the water until next June when, scraped
and caulked, patched and painted, they will be sent back by
their skippers onto the green Maine tides.

After we've ordered—Pru's Cobb salad with Green God-
dess, my last lobster roll for some time to come—we sit over
our glasses of white wine and act self-conscious. She worries
her napkin; I poke the lemon wedge deeper into my water glass.

"Webb brought me here once," she says. "Did he discover
it and tell you, or was it vice versa?"

"I don't recall. We might have found it together."

"I hope so. For symmetry."

"What about this husband of yours?" It is a subject that
abruptly crosses my mind, and I open it almost without hesi-
tation. "This Mackenzie fellow."

Pru raises an eyebrow. "What made you think of him?" she wants to know.

"Another kind of symmetry, I suppose."

"But so far in the past."

"You don't have to respond," I say.

She shrugs. "I don't mind. I met him one summer while I was still at UMass. I was waitressing in Kennebunkport; he had a rock band that played the hotel on Saturday nights. I was sort of a groupie. You could say that the marriage wasn't much more than trying to make a one-night stand legitimate."

"How long did it last?"

"Three months. Four. What's interesting is that a few years back he decided to go into politics. Now he's in the Maine legislature—lives in Augusta with a blond wife and three kids."

"You kept track?"

"He sends me Christmas cards," she says. "I think he wants to run for governor." She leans back while the waitress sets her salad in front of her.

"Will you vote for him?" I see there's too much lettuce in my lobster roll. If Pru weren't with me, I would probably complain.

"Why not?" she is saying. "If it keeps him out of the clubs."

"So generous."

She considers me. "You're not happy with your food," she says. "I can tell."

"I'm too fussy," I admit.

"Let me take your mind off it," she says. She picks her purse up from the floor and pokes through it until she brings out a snapshot. She lays the picture face down beside my wineglass.

"What is it?" I ask.

"Turn it over."

I turn it face up; I almost laugh. It is a photograph of Webb, stark naked, standing at the doorway of the studio. He's facing the camera, hands at his sides, looking faintly embarrassed despite the camouflage of his beard—a man just slightly past his prime, a bit on the heavy side, somewhat soft of flesh. His genitals seem prominent, the penis flaccid but—I'm certain— ever ready to be blooded, potent.

"I made him pose like this," Pru says. "For two reasons. I told him I wanted to have it so I could refer to it and remind myself how he excited me. And I wanted it to remind him that he wasn't as old as he tried to be."

"Understood." *Lucky Webster,* I'm thinking.

"I know. He doesn't look like the best lover in the Northern Hemisphere, does he?" She catches her lower lip under her teeth for a moment; her eyes glisten. "But he was," she says. "He was remarkable. He was perfect for me, perfect for fatherhood."

"Did he try to be old?"

She slips the photo back into her purse and sets the purse on the floor beside her. "He'd sit beside me and hold up his arm, pull at the skin around his elbow. 'See how loose this is? All this flab? How can you lose muscle tone at an elbow joint; it isn't as if it didn't get all the exercise in the world.' 'Bending the elbow' is how he described his drinking."

"Yes," I say. Of course I'm thinking of myself, my own fears and doubts about mortality—the staple of every man's life when he turns the corner into his sixties.

" 'I feel like old furniture,' he'd say, 'losing all its stuffing, like grandmother's chair.' " Pru sighs and takes a sip of her wine. "You know that old leather chair of his?"

"In the front parlor. Of course."

"Webb called it his alter ego. 'That's the me that is to come,' he'd say. Then he'd make love to me in it, and it was as if he'd forgotten all about his gloomy mortality."

"The mortality part came true."

And that kills the lunch. After that, conversation comes hard.

"So you're keeping the baby," I finally volunteer.

She seems startled. "Why wouldn't I?" she says.

"Robert told me you'd asked him about giving it up."

"Oh." She makes a dismissive sweep of one hand. "Right after the death, when I was crazy and afraid, I remembered reading somewhere that childless couples would pay a ton of money to adopt. *That would solve everything,* I thought. But no; I'd never do that to Webb—to his memory. Never."

I nod. *God damn lawyer Robert,* crosses my mind. "It was none of my business," I say.

"I don't mind."

"And I'm sorry I'm leaving tomorrow," I tell her.

"So am I," she says. "I hope you'll visit me, I hope you won't feel awkward about me when you do."

"Awkward?" I say. It's a strange word; its sound so perfectly fits what it describes that my mind lingers on it, turns it over and over like a child's alphabet block, trying to pull softer words out of its harshness. *Dark. Draw. Ward. Raw. Ark. War.* "I don't feel awkward."

"You could even stay a while longer now." She finds the Salem package in her purse and taps out one cigarette. "I'm not planning to go back to the bookshop. You're welcome, you know."

"I know." I watch her light the cigarette. "Are you smoking a little too much?"

The words are out before I can catch them. Pru looks at me, looks at the tip of the cigarette, then stubs it out in the ashtray.

"Thanks," she says. "Thanks for caring. But I do follow the rules. I only have two or three cigarettes a day, at most. I take the pills. I do the breathing exercises and get my sleep and put my feet up."

"Let's have coffee," I say. I have to stop fretting, do I not? "Will we have dessert?"

"Coffee, yes, but dessert, no." She shakes a finger at me. "Be consistent."

While we linger over coffee—I think neither of us truly looks forward to my leaving Maine—there is activity under our window. A man and a young woman I take to be father and daughter appear on the dock and board the *Nautigal*. We watch the man go to the cockpit; the daughter waits on deck, brushing the snow off a gunwale so she can lean looking out toward the harbor mouth. Shortly, Pru and I see a burst of blue smoke from the *Nautigal*'s stern as the inboard engine fires up; a disturbance of black water boils white, steaming on the cold air. The girl vaults to the dock and casts off the lines, then hops back aboard to take the tiller. Her father gives her a small salute, then turns to the wheel. The *Nautigal* motors away from us, her mast a distorted shadow on the shimmery surface of the harbor. The *Polo II* and the *Sally Ann* bob in her wash, waiting for their own skippers to rescue them from the impending winter.

f i v e

∎

HARRIET if she were alive would understand nothing of
what I have been telling—not what it was that drew Webster
Hartley to women regardless of age, of station, of water or
blood, and certainly not what drew those women to him; not
what I admired about him even while I was appalled by his
doing and saying; not whatever it was that made, and still makes,
Prudence Amanda Mackenzie more than an immoral woman
unbothered by adultery or the tincture of incest. It isn't that my
poor dear wife was incapable of imagination, of realizing that

there were in the world people who justified living outside the rule book, and she would even have accepted that such people were male more often than not—because that is the slant of our Western culture, for better or worse, like it or not. No, it is only the particular that would have baffled her, as in a very real way it continues to baffle me. "You can't have every pretty woman you see," Webb said once, but you could see he regretted the fact; he said it with a sigh suggesting that the world ought to be different—that one *ought* to be allowed to have every pretty woman one saw.

NOW THAT I KNOW EVERYTHING—or almost everything—I wonder if Webb would feel apologetic for the phony mystery, the cloak-and-dagger borrowed from our olden days in the service of Uncle Sam. Back then we frightened ourselves with worst-case tales we told in letters home, Webb fretting in longhand over the prospects for torture at the hands of the Red Chinese, no worse than me telling my parents I was a mere ten minutes from the Soviet Zone, and that in case of attack, ships were waiting in the harbor to evacuate us security forces ahead of the women and dependent children.

But that was adolescent ego, and this was something more delicate, though Jenny's version was not to be so delicately phrased.

Webb was sure he had a goodly number of years left to him—a lot of paintings, a lot of lovemaking. And now I remember old Coxie, a poet-professor of ours at Bowdoin, saying, "The muse can't just be laid; she has to be seduced every time, and sometimes a man gets tired of all that lovemaking." Webb saw that there *is* a connection. *And damn well lived it,* Jenny would say—and Harriet would have agreed.

Yet I saw, firsthand, how much Webb loved Prudence, how tangled up he was in all her youth and beauty. I believe now that it was the perfect attraction of kinship, of blood calling to blood, daughter to father, father to daughter. It must have come as close to what he'd searched for, his whole life through, as he could have imagined.

And what was that? An ideal, or at least *ideal* as Webb defined it: the perfection, the paradigm, the clay mold God broke Eve out of and that (naturally) could never be re-used. There was only one original—one Eve, one Adam, the rest of us clever copies, Webb would have argued—some more authentic than others.

He must have believed he had gotten close to the secret of that perfect copy. It had to do with how the everyday strips us of our *deep* humanity and substitutes a veneer of civilization. It's a prissy civilization, by Webb's lights: monogamous, monotonous. That was all right for most men, but not for Webb. Affairs with pretty women—dear God, what a lot of them— canceled all that: for him they were outside time, outside the everyday. James Dickey has a poem, "Adultery," that begins, "Some places we cannot die. . . ." I'm not sure Webb knew that verse. It means that the adultery is timeless, that it immortalizes the lovers because it is apart from the commonplace world of conventions and obligations; but it also means that it would be too humiliating to everyone concerned for one of the lovers to drop dead in the other's bed, or in a sleazy motel room—and of course that happens all the time, as we see by the exposés of famous people in the tabloids. Webb might not have accepted that meaning: how terrible for our survivors are the sins we get caught at.

So he made love to many women, had the best of them, intimately, irresponsibly, and outside the ordinary schedules of their lives. Removed from their husbands, their legitimate boyfriends. Perhaps he thought if he loved enough of them he might find Perfection in a single package instead of in those stolen bits and pieces. ("There's plenty of morbid interest in America in serial killers; but who's written a book lately about a serial lover?") Or was he only restless, and did the women get to be faceless, even tedious?

Until Prudence.

Jennifer had told me—and my own visits had confirmed—what the girl meant to Webb, how he doted on her, how Jenny disapproved in no uncertain terms. But that may have been his real secret: *the most nearly perfect object of a man's love is that which is simultaneously self and other, other and self*. Prudence was Webb and not-Webb, and so she had the dimension no other love of his could have had.

Harriet would have called it outrageous. I know; it was. And now Prudence is Alec and not-Alec.

WHAT KEPT US—Webb and I—friends over forty-odd years through thick and thin and fat and lean was Jennifer. Was Pru's mother. Was my rage and his guilt over Baltimore. Webb knew his guiltiness, of course, but he also knew my residual anger at him; how else explain what Prudence referred to as "the famous car-radio incident"? Rage and guilt—they kept us together like a textbook marriage. He may have felt sorry for the hurt he inflicted on me, and yet . . . I had a full life with Harriet; God knows Webb had a full one with Jenny—more full than ever I could have had. The night that poor derelict was murdered on the library steps, I realize now, she stopped being a librarian and became a woman; the fear, the horror of it all stripped "job" from her and turned her into something elemental. She had needs, and Webb was there to supply them. With me she had desires, and plans, and love in the kids/house/station wagon sense. With him, that night—and she was never the same, after—she absolutely required the healing of passion.

BUT "the famous car-radio incident":

Once—it was a while ago and Webb might have forgotten this, for I never heard him refer to it—I drove him and a stack of his paintings to a gallery in Ogunquit.

It was high summer in Maine, the roads and beaches clotted with tourists, cars carrying Massachusetts and Connecticut and New York license tags, leggy college girls in bikinis and silky pastel overblouses strolling in twos and threes along the Shore Road between Perkins Cove and Ogunquit—"Gunkit," we called it, after a stupid song we'd sung during hot vacations from Bowdoin:

It's Gunkit,
It's Gunkit,
It's Gunkit makes the world go 'round.

Almost ad infinitum, but ending:

Sing Halleluia,

Sing Halleluia,

Put a nickel on the drum and you'll be saved.

It was mindless and it was stolen from an old Salvation Army song, but it's the mindless, stolen things that become true nostalgia, isn't it? Anyway, we had left Pru behind with the infant Mindy asleep, and we were traveling from Ogunquit toward York on the Shore Road, a two-lane blacktop winding past numerous resort hotels— Sparhawk Hall sticks in my mind because we had another song about The Girls of Sparhawk Hall, meaning the college-girl waitresses and chambermaids who worked there and who walked on the beach with us and necked with us on the summer lawns in the lovely sport we called "grassing" and who were too benevolent to ask of us anything in the way of lasting attachment—and, by that late date, also winding past white-frame condominiums and myriad tiny art galleries, one of which was where Webb and I were headed on that particular afternoon.

We got to the place around two thirty; I parked close to a back entrance and we both hopped out and unloaded Webb's canvases into a sort of shed where a lot of other canvases were stored, all of them seascapes—the water ranging from moss green to aquamarine to angry violet, and the rocks from yellow to muddy brown to black, but all of them, every blesséd painting in that good-sized shed, rife with foaming breakers that crashed and hurled themselves against those rocks out of that surging ocean. You'd have thought, if you were a stranger to

Maine, that the sea was never calm and that even to wade gingerly into it was to say farewell forever to life on earth.

But it sold, that stuff. Webb despised it, of course. We were there that day only because Webb knew the proprietor—they were drinking buddies from some earlier time—who had volunteered to put his work on show at what was surely the best time of the year to *be* on show. "I don't have any pictures of the snotgreen sea," I'd heard Webb say over the phone the day before, "but I'll bring along some things that won't embarrass you." So there we were. The proprietor pointed out an anteroom where Webb's work could be somewhat segregated from the Pounding-Waves School, and after we'd hung the canvases we sat a while in the man's kitchen and among us finished off a nice bottle of a California Chardonnay whose label I meant to remember, but of course forgot. The proprietor was bald and gravel-voiced and wore red patent-leather shoes; I wondered where Webb had met him, and how they had happened ever to go drinking together. It turned out he was a friend of one of Webb's wives; that answered one question, but raised others I chose not to pursue.

On the way back home was when I got another reminder of Webb's temper. I realize now that what triggered its explosion was not only a slight perverseness in myself—as if I wasn't going to let myself be browbeaten again by this "artistic" friend of mine—but a day-long compiling of his own dissatisfaction and impatience with the world as it is, especially the art world of Maine in the summertime, when the audience for art is fatuous and shallow and rich merely in money. How I remembered the blue mailbox and the Kennebunk witch!

Both of us were silent in the car for perhaps a dozen miles, and it was to counter that silence that I reached over to switch on the radio. I fiddled with the tuning knob—we were at that point perhaps ten miles away from Ogunquit, already mercifully out of the tourist traffic on Route 1 and cruising along Route 109 toward Scoggin—and eventually I found a music station I thought was worth attending to. It was a Top Twenty station out of Boston, doing its weekly countdown of the most-played songs of this moment of the current millennium. It was bearable, if not Great Art.

Webb, without a word, reached over and turned the radio off.

I turned it back on.

Webb turned it off.

"What's the matter?" I said.

"It's crap," he said. "I won't listen to it."

"Hey," I said, "*I'm* listening to it."

"But *I* don't want to," he said.

"It's my car," I said. Not true—it was a rental—but surely I was the machine's proprietor.

"Then be a good host," Webb said.

I turned the radio back on. "Screw you," I said. "I happen to like this station."

"Screw yourself," Webb said. "Stop the car."

"What?"

"Stop the fucking car. I don't want to ride with this crappy music."

"Whatever you say."

I slowed the car, drifted onto the shoulder, stopped. Webb opened his door.

"What the hell is the matter with you?" I said.

"Nothing," Webb said. "I just happen to have good taste, and I don't have to be trapped into listening to rotten music." He got out of the car.

"You're crazy," I said.

He leaned into the car. "Maybe. But I'm not rude." He slammed the door and walked away in the direction we'd come from.

I sat for a minute or two, considering matters. In the rear-view mirror I could see Webb trudging along the shoulder as if he had a purpose. I shifted into reverse and backed up after him. Once I was alongside him, Webb stopped. I leaned across the seat and rolled down the window. He looked in at me.

"What now?" he said. "You trying to run over me?"

"Get in the car," I said.

"Are you going to listen to the radio?"

"Yes."

"Then piss off," he said. He resumed walking toward the ocean we had left behind.

If that's what he wants, I thought. I really did. That's the kind of best friend I was being. I pushed the shift lever into first and floored the accelerator. The tires shrieked; gravel sprayed in Webb's direction; I drove until he was no longer an image in my mirror.

After about five or six miles, I slowed down, turned around in somebody's front yard, and drove back toward Webb. I saw him from a half-mile off; now he was walking away from Ogunquit, toward me. He walked half frontward, half back-ward, watching for cars, his thumb cocked to hitch a ride from any passing stranger. I drove past him without slowing down; in the rearview mirror I saw the thumb of his right hand still soliciting a ride, the longest finger of his left hand delivering a personal message to me and my radio.

I waited until Webb was again out of view, then turned back. I pulled up beside him. "Going my way?" I said.

He looked in.

"You going to keep playing that frigging radio?" he said.

I shook my head. "No."

He opened the door and got in. We drove to Scoggin in dead silence, drove through the heart of town, drove to the lake and beyond, drove into his own driveway, where Prudence, who'd arrived on the day of the blue mailbox—a far smarter disagreement—sat on the porch steps shelling beans, watching the two of us like a mother wondering what her foolish little boys had been up to this time.

"YOU ALWAYS PERPLEXED ME, you two," Prudence says now. "I think you ought to have been twins."

"Webb would resist that," I say. We are in the kitchen, late morning, saying our good-byes.

"It's beyond his control." She clasps her hands over her stomach and smiles—whether at me or her unborn, I can't tell. "When you come back next summer," she says, "we'll drive to Ogunquit, the four of us."

"All right."

"We'll give Webb's ashes to the ocean, off that cliff where Sheila What's-her-name taught you two to drink."

THE LAST THING I load into the car is Webb's blue mailbox; I'll stop at a frame shop in town, have them crate it and ship it to Evanston. All around me is winter, its dominion, its threats. The sky is colorless, seamless. The air smells of snow. I'm not sure I look forward to scattering what remains of Webb's ashes; how can it not remind Pru of what she has lost, dredge up the hurt? But I can't say any of that. I can only dread the eventual occasion.

And what if I don't come back at all, even to the marvelous Maine summer? Suppose I content myself with my retired existence in Evanston, with the lake nearby, the pulse of Chicago—its music, its theater, its galleries and art museums I have never visited often enough or long enough—a happy presence in my life, my former colleagues and a few old friends close at hand?

Or suppose I do something brazen, as Webb might have been brazen: suppose I pack up and move to California? Not to Jenny, who can never ever be more than a mismanaged past time, but to Natalie Kramer—Natalie and the know-it-all Esther; Natalie and the taunting ex-husband and the lisping Billy; Natalie and the expensive stereo speakers and the unmentionables catalogs and the thick magazines whose tables of contents are lost among glossy and suggestive advertising; Natalie of the posturing, the vanity, the practiced, elitist graciousness?

I lodge the blue mailbox carefully behind the car's front seats and slam the door shut. My life is rich with possibilities. The world, as they say, is my oyster.

When I come back in from the car, the house is quiet. I presume Mindy has been put down for her nap, and when I look into the living room I see Pru taking her own habitual rest. She is lying on her back in the middle of the room, a sofa pillow under her head, her arms at her sides. I think the burden of the sixth month of pregnancy gives her backaches; lying supine like this must relieve the pain, must truly relax her. Her eyes are closed. I can't tell if she is asleep, if she knows I am in the doorway watching her.

She is wearing the black tights and one of Webb's tentlike dress shirts—a pale blue one with thin red stripes widely spaced. She is barefoot. In her shorter haircut Pru's face seems more open, younger, irresistibly innocent. Her child, the fatherless child, is a roundness that partly opens the long blue shirttails to show a triangle of pale skin. I feel remarkably protective of this fertile woman, so many years a stranger to me. The feeling is genuine, and surely it is proper.

But much more than that, I feel *desire* for her, and though this is a feeling just as genuine as the urge to protect, I know now it is *not* proper, not acceptable. Even Webb would remind me: propriety; love. And yet in my mind's eye, this instant, I see myself entering the room, kneeling beside this dear woman, bending to kiss her half-parted mouth, her closed eyelids, her unclouded brow. I see my hands parting her man's shirt, drawing down the loose elastic of the waistband to conform my hands to the hardening globe of her belly. I kiss the distended navel, whisper affections against the heartbeat of the child attached beneath it.

But the entire image is fantasy, the sheerest intimate fantasy, though I feel such ambiguity of desire as I have never in my life felt for another woman. The usual beauty of ambiguity, as I have lectured my students a thousand times, is that one need not choose either/or, but is permitted to luxuriate in both/and. Yet erotic fantasy is all a father—ambiguous or not—is allowed for a daughter, and even Webster Hartley, girl-crazy as he was, must have realized the perverse excess of love before he died, before he conveyed all his curious legacies for good or ill to his naïve, helpless, best and dearest twin.

I wish I could confess to Pru my feelings, my hunger, how deeply and achingly I am drawn to her. But would the world be better if we were always honest? Would life be happier if we admitted our weaknesses? And besides, who can possibly argue that she is not, more than ever, mine?

TUCKER-REID H. COFER 4/04